Designated Driver

Designated Driver

A Jewel Cruise Line Adventure

Christine R. Whitlock

DEDICATION

To my amazing son, Alex.

God gave us another day together!

"Don't bother to give God instructions; just report for duty."
—Corrie ten Boom

PART ONE

High Seas

Lord, I know that people's lives are not their own;
it is not for them to direct their steps.

—Jeremiah 10:23

CHAPTER ONE

Saturday, April 12

2025

"Kiss! Kiss!"

The sound of silverware clanking on sweet-tea glasses thrilled Anna. She and her husband, Jude, were celebrating their twenty-fifth wedding anniversary, and the evening was going perfectly. Anna had reserved the best reception hall in Wonder, Alabama, one year ago and began making plans immediately. She invited fifty-two guests, and by the looks of the full tables and the sounds of the clanking glassware, most of them were present. The fresh daisies on the tables looked beautiful, and the volume of the three-piece band was suitable for table conversation. Yes, the evening was perfect.

Anna Yearling was a part-time writer and full-time control freak. She liked things in their places and would lose sleep to make sure they stayed that way. Anna preferred the term "stickler," but had to admit to herself and to her friends that she was a drill sergeant in all areas of her life. From her morning routine to her diet, Anna was always in control.

When the clanking stopped, Anna pecked Jude on the lips and surveyed the smiling crowd. From the head table, she could see relatives, friends from church, and coworkers. The tables were set up in a grid design for easy walking flow with buffet tables set on two sides. Desserts were displayed at the back of the hall as were large containers of sweet tea, water, and lemonade. Space for a makeshift dance floor was to the left of the head table, and a three-piece band was to the right. Perfect!

"Tell us again how you met?" Justin, Jude's best friend, yelled the request from a nearby table.

Jude laughed. "You know the story. We don't need to go over that again."

"We want to hear it." Justin was standing now, and the guests began a soft clap. "I bet some of you haven't heard about the explosion."

Anna waited a socially appropriate ten seconds before she stood. Her straight blonde hair was pulled back in a twist. She thought it would be better for dancing but regretted it as soon as her best friend, Meg, started taking pictures. Her face would look oversized in all the pictures. "Okay. If you insist." Jude dropped his head to his hands, and Anna laughed. She loved telling this story.

"As you know, Jude and I were students at Oakmont College at the same time, but we didn't meet until our sophomore year. He was in the business school, and I was in creative writing. In the spring, we both signed up to volunteer at the annual Lollipops on the Lawn Festival. Each year, Oakmont invites local foster children to a big carnival on campus—complete with hot dogs, face painting, and kiddie rides." At the last word, she looked at Jude. He rolled his eyes, and the crowd laughed.

"The festival lasted most of the day and ended with the children attending a dance party on the lawn. Somehow, Jude had eaten four hot dogs during lunch and was then moved to help with the swirling chair ride where I was working. It was called the Flying Pigs, because children sat in swings that went around in a circle. Spoiler alert: Jude has problems with motion sickness. That's why we can't take a fabulous cruise to celebrate our anniversary. We're spending a week in Destin this summer instead.

"Anyways . . ." Anna side hugged Jude and continued the story. "A girl around five years old asked one of us to ride with her because she was too scared to ride on her own. I was wearing new white linen pants, so I obviously couldn't ride on the Flying Pigs. Jude tried his best to get out of going on the ride, but I'd practically pushed him into a chair. Nothing seemed out of the ordinary until Jude bolted out of his seat and off the ride when it stopped. He rushed toward me to tell me that he was going to the restroom, when *splat!* He threw up all over me and my white pants. He practically exploded."

At the word *exploded*, the crowd erupted in laughter. Most knew the end of the story and Jude's famous last words. "I was horrified," Anna continued. "When I looked at him, he just said, 'My bad.'" Many in the audience recited the famous words along with Anna. "'My bad.' That was all he could say." Jude was laughing now.

"Jude was horrified, as were the children exiting the ride. He quickly found some paper towels and handed them to me. What he did next won my heart. He asked to pray for me and my clothes. It was the sweetest thing anyone had ever done for me. I knew while he was stuttering through the prayer that I would marry that man. And I did one year after we graduated on the first Saturday after tax season. And here we are twenty-five years later with three beautiful children and a bustling accounting practice." Jude stood and hugged his wife. But he wasn't wearing his usual smile. Only Anna would notice, but something didn't seem right.

The band started playing, and the anniversary party continued. Anna walked among the guests and thanked everyone for attending.

Jude stood in a corner, joking with three of his friends. Justin Young had been Jude's best friend since they were seated together in sixth grade homeroom. Their families had shared weddings, births, and vacations together for decades. The two other men deep in discussion with Jude and Justin were friends from church, BB and Jay. Anna assumed that the quartet was either discussing bass fishing or the Alabama football spring game. No. They were discussing the A-Day game. They wouldn't be talking about anything else today.

Before the celebration ended, the Yearling children presented their parents with a large family portrait in a beautiful silver frame. Anna beamed at her picture-perfect family. She and Jude named their children after times of the year to go with the Yearling last name. Anna decided that her name sounded like the word *annual*, and Jude's full name of Julian sounded like *July*, so a calendar naming theme was inevitable.

Maya was the oldest at twenty-three and was a near-carbon copy of Anna. She graduated with a degree in logistics in three years and led a very organized life. She worked as a purchasing coordinator for a large shipping company and was engaged to Hunter Day, which thrilled Anna. The calendar-themed names would continue. Maya and Hunter were to be married in early June, and the Yearling home had been "wedding central" for over a year.

Adding to their exciting year, Anna and Jude's only son, Jan, would be graduating with a biochemistry degree from the University of Alabama in two weeks. He had secured a coveted internship with Carbolytic Pharmaceuticals in Atlanta and would be moving to the big city over Memorial Weekend. The family had traveled to Atlanta in March find the perfect apartment for Jan to rent during his internship year. If everything went well, he would be offered a permanent position this time next year. Jan was the carbon copy of his dad. Both loved numbers and college football, but not necessarily in that order.

The youngest Yearling was the wildcard of the family. Winter kept her parents on their toes. She was a junior in high school and refused to make plans for after graduation. She would not even talk about them. Instead, she vowed to enjoy high school "in the moment." To Anna's frustration, Winnie was a free spirit who loved life and lived it without regard for the future. Her motto was "no strings." She did not want to be tied down. More importantly, she did not want to be controlled. Winnie was dedicated to her role as editor of the school newspaper, and Anna hoped that meant she would follow in her own footsteps as a writer.

After carefully packing the family portrait back into its box, Anna convinced her husband and children to join her in a fun dance on the dance floor. Jude was reluctant but would do anything for the children. The five of them began bouncing around to Kool & the Gang's "Celebration," and soon half of their family and friends joined in. Anna scanned those seated and made a camera motion to ask them to take pictures. Pictures of her perfect moment.

As the guests slowly began leaving, Anna walked toward Jude and his group of friends. "We haven't slow-danced yet. Wanna join me?" She would never forget the look on Jude's face as he halfheartedly agreed to dance. Yep. Something was definitely wrong.

"Are you having fun?" Jude asked. "We don't do this very often." He led Anna onto the dance floor.

"I am. Everything is perfect. And the shrimp toast tastes better than I expected. Are you having fun?"

"Sure. But you know this isn't my scene. I'd rather be sitting by the firepit in the backyard making s'mores."

Anna knew that Jude didn't enjoy dressing up for parties. But he was willing to keep her happy. "I know. We won't have to do this again until our fiftieth anniversary. I promise."

Jude laughed. "Except for the big shindig in June. The wedding is only seven weeks away, you know."

"Oh that. I guess that will be even fancier than tonight. But then we are clear until our fiftieth. Well, of course we will have two more weddings in the meantime, unless Winnie tries to annoy me by eloping. And we will be turning the big five oh in two years. That calls for some sort of shindig. After *that*, we can take a break from big parties. That will be it—maybe." Anna shot her million-dollar smile that usually melted Jude. He barely grinned.

After the dance, Anna and Jude said good-bye to the remaining guests. Their three children and Jude's parents helped wrap up the leftover food to take home. The stash should keep the family fed for a day or two. The kids rode separately and left with the food and the daisy decorations. Anna and Jude stayed behind with his parents to clean up and to ensure that the hall was in adequate shape to receive their deposit in return.

Jude's mom, Sylvia, walked up to Anna and gave her a hug. "What a lovely evening. The turnout was great. Did you see that Uncle Rudy was here? I didn't think he would get out after Aunt Louise passed."

"Yes, I saw him. He looked good. Thank you so much for your help, Sylvia. We couldn't have made it twenty-five years without you and Tom." Anna's parents died seven months apart one year after she and Jude were married. They never met their grandchildren. The back-to-back losses were devastating to Anna, but her in-laws picked up the slack and loved her as their own. They gave the couple much-needed date nights and hosted most of the holiday meals. They helped shuttle kids to ball games and dance recitals. And they celebrated every milestone with the family. Jude's brother, Dorian, and his wife, Kara, had no children, so Maya, Jan, and Winnie got the grandparents all to themselves. Yes. Anna scored well in the in-law department.

As his parents drove off, Jude turned to Anna. "Ready?"

"Yep. Let's go. I hope the kids realized they need to unload all that food."

Jude laughed. "It's probably still in Jan's car. We better check on it." Anna would have liked one more dance or even a moment of reflection before they left. But Jude just fiddled with his keys and waited for her to walk through the doorway.

On the way home, both were quiet until Jude brought up the Oakmont story. "Why does Justin have to bring up 'my bad' every time we are around other people? It's getting old."

"Oh, he's just having fun. You are so wonderful that it's interesting to hear something about you that is less-than perfect. I love that story."

"Well, I don't. Please stop telling it." With that, Jude cut off their discussion and ended the evening on a sour note. He and Anna got the food put away and found containers with water for the daisies. The children were watching YouTube videos in the family room when they finished. Anna appreciated that her children got along well. She hugged each good night and headed upstairs for bed. Jude fell into his recliner and asked the kids what they were watching.

As Anna neared the top of the staircase, Jan called out, "Mom, I'm glad that Dad threw up all over you! If he had a stronger stomach, we wouldn't be here."

Maya slapped Jan's knee. "No, Jan, we'd still be here. Dad would have managed to do something else embarrassing to get Mom's attention. I'm sure of it."

"Hey," Jude inserted, "maybe *Mom* would have done something embarrassing." The rest of the group laughed.

"Mom? Never," Jan challenged. "She's too much of a perfectionist to embarrass herself. It had to be you. No worries, Dad. We're glad you puked on Mom. The bar has been set low for the rest of us." At that final comment, Anna called it a night. The party was perfect. Her children were perfect. And her husband was perfect. He was always exhausted after tax season. That must be why he didn't seem as happy as he usually was.

"Good night, everyone. Don't stay up too late. I will not have anyone yawning at church tomorrow."

"Night, Mom!" came a small voice.

Anna looked back, and Winnie was smiling at her. Her youngest child didn't speak much. But when she did, she left an impact. Anna gave her a wink and padded to her bedroom. She quickly washed her face, brushed her teeth, and changed into a comfy nightgown. Downstairs, she heard the sounds of her perfect family laughing at videos of people falling in hilarious manners. Their voices created a sense of safety and sent her off to sleep in moments.

1851

"Kiss! Kiss!"

The guests began stomping their feet. Sarah Wilkes was beaming with pride as she watched her youngest sister, Mae, shyly kiss her new husband. Sarah had single-handedly raised her three sisters after their parents were killed in a barn fire twenty years ago. She remembered the huge flames and the bucket brigade, but she didn't remember much else of that terrible night. The pastor of their church and his wife took the girls in by providing food and shelter, but not much else. Sarah knew that her mother was watching from heaven and didn't want to disappoint her. Sarah ensured that the girls completed their schooling and found proper mates. Mae, with porcelain skin and coal-black hair, was the last to marry. She fell in love with the new schoolmaster only three weeks after he moved to town.

Now that the sisters were married, Sarah and her husband, Asher, would take on the arduous task of traversing the Oregon Trail from their home in Oak Grove, Missouri. The promise of free farmland in the Oregon Territory was too much to resist. Asher had worked for John Morgan for fifteen years and still had not received the crop-share property he had been promised. After much prayer, he and Sarah made the decision to move their family to a more prosperous territory. They would leave one week from today. The thought of permanently leaving her sisters was heartbreaking. But Sarah and Asher had the responsibility of providing for their five children. And their current situation was leaving the family at risk.

Sarah met Asher Wilkes at a church picnic in the early spring. She had been eleven when her parents died and had no expectations for a happy future. Shortly after Sarah turned eighteen, Asher's family moved from nearby Harrisburg when his father accepted a position as the town's dentist and barber. He was exactly three years older than

Sarah and needed a wife. Sarah was the logical choice, and the two were married without much discussion. Through God's providence, Asher was an ideal husband. He treated Sarah with kindness and patience. He insisted that her sisters move in with them in their bunk house. And he read passages from the Bible to the women every night. Sarah couldn't love him more.

After a painful miscarriage, Sarah gave birth to their first son when she was nineteen years old. Luke was a large baby with a gentle temperament. He was so much like Asher that Sarah joked that they were "distant twins." Luke was now seventeen and worked beside his father every day. He never complained, but Sarah knew that the work was difficult and the rewards were small. The Oregon Territory offered a new hope of land for Luke too. Sarah prayed that he would find a wife soon after they were settled on their new property.

A year after Luke was born, the twins, Jewel and Jade, arrived. The girls were oddly close, even speaking their own imaginary language. They would turn sixteen on the Trail and begged Sarah nearly every day to wear rouge to darken their lips. Jewel and Jade had matured quickly, but Sarah was determined to keep them children as long as she could.

When Sarah was twenty-three, Trenton was born. He was sickly from birth, and there were several sleepless nights when his parents thought they would lose him. But God had protected him for thirteen years thus far. He worked with Asher on the farm but tired easily and needed frequent rest. Over time, his father taught him how to keep husbandry and financial records for Mr. Morgan. Trenton took to the accounting quickly and became an asset to his family.

The wildcard of the family was Jeremiah. Sarah thought she was finished bearing children after falling sick with scarlet fever. She recovered quickly and thanked God daily that she was still working with Asher to raise their family. Thinking that her daily sickness was a residue from the fever, Sarah did not suspect that she was pregnant until late in the pregnancy. In 1846, God blessed their family with Jeremiah. He would turn five on the Trail. Nicknamed Fidget, Jeremiah rarely sat still. He helped with the farm where he could and stayed underfoot of Sarah when he couldn't. Sarah knew in her heart that God had a special plan for Fidget. She envisioned him becoming a preacher or a traveling salesman. Or maybe an acrobat like those at the 1850 World's Fair.

 Sarah helped her sisters, Meg and Amelia, serve cake to the four-dozen wedding guests. Widow Cooper provided the three wedding cakes: a white cake for the bride, a fruitcake for the groom, and a bundt cake for the guests. The reception was held on the back lawn of the town's largest church in Oak Grove, and the weather was pleasantly warm for late April. Sarah couldn't help but think about how much her parents would enjoy the wedding of their youngest daughter. Then she laughed at the thought of Jewel and Jade getting married. They would probably want to have a joint wedding wearing elaborate dresses and jewelry. She said a quick prayer for the future husbands of her growing girls.

 After the ceremony, Asher drove the family home in their new prairie schooner. He was warned by the wagon master that their Conestoga wagon would be too heavy for the oxen to pull all the way to Oregon. The schooner would carry their worldly possessions the two thousand miles from Oak Grove to Oregon City. Sarah had been pruning their cargo by giving what could not be carried to her sisters. She would keep beds for the children and a change of clothing for each person. Plus cookware, mementos, and ammunition.

At their house, Jewel and Jade talked in their special language. The others could not interpret their words but generally understood the topics. Sarah knew the girls were talking about Mae's wedding and their own future weddings—or wedding. The older boys settled quickly, but Jeremiah was pretending to hunt buffalo in their front room.

"Time for bed, Fidget," Sarah warned. "We don't want to be yawning at church tomorrow."

"Yes, ma'am. I need to fell this last bison. He's a tricky one."

Sarah chuckled to herself. This boy would keep her on her toes this summer. He just might run to Oregon ahead of the family on his own. "Get the last one and change into your nightshirt soon."

Asher was sitting at the dining table with Trenton. They were discussing the sale of four donkeys that would not make the trip west. Sarah ran her hand along the top of the table. Asher had made the table for Sarah as a wedding present. He also made six simple chairs and promised to fill them with enough children. With the arrival of Jeremiah, he surprised Sarah with another matching chair shortly after he was born. They would not be able to take the table and chairs with them on the schooner, so she decided to give them to Meg, who promised to use the handcrafted set with care. She was expecting her third child and was grateful to have seating for their growing family. Sarah had asked Asher if they could tie the table below the wagon, but he'd convinced her that it would be too heavy for the oxen to pull. She didn't like change and knew that the decision to relocate to the West would present many changes.

Please provide me with courage, Lord.

CHAPTER TWO

Sunday, April 13
2025

Anna and Jude found their seats in their usual pew at church—center right near the middle. Jan and Winnie arrived with them. Maya rode with Hunter on Sundays and was usually a few minutes late. After lunch, Jan would return to Tuscaloosa for the end of his final semester. But this morning was perfect. All of Anna's birdies were in the nest.

Today's message was from a guest missionary serving at an orphanage in Honduras. He and his wife were home for a month on a prescribed leave. The man shared stories of violence and poverty. The sanctuary was quiet as he displayed images of men walking the streets with machine guns and machetes. And the information about gang murders was shocking. But . . . God. The gospel was being spread in this troubled nation. And new churches were being planted. The beautiful people of Honduras were finding hope in Jesus.

Anna couldn't imagine a never-ending life of violence, much less poverty. How do parents grow and raise their families under such fear? How do children live into the future? Yes, she should do something to help. Everyone should do something to help.

After the service, the family—plus Hunter—met at Say Cheese for lunch. Known for putting cheese on everything, even desserts, the restaurant was a favorite of most citizens of Wonder. Anna favored the cheesy broccoli soup, and Jude usually ordered the parmesan pork chops. On special occasions he ordered a slice of apple pie topped with cheddar cheese. The Yearlings found a table outside, and all began talking about Honduras at once.

"We should do something. Pastor Ed said that the church is sending a team in July." Winnie was clearly moved by the pictures and stories that the missionary shared.

"No," Anna interjected. "We can't just all just go to Honduras. We have a wedding soon. And Jan will be starting his internship. I have a book deadline of August first, and Dad has a full-time job. Plus, we scheduled our family vacation to the Gulf the week after the fourth again. It just wouldn't work."

Jude agreed. "We'll donate to the mission. I'm sure there is a huge need for money."

"But it's not the same. I want to do something." Winnie stopped talking as the food arrived and was visibly unhappy at the dismissal from her parents.

"Look, it's not safe for any of us to travel to that country right now. And we certainly aren't going to let our seventeen-year-old daughter go without us. We'll pray and send some money. Maybe a local opportunity will pop up. That would be more practical," Jude pushed back.

Jude prayed a blessing over the food, and talk turned to the previous night's anniversary party. Apparently, the shrimp toast was a hit, but the watermelon soup was not. Jan asked about having a band for his graduation party. Anna cleared up any confusion by declaring that they were not having a full-blown party for his graduation. They were keeping the family tradition by eating at Dreamland BBQ after the ceremony.

Jan smiled. "Ha! It almost worked. I thought I could sneak in a little party without you noticing."

Jude patted him on the shoulder. "You know we are proud of you, son. But we are a little partied out right now. And we did a restaurant for Maya's graduation. It'll be fun. Any word on the apartment? You need to get a deposit down before you lose it."

"No. I'll try to call tomorrow. The guy said it was mine. They just have to 'prepare the documents.' It's all digital."

"Sounds good," Anna said. "Now, how many RSVPs do we have today?" Maya's church wedding shower was on Saturday. Thankfully, three ladies from Anna and Jude's Sunday school class were planning everything.

"I think we are at thirty-two. I can't wait!" Maya hugged Hunter's nearest arm, and he smiled obligingly.

"Not a bad turnout. And that will be it. The next wedding event will be the rehearsal dinner. Hunter, was your mom able to get the fish *and* the chicken?" Anna asked.

"Yes, ma'am. She said that everything is all set." Hunter was not excited about the wedding details but knew Anna would freak out if things weren't perfect.

"Miss Grace said that the menu is set," Maya spoke up. "She is still going with simple flowers on the tables. And the Potter House is letting her go in early to decorate. She and Mr. Gene will leave the rehearsal ceremony and rush to the restaurant early to make sure that everything is set."

Anna exhaled. "That sounds great. If we have fish *and* chicken, I'm happy. You know the trouble we had with Aunt Catherine and Uncle Carl at the New Year's party two years ago. We don't want that to happen again. Oh, that reminds me. I need to change their hotel reservation. They are arriving a day earlier." Anna pulled out her phone and made a digital note to call the hotel.

After lunch, the family went their separate ways. Maya and Hunter went over to his parents' house to help paint their garage. Jan played a video game in his room for an hour before driving back to Tuscaloosa for his last two weeks of college. Winnie got lost in a book on the back deck, still sulking from the veto of the Honduras trip.

Anna decided that she needed a few more plants for the flower bed on the side of the house and talked Jude into taking her to the garden nursery. He was quiet until Anna brought up work. As soon as she asked about his upcoming week, he talked nonstop about "late filers" and "month-end reports." She loved that her husband shared the stresses of his accounting job with her but wished that he would share his emotions and feelings a little more. She figured it was a "guy thing" and listened with interest to his busy schedule.

When Jude didn't ask about her week, she casually mentioned that she really needed to fit some writing in—and soon. "I'm a little stuck. I love my characters and their journey, but their lives are so routine and predictable. How interesting is a batch of cornbread? Or a broken axle?" Anna's current project was a fictional story about a family living in Boston in the early 1800s. She loved that time period and had written several novels about early American families. Most of her stories were light and fun to read, but one involved a cholera outbreak that devastated the citizens of a small town.

Jude answered without looking over. "It will come to you. It always does." And that was the end of her sharing. Jude had too much on his mind to add her latest novel to his list. Plus, he was right. The stories did always come to Anna. August was only three months away. This one better come soon.

Later that night, after planting some Gerber daisies and showering, Anna texted Jan. He had made it to his dorm safely. She then sat on the couch in the family room while Jude was watching a documentary about Pompeii from his ever-reliable recliner. Maya was still out with Hunter, and Winnie was working on an article for the school paper. Anna took out a notepad and tried to brainstorm her story. Sometimes, throwing words onto paper would create a semi-complete narrative. Unfortunately, it wasn't working tonight. She put the pad down and joined Jude at "TV staring." They watched three episodes of *Newhart* and went to bed. Another day closer to the Yearling-Day wedding gala.

1851

Sundays were Sarah's favorite day of the week. Asher observed the Sabbath and only worked when necessary, such as feeding the animals or repairing their home. The rest of the day was spent together as a family. They played games and read stories from the Bible. Sometimes the girls would put on plays for the others, which always involved makeup and singing.

Today, the Wilkes' church family was honoring them with a potluck lunch after the service. Pastor Brown's wife, Mary, organized the placement of tables and chairs on the back lawn. Sarah would bring leftover food from the wedding and vegetables from the winter garden that would not survive the five-month trip to Oregon.

"Is everyone ready?" Asher had pulled the family's wagon near the front porch. Jeremiah bounded out of the house without his shoes.

Sarah had spent precious money on new shoes for her youngest. He would probably walk twice as far as the others in his exuberance. Anna tied her bonnet on her head and found Jeremiah's shoes. The girls walked toward the wagon carrying on a conversation with themselves. Sweet Luke stood by the wagon and waited for the women to enter first. He seemed melancholy these days, and Sarah feared he was down over the upcoming move. She noticed he had been speaking to Kate Campbell recently and wondered if he was developing a fondness for her. She silently asked God to provide peace to all her children for the upcoming changes.

At the church, the Wilkes family filled their usual pew on the right side of the church. Sarah's grandfather was a sailor and had taught her sailing lingo whenever he visited. She knew that the right side of a ship was the starboard side, and she felt connected to him whenever she sat in their pew.

The church members sang "Amazing Grace," Sarah's favorite, and the pianist played "Rock of Ages" as a solo. The music fed Sarah's soul, and she found herself smiling. She reached for Asher's hand and gave it a squeeze. God would care for her family, and Sarah felt a comforting peace knowing that truth.

"Do you like to worry?" Pastor Brown began. The congregation nodded. They were familiar with his blunt preaching style. "Do you feel that worrying helps the situation? Well, I'm here to tell you that fussing and fretting are of the devil. Isaiah chapter twenty-six, verse three tells us that 'You will keep in perfect peace those whose minds are steadfast because they trust in you.' Think about that. Perfect peace. What does that look like?" Sarah pictured a spring meadow in her mind. "Not a little bit of peace. Or peace about a few things. But *perfect peace.* Perfect, tranquil peace. That's *shalom* in Hebrew. And it doesn't stop there."

Sarah noticed that the congregation was listening intently. Pastor Brown had a way of making the Word come alive. But he hit on a need today. The world didn't allow for much peace these days. President Taylor died last year. The Gold Rush had begun. And the country was divided over the interest of slaves. Sarah had to admit that she did a lot of worrying. She asked God for provisions daily but immediately began worrying as soon as she finished. Today's message was an unexpected blessing.

"Isaiah tells us that we can stay in perfect peace . . . here on Earth," Pastor Brown continued. "Notice the word *keep* in the passage. Our God promises—yes, promises—to *keep* us in peace. And not a partial peace. A perfect peace. How do we claim that promise?"

Elliott Sutter startled the crowd by yelling to the pastor, "With the blood!"

"Amen, Brother Elliott. That is correct. The second part of verse three states, 'because they trust in you.' That is the secret to a peaceful life. That is the answer you have been looking for today. It is your mind. What is your mind dwelling on this morning? Where are you abiding in thought? To have perfect peace, your mind must be on our Savior Jesus Christ. And nothing else."

The pastor continued speaking about controlling the mind, but Sarah was ironically distracted. She began thinking about the growing list of preparations needed for the upcoming trip. And the even longer list of dangers they would face. Could she simply stop her mind from thinking about them and focus on Jesus? That seemed impossible, but certainly worth trying. Sarah consciously stopped thinking about the trip and absorbed Pastor Brown's words into her mind. She could feel her jaw loosening and knew she needed to live Isaiah 26:3 today and forever.

Thank you, Lord, for speaking to me this morning.

The church picnic was wonderful and painful at the same time. The Wilkes family would probably never see their precious friends again. Abe Taylor declared that he would follow them to the Oregon Territory next spring, but Sarah knew that would not likely happen. She would write her close friends when she could, but friendships through the mail system were not the same. She would never hear Callie Davis's high-pitched laugh again. Or taste Norah Bell's blueberry cobbler. The good-byes were overwhelming, and Sarah tried her best to take her mind captive and focus on the good that was coming. And the trouble they would be in if they stayed in Oak Grove. John Morgan was becoming meaner and had threatened to hire local Otoe Indians to farm his land instead of the "lazy white men." Walking toward her husband, Sarah mentally listed off her blessings. Asher and the children were her biggest ones. She wouldn't let herself be sad today.

Back home, the family entered their sparce house. Everything needed for the journey was strategically placed near the front door. Mary Brown sent the family enough food for supper and breakfast, so Sarah would not need to light the stove again. Fidget asked to play outside, and his parents obliged. Asher tried not to work too much but needed to check on the integrity of the wagon and the animals. He enlisted Luke and Trenton to help. Sarah and the girls looked over the food supplies and wrote goodbye letters to their friends. Everyone tried not to think about the life they were about to leave behind.

CHAPTER THREE

Saturday, April 19

2025

Precisely at 1:45, Anna drove Maya and Winnie to the church. She had chosen to wear a pale-blue fitted dress with navy sandals. Maya wore a beautiful white dress with bell sleeves. Anna warned her that the sleeves would become a nuisance when opening gifts, but Maya didn't listen. She insisted on wearing the new dress anyway. Winnie wore Army green pants with a white button-up top—her getting-dressed-up uniform.

Anna was quiet on the drive. She realized that trips like this would become rare in six weeks. Maya and Hunter had purchased a two-bedroom starter home in nearby Amber Falls. Anna vowed to follow the no-visiting-the-newlyweds-for-the-first-year rule, so she would be at the mercy of Maya to visit. And she suspected that her daughter would be too busy to visit as much as Anna would like. To overcome that, Anna would plan a few more family gatherings than usual. Those would also lure Jan to drive home from Atlanta.

The church parking lot was filled with a suitable number of cars, and Anna was relieved. She let Maya walk in first to receive the gushing attention from the guests. After a few minutes, she and Winnie walked in. They found Maya already seated at the middle of a circle of chairs, talking with some of her friends. The girls had grown up together, attending Vacation Bible School, youth retreats, and college praise concerts over the years. Anna took a mental picture of the entire scene. Her oldest was getting married. The "fab five" would forever be separated. She couldn't be happier for Maya, but watching two of her birdies leave the nest forever was brutal. Strangely, Anna hadn't thought about the effect the wedding would have on Winnie. Maya and Jan had been out of the house to attend college, but they were still home for holidays, summers, and random weekends. This may be as hard on Winnie as anyone else. Of course, it could also be Winnie's greatest wish. She would effectively be an only child for a year. Well, *if* she left for school or something next year. To Anna's torment, Winter Yearling still had no concrete plans for her future.

"Look, Mom! A gravy boat. I have my own gravy boat." Anna started to laugh, but quickly realized that Maya was serious. A fancy gravy boat was every woman's wifely rite of passage. Of course, Anna still used a large measuring cup to serve gravy on holidays. But a downright, authentic gravy boat was a telltale standard for a good hostess. Anna suddenly saw Maya as a four-year-old pouring all the gravy onto her green beans on Christmas. She scolded her daughter as she jumped up and made more gravy. Anna cringed as she remembered her exasperation over the gravy. Did it really matter? What could have been a sweet memory was now a regret. Hopefully, Maya did not remember it at all.

"Remember when you yelled at me for pouring a whole boat of gravy on my plate?" Maya yelled the question across the room.

Cringe. Cringe. "Oh, I don't know if I actually yelled. You'll see, sweetheart. Holidays are stressful for the women. And lump-free gravy is like gold on the holidays." Some of the older women nodded in agreement. Meg, a loyal best friend, put her arm around Anna in agreement.

Maya continued opening gifts while the guests enjoyed delightful finger foods and Jane Nelson's famous rhubarb punch. The afternoon was lovely, and she even caught Winnie engaging in conversation. This is what Anna dreamed about when Maya was a baby.

As the first guests began to leave, Maya stood. "Before we end today, I would like to make a toast to my lifelong role model. Mom, you taught me what a godly woman should be. And I hope I can be half the wife you are. Congratulations on twenty-five years with Dad. And I can't wait to watch the next twenty-five."

Nellie Campbell raised her punch glass with the shaky arm of an eighty-seven-year-old widow. "Don't forget that the first fifty years are the hardest." The crowd of ladies laughed and began picking up loose wrapping paper. Anna rushed to her daughter and hugged her for a full ten seconds. Maya had never called her a "role model" before, and the words were cemented into Anna's heart. The church shower was officially perfect, just as Anna had prayed it would be.

After loading every gift into Anna's SUV, the Yearling women drove home. Maya talked nonstop about the kitchenware she received. She marveled at the new recipes she could try and planned to have her family, including Grandpa Tom and Grandma Sylvia, over for a cookout as soon as she and Hunter returned from their honeymoon.

Hunter's parents, Grace and Gene Day, had surprised their son and his fiancé at Christmas with a weeklong honeymoon cruise on *Plunder*, the newest ship in the Jewel Cruise Line fleet. The trip was scheduled for the day after the wedding, so the couple would fly to Miami from Birmingham three hours after the reception. They would stay at a newer hotel near the cruise port and board the ship before lunch the next day. It was a tight schedule, but they agreed to do whatever it took to sail on the marvelous treasure ship.

Identical in design to its sister ship, *Golden Fortune*, *Plunder* was a mega ship designed to look like an authentic pirate ship. Billed as the only "treasure ships" in the world, *Golden Fortune* and *Plunder* offered passengers the chance to win $50,000 in gold each week. Members of the purser's offices provided clues during the cruises that led to a treasure box filled with gold coins hidden each week. Media coverage of winners, complete with pictures and video clippings of ornate boxes being found, had skyrocketed the cruise line's success. Cabins on the two ships were selling quickly, and the line recently announced plans for a third ship, *Buccaneer Bounty*, to be launched in 2026.

The Days booked directly from the line's website after Gene's brother and sister-in-law raved about their experience on *Golden Fortune*. Maya and Hunter did not plan to spend much energy treasure hunting but were becoming increasingly excited about solving the clues. Maya read that the first clue would be placed in each cabin at embarkation. She could only imagine the cryptic hint they would find on the first day.

When the girls arrived home, Jude helped bring the gifts into the house. Maya and Hunter would close on their home the Monday before the wedding, so they had no place to store wedding gifts but their parents' homes. Their new furniture and appliances would be delivered the day after closing, as space was becoming tight. The timing of the deliveries was not ideal but would work.

Today's haul was stored in Jan's room. Once Jude had brought in the last of the gifts, Maya and Winnie sat down and went through every box and visualized each item being used in the Day household. Anna and Jude sat in the living room, and she recounted the details of the final wedding shower. "It was perfect. Maya has pretty much everything she needs to get started. Someone from her company gave them an adorable welcome mat with "One of those Days" printed on it. I don't know how I feel about all of this. She'll only be thirty minutes away. But Jan will be four hours away. We're one month away from the 'big Yearling break-up.'"

"No," Jude countered. "We're one month away from our children fulfilling their purposes. Don't be so dramatic. Maya and Hunter are successful in their jobs. It's time for them to launch out into their own lives. Pun intended. And Jan will be great. That internship was quite competitive. He will be working for a major pharmaceutical company one month from now. We did exactly what we were supposed to do. We raised independent, caring children who love Jesus. We guided them into their futures. Well, two out of three. Winnie doesn't believe in the concept of *future*."

"Ha! She does believe in the future. She just doesn't want to think about it in the present."

Jude found a Bogart movie for the couple to watch, and eventually their daughters joined. When the movie ended, Anna set out sandwich fixings for the family—minus Jan—to eat on the deck. The weather in May was beautiful. Soon, the humidity and mosquitoes would become a nuisance. But not yet. May was perfect.

1851

Today was the day. The Wilkes family would be leaving Oak Grove forever. They would meet the wagon train in Independence tomorrow.

Families traveled in large groups for safety and to get extra help with chores and animal care. The group collectively hired a wagon master who knew the trail extensively. Usually former fur traders, the wagon masters had traveled the terrain back and forth many times.

While Asher focused on the tangible aspects of the trip, such as provisions and transportation, Sarah focused on the psychological aspects. They made an efficient team. Thinking of the emotional toll the long journey would take, Sarah stored two ribbons and a whistle as birthday gifts for Jade, Jewel, and Jeremiah. She reassured Luke that God would provide him a wife in Oregon.

She walked around with a smile as Asher loaded everything they owned into their wagon. "This is the day!" she repeated over and over like a mantra.

But Trenton was not buying it. Her middle son was a worrier like his mother. Sarah tried to reassure him by encouraging him to give his concerns to God and leave them there. But his mind continued to focus on potential problems. *What if we get sick? Who will take care of us? What if we get lost? I'm not a strong swimmer.* To preempt his swirling mind, Sarah purchased a large leather satchel for him to carry on the trip. She filled it with loose paper, pens, and three bottles of ink. When they arrived at Independence tomorrow, she would ask him to be the family recorder. Hopefully, with an ongoing task to be completed each day, Trenton would not dwell on his worries as much. Sarah planned to dictate her thoughts to him at night and have him write them on the pages. He had beautiful penmanship—better than Sarah's—and would unknowingly help her create a detailed record of their trip. She would fill in details when Trenton was busy.

"Come here, Star," Asher called to his wife. He had called her Star for as long as Sarah could remember. She loved the nickname, especially because Asher claimed that she lit up his dark life when she was around. "Look at the bedding. Am I forgetting anything?"

Sarah walked around the schooner and counted the pillows and blankets in the early morning darkness. They were tied in bundles around the perimeter of the wagon, and she confirmed that there were enough for the family. Traveling in the late spring might be warm, but evenings, especially in the mountains, would be cool regardless of the date.

Emigrants must wisely time their departure for the West. The trip took approximately five months and was carefully navigated. The travelers must leave late enough for the grass to have grown plentiful enough to feed their livestock, but early enough to cross the Rockies before snow set in. Most families left in late April or early May. They aimed to cross Independence Rock by July fourth.

The prairie schooner was for carrying supplies, not people. Family members would travel the entire two-thousand-mile route on foot unless they were deemed too sick to stand. They would walk up to twenty miles each day. Sarah prayed that the children's shoes would not wear out before Oregon. They only had one pair each. She also prayed that their feet would not grow much over the summer.

Sarah watched Asher survey their supplies. Trenton was carefully logging the information his dad was voicing. "Flour: eight hundred pounds. Sugar: one hundred pounds. Eggs: two barrels. Coffee: one hundred pounds. Tea: six pounds. Bacon: four barrels. Pickles: one keg. Beans: twelve sacks. Dried peaches: four sacks. Lard: two and a half pounds."

Asher looked up to survey everything, then resumed. "Now for the supplies." Trenton turned a page in the ledger. "One chest of clothing and blankets. Tents and supplies. Ax. Hatchet. Knives: six. Rope. Axle grease. Water keg. Candles. Pans and stove." The list went on. Anything that could melt or break, such as bacon or eggs, was packed in containers of grains. Luke was responsible for sorting and maintaining seeds and planting tools. They would be critical to begin the fall and spring crops in the Oregon Territory.

Church members had provided a substantial donation of money for the Wilkes to use at Fort Kearny and Fort Laramie for replenished supplies. Sarah and Asher had promised their house and land to Meg, Sarah's oldest sister. Her husband, in turn, gave them a milk cow, two goats, and two mules. The mules would carry supplies on their backs and help the two oxen pull the wagon when needed, and the cow would provide milk and possibly fresh meat if game and buffalo became scarce. Asher kept two horses, Remy and Red, and sold the rest. He and Luke were the only ones proficient enough to ride them up and down slopes.

Just as the sun began lighting the sky, Asher gathered the group in a circle. They had said their goodbyes to family and friends the previous day. Today, they would say goodbye to their Missouri life. "Heavenly Father," Asher began, "we thank You for the provisions You provided. It is everything we need. We pray for Your protection on the Trail, and Your extra provision of strength and endurance. Bless the wagon master with knowledge and the others in the company with patience. In Your mighty name we pray. Amen." The others added soft "amens" in unison.

As Sarah looked back at her house one more time, Asher and Luke led their family northwest toward Independence. They would meet up with the wagon company tonight and begin the trek west on Monday morning.

The girls had already started chattering, and Fidget was wielding a stick like a sword when Sarah heard a cry from behind her house. Her former house.

"Wait! Wait!" It was Amelia, Sarah's middle sister. Amelia was the quietest in the family. She preferred reading books to talking and made the world's best rabbit stew. "I have something to give you."

As Sarah walked toward her sister, a tear ran down her cheek. She had managed to control her emotions yesterday. Today was a different test. Today she was leaving Missouri forever. "Amelia. What are you doing up so early? Did you walk here all by yourself?"

"Yes. I couldn't let you leave without one more hug. And to give you this." Amelia held out a beautiful hardbound journal. It had a leather cover and blank pages inside. "I thought you could keep a diary of your travels and your new life. Maybe we will visit someday, and you can read it to me. I sold one of our hens to buy it. But you are worth it. You are the best mom a bashful orphan could have ever wanted."

Sarah began crying heavily and hugged her sister. "Thank you for this. I will write you when I can, sweet Amelia. Asher said that there's a post at Fort Kearny. I promise to send a note when we are there. And I will send a longer report with the wagon master when he heads back to Missouri." She hugged Amelia one more time and turned toward her family. "I love you!"

"I love you too!" Amelia sat on the front porch of the house and watched Sarah's family walk away. Their schooner was loaded to the brim, and the children and livestock were walking at a good pace. She prayed for the protection of her oldest sister. The one who took on the burden of caring for her sisters when tragedy struck.

When Sarah rejoined her family, she discovered that they were playing a walking game. Asher had started them on the alphabet game. Sarah laughed to herself realizing that the family was already bored after only five minutes of walking.

Trenton reported that Jade had found "Asher" and Jewel had found "boots." He himself found "cow," and the family was now waiting for Fidget to find something that started with the letter *D*.

"Sound it out, Jeremiah," Sarah encouraged. "You know what a *D* sounds like."

"Duh . . . duh . . . Daddy," Fidget exclaimed. "I found Daddy!"

"Well, I didn't know I was lost," Asher added. "Thank you for finding me." The children giggled, and Trenton declared that it was Papa's turn. "Everything. I see everything."

"No, Papa," Jade chided. "You can't find everything. Only one thing."

"Very well then," Asher continued. "I see an embrace." He then walked to his wife and gave her a hug before she could stop walking. The girls aahed, and the boys eewed. And Sarah cried.

"I see my family," Sarah added for her word. "The most wonderful family God ever created."

CHAPTER FOUR

Monday, April 21
2025

Easter Sunday had been a restful day, and the entire family appreciated it. Pastor Ed spoke about the need for margins in the lives of the congregation, and Anna felt less guilty about enjoying the Sabbath by worshipping with fellow believers, napping, and watering her garden. Winnie brought up Honduras again at the family lunch, and Jude patiently explained that this year was not the time to fly to another part of the world. He promised to investigate possibilities when their lives "calmed down a bit." He switched the subject by asking Winnie if she would like to work part-time for the summer in his office. He always had a need for filing. She tried not to appear insulted but made it clear that she was not a "numbers person." She worked with ideas. Of course, Jude and Anna kept their frustration hidden. But later they discussed their rudderless daughter while getting ready for bed.

"She's running out of time, Jude. Maya had visited three colleges before the end of her junior year. Winnie doesn't even want to talk about college."

Jude sat beside Anna on the bed. "We are going to have to give this one to God, Ann. He loves Winnie even more than we do. And He has a perfect plan for her. We just have to pray she finds that path. We can't drag her kicking and screaming where we want her to go."

"You make me sound like an ogre," Anna said.

"No. I'm not saying that. We just can't control everything. I like to think that Winnie is being extra careful with her future."

Anna sighed. "It feels to me that Winnie is being extra careless. I'm glad she has another year. We can give her this summer to be carefree. But she will have to get serious when school starts back in the fall."

Jude looked at Anna and put his hand on her shoulder. "It's her life, whether we like it or not. Give it to God and sleep well."

"You're right. But that's not easy for me. Thanks for sailing through life with me. Well, for walking through life. We don't want you to get motion sickness." Jude hugged his wife and laughed at her joke. Then he asked God to steer his youngest child to her perfect future.

The house was buzzing as usual on Monday morning. Jude and Maya were getting ready to go to work, and Winnie had already left for school. Anna had a morning full of errands, which would cut down the amount of writing she would get done that day.

As she was walking to her car thirty minutes later, Anna's phone buzzed. She cringed when she saw her editor's name pop on the screen. *Laney Oates.* Her first impulse was to ignore the call, but she knew that would be a mistake. She had a contract to complete her next novel by August first and was grateful to have a publisher willing to pay for her work. But her latest novel was going nowhere. Anna's creative legs were walking in quicksand. When she began writing about a family traveling from Boston in 1822, she saw a sweet story of a mother keeping a family of seven healthy and happy. But that story quickly became boring. With no technology and very little personal interactions on their journey, the story didn't write itself like Anna's previous books had. But Witness Publishing wanted a story from the early American period, and Anna Yearling promised them an amazing tale. Unfortunately, August first was coming quickly. And this summer was going to be the busiest of her life.

Anna pressed the image of the green phone receiver on her screen. "Hey, Laney. How was Indianapolis?"

"Hi there. It was great! We picked up a chain bookstore, but I can't tell you about that yet. How is the Boston family?"

"Still in Boston. I haven't gotten them out of their house yet. This one has me stumped. But don't worry. I will meet the deadline. This week and next are uneventful, except for the weekend. Jan is graduating on Saturday, and Mother's Day is Sunday. But I will devote the rest of my time to the happy family. I promise."

"You don't have to promise. I know you will make the deadline. You always do. Congratulations on the graduation. Two through college is a big feat. Pat yourself on the back for that one."

Anna rolled her eyes. Maya and Jan had done all of the work. She couldn't help them with logistics and biochemistry. She wasn't even sure what they did in their jobs. "Thanks, but those kids did it themselves. I will keep you updated. At the very least, I'll let you know when the family hits the road."

"Sounds good. Happy Mother's Day! Talk to you soon."

"Bye." As the pressure to write mounted, Anna's clock sped up. She rushed through her grocery shopping and Amazon returns before skipping hot cocoa at the Beanery. Once home, she put the groceries away quickly and sat at her desk. "Let's get you packed up, unnamed family."

Anna worked through lunch and managed to sketch out a timeline for the journey and write over one thousand words. She was still a little behind schedule but should be able to catch up over the next few weeks.

1851

The walk to Independence was thankfully pleasant. The children were in good spirits, and the animals pulled their weight with ease. Asher was pleased; therefore Sarah was pleased. The family met the wagon company a mile north of the town square shortly before suppertime on Saturday. There they waited for the rest of the families to gather before readying to leave for the Oregon Territory on Monday.

Twelve families would be traveling together. Ten were heading to the Oregon Territory, and two would separate at the "parting of the ways" near Fort Hall and head to California with dreams of golden riches. The second group would join another group if all went as planned. Half of the families travelled with one schooner, while the other half had two. Two of the schooners had family names painted on the covers. Those with two wagons carried food in one and supplies in the other. Sarah tried not to envy those who were able to carry furniture. She wished she could have brought the table the Asher had made her, but quickly gave thanks to God for what she could bring, especially her husband and children.

The Wilkes made camp near the Montgomery family. Sarah was thankful for the friendliness of Betsy Montgomery. The woman had curly brown hair with round, rosy cheeks and walked everywhere with a perpetual smile. She introduced herself promptly and named her children for Sarah. "That's Tyler. He's seventeen. And strong as an ox. My next boy is Gomer. He's a dreamer. Job is next. He's twelve. And Annie is eight. They are excited to travel. We can't wait to see the Oregon Territory and the mountains. Did you hear that the soil is as black as coal? God willing, we will be tending winter crops by October."

Sarah introduced her family to Betsy in chronological order and shared her excitement about the fertile soil. Luke and Tyler were already talking intently by the Wilkes' wagon. Being close in age, they would surely become close friends. After the introductions, Betsy excused herself to go check on their wagon. Sarah thought it odd that Betsy did not mention her husband but quickly pushed the thought away. Today was an unusual day. None of the travelers would be in their right minds for the next few months.

As Sarah was looking for folding chairs, Asher walked up with a tall, wiry man sporting a patchwork vest and white hair sticking in every direction. Her husband explained that he was the wagon master and his name was Spit. Sarah quickly figured out why.

"It's so nice to meet you, sir. Thank you for leading our group. Do you have a formal name?"

Spit chuckled to himself. "No, ma'am. Ain't never been called nothin' but Spit. You just holler if you be needing anything. But not in the early morning. That's when I be speaking to my Maker."

Sarah thanked Spit again and watched him walk off with Asher. Her entire family's lives depended upon Spit's knowledge of the treacherous terrain. Doubt began to creep in, but Sarah reminded herself that there was no turning back now. They had nowhere to live, and Asher had nowhere to work back in Oak Grove. Onward, ho!

Sunday had been a relatively relaxing day for the women. The men were purchasing final provisions and securing their schooners. They were also filling their water kegs from a nearby spring. There was a blanket of excitement over the camp, and the children were quickly becoming friends with one another. Tyler and Luke were usually standing beside each other, and little Annie Montgomery followed Jewel and Jade everywhere. Trenton didn't talk much and kept to himself. He spent most of the day sitting by three other boys his age. They were whittling sharp points onto the ends of sticks, while Trenton pretended to be adding figures on a blank piece of paper. He was so tentative, and Sarah wondered if this trip would bring him out of his shell a little.

As always, Fidget did not sit still. He went from wagon to wagon introducing himself and asking for candy. When a new family arrived, he was at the front of the welcoming party looking for children his age. Sarah laughed to herself as she thought about tying a bell to one of his shoes so she could keep up with him.

Sarah was amazed that three of the women in the camp were with child. They would be expected to walk the Trail with the others and pull their weight making camp each night. Susan Franklin expected to give birth in a few weeks. Caring for a newborn would be exhausting, but "many hands made light work." The others would step in and help, even providing goat milk to keep the baby fed.

Sarah didn't roam around to meet the other families. She expected to get to know them quite well on the journey. In fact, the ten families traveling to the Oregon Territory would be the only family she would have soon. They would celebrate their milestones and mourn their losses together. Sarah hoped for a new best friend she could consider a sister.

When the last family arrived, Spit gathered the group together to discuss the plans. "Welcome to Spit's great adventure." No one laughed. "This here trail is dangerous and ugly. We will be exhausted every night. But if you follow my directions, you will make it out West safely. If any of you bought one of them fancy guidebooks, burn it now. You wasted yer money. I've been traveling the trail for twenty-five years. First as a trapper and later as a guide. You must follow my commands to stay safe." A murmur fell over the camp. Decisions were made to place lives into Spit's weathered hands. Young and old would depend upon him to lead them, feed them, and protect them. The crowd finally quieted. "We aim to make it to Fort Kearny in two weeks and Fort Laramie by the middle of June. In between the forts, we'll cross the South Platte. If we can make it to Independence Rock by July fourth, we will avoid the heavy snows and git to Oregon City by early September. That's a lot of time we'll spend together. So, git to knowin' each other. And look out fer each other. We are our only protection till the next fort."

Spit paused and allowed the group to chatter a moment, then he resumed. "Tomorrow we will cross the Missouri River. We will ferry the wagons, women, and children. Men should swim your horses and mules across. The price is five dollars a head—person and animal—to take the ferry, but the Marshall landing charges my groups three dollars and fifty cents. Have your money ready. Buckaroos, stay close to the middle and hold on. If you fall in, no one will come to getcha."

Sarah cringed at the last remark. She would have to hold Fidget with both arms. Luke and Trenton would swim the horses, and Asher would swim the mules. The girls would sit quietly beside the schooner. *Father, please be with us tomorrow. Slow the waters for every family. Amen.*

"Git a good night's sleep. We'll leave early in the morning. A representative of the state will be walking around taking names. Make sure that your names are on the list so your departure will be doc-ee-mented."

Monday began with calm breezes and chirping birds. As he forewarned, Spit sat away from the camp, talking to God with an open Bible on his lap. Asher gathered his family for a traveling prayer, and Sarah served her husband and children bacon and beans. Nearly every meal on the Trail would consist of bacon and beans. The women would sometimes prepare dough in the mornings and allow it to rise during the day so bread could be eaten at suppertime. But the treat of fresh bread would be rare. Coffee was had by everyone, including the animals. The rich flavor masked the strong mineral taste of the stream and river waters. Cows and goats provided milk, which would occasionally be hung below the wagons to be churned into butter over the course of the day.

As the individual families were finishing their morning meals, winds began to whip. Sarah hoped this wasn't a sign of storms to come. She had heard stories of wagons being blown into rocks and people being struck by lightning as they walked. She felt her worry about the storms increasing, then remembered Pastor Brown's message. Abiding in Jesus would keep her in perfect peace, so she began softly singing her favorite hymn. It worked. Her uneasiness abated—for now.

Spit sent word among the travelers that they would be leaving in "three shakes of a coyote's tail." Sarah had no idea what that meant, but figured it was time to load up and move out. She quickly rinsed the breakfast dishes and secured them in a small crate on the wagon. The children gathered around her, and Sarah noticed that each was smiling. People, especially children, were adventurers by nature.

Maybe this move will be the start of a beautiful chapter for our family.

Before the wagons began moving, Brother Barton said a word of prayer. He was traveling alone with his sister's family. His wife and two children had died when dysentery spread through St. Joseph, Missouri. His sister also lost an infant in the outbreak. She was traveling with her much-older husband and his three daughters.

When the prayer was finished, the group broke into three verses of "My Faith Looks up to Thee." As soon as the hymn was completed, families headed to their wagons. The time was now. Those with fewer oxen went first. The large animals trampled valuable grass and created large ruts in the mud. With two oxen, the Wilkes family started fourth in line. Over time, stops and starts would vary, but the group would plan to stop for lunches, or nooning, and dinners together at one time and location.

"Wagons, ho!" Spit started the convoy. He was traveling on a dark-brown mare with oversized saddle bags. He claimed to have enough beans and dried fruit to make it to Fort Kearny, but traveling families would regularly invite him to join their meals.

The first hour of the trip was surprisingly quiet. Most of the adults were pondering the long journey and their new life. The children were figuring out their new routines. Sarah noticed that Jade was smiling broadly and looking from side to side. The other children's gazes were focused on the ground. But Jade was taking everything in. She had always been inquisitive, and Sarah marveled at how her daughter's eyes scanned everything in front of her. Asher and

Luke were directing the oxen on horseback, and from what Sarah could tell, they were not needed. The large beasts were following the wagon in front of them at a steady pace.

The group heard the Missouri River before they saw it. They had traveled six miles west before they encountered their first major hurdle. The first ferry they saw at the Independence Crossing had a line of about forty schooners. Sarah figured that it would take two days for the people in line to cross. But Spit led their company to the right, or north to the Marshall Ferry. It took thirty minutes to get the group to that ferry, but the line was much shorter. Sarah counted eleven wagons waiting.

Spit's company fell in line, and Sarah was relieved to see wagons crossing with seeming ease. She and the children sat inside their schooner while they waited to cross. Spit warned that they shouldn't unpack any supplies or food until they were safely across and over the state line into the Kansas Territory.

"Where's Papa?" Fidget asked.

"He's with Spit," Sarah replied. "They have to pay the operator and secure our place in line." She noticed that the children seemed uneasy about the upcoming crossing. "I am excited about crossing the river. Is anyone else?"

Jade immediately raised her hand. "I am. It will be like we are crossing the Red Sea with Moses."

Trenton laughed. "Maybe God will part it for us, and we can walk through the mud."

"Nonsense, children." Their mother laughed. "We will ride safely by the schooner. The operators know how to get us across. We just need to be quiet so the oxen don't get spooked. We don't want them moving and tipping over the ferry."

Jewel gasped. "It can tip over?"

"Well, it could if we all ran to one side," Sarah explained. "But we won't do that. And Trenton and Luke will be right by us on the horses. Papa will be behind with the mules. This will be the first wonderful story to tell of our travels."

The children quieted for the hour it took to move to the head of the line. Asher appeared at the back of the wagon and asked for Luke and Trenton to join him. Sarah said a prayer with the remaining children and tried to keep them distracted as their schooner was slowly led onto the ferry. Another wagon was brought on behind them.

With a sudden lurch, the ferry began to move. Water splashed over the sides, but the wagon remained steady. Luke spoke to the oxen from his swimming horse, and all involved remained calm. Sarah could see that Trenton was straining to keep his horse from stopping, but Asher urged it on as he swam with the mules. In what seemed like less than ten minutes, the ferry was stopped, and Luke was calling the oxen to move forward. The daunting task was over. The family was reunited and began the hour trek to their nooning spot just over the Kansas territory line.

At lunch, the children ate in silence. Sarah did not expect such calm. She could only assume that the change was still new. It was still ongoing. And the children were processing their new lives. Sarah regretted that she hadn't prepared them better.

At dinnertime, Fidget declared that he couldn't eat another bean.

"This is our third day traveling, boy," Asher reminded. "You will starve if you don't eat another bean."

The reply was not acceptable to Fidget. "I don't like beans anymore. May I have rabbit stew instead?"

Fidget's four siblings looked up in shock. Sarah, knowing how to appease the boy, scooped more beans onto his plate. "Here you go. Fresh rabbit stew." The family laughed, and Fidget made a performance out of eating the remaining beans.

"Yum," Fidget declared. "This rabbit stew is delicious. Better than Aunt Melia's. Look out, rabbit stew. I'm gonna eat-cha."

Sarah looked at Asher. He grinned back. That boy would keep both of them busy for the next ten years or so.

CHAPTER FIVE

Tuesday, April 22
2025

Tuesday began as a normal day. The family was buzzing with their usual morning routines. Anna got up thirty minutes earlier to spend a little more time on her book. As she was taking a bagel out of a bag, she heard Maya call. "Mom! Get in here!" Anna rushed to the living room to find Winnie standing face-to-face with Maya. Nothing seemed out of the ordinary until Winnie turned around.

Winnie's eyebrows were missing. Anna gasped. "What happened? Did you do this?"

"Yes, I did. If the family is going to treat me like a child, I'm going to act like a child. I shaved them off."

Anna was speechless.

Maya spoke next. "I really must get going. We have two vendors coming at the same time this morning. Don't flip out, Mom. It will be fine."

Anna was still speechless, and Winnie marched off to grab a protein drink to down on the way to school. "Jude, would you please come down here? Now!" Anna had found her voice.

When Jude casually appeared in the kitchen, he didn't even notice that Winnie was missing eyebrows. Anna pointed them out, and Winnie again declared that she was acting like a child because she was being treated like a child.

In his no-nonsense manner, Jude let the incident roll over. "Very well. Your curfew is now ten o'clock."

"Jude! This is a big deal! What will everyone think? What about the wedding pictures? Her eyebrows won't grow back in six weeks. The wedding is in less than six weeks. This is a disaster!"

"No, Mom. Children in Honduras living in dumpsters is a disaster. This is an annoyance. There is a difference."

Jude looked up. "She has a point, Anna. Winnie feels the need to annoy us right now. Let her do it. But remember this when she asks to go to Six Flags with Macy on Memorial Day. I think it would be better for her to help us work around the house that day." Winnie let out a sigh and marched off to her car. When she slammed the front door, Anna began crying.

"Why does she push my buttons? We have so much going on right now. I can't deal with her tantrums."

"Anna, this isn't about you. Winnie doesn't feel heard. She doesn't feel seen. We have spent so much time this past year talking about the wedding and Jan's internship, she must feel left out. Let her have her statement. Stop crying. The eyebrows will grow back."

Anna dabbed her eyes with a napkin. "I hear you. That sounds great. But Winnie doesn't want to do anything. There is nothing we can do to include her. She acts like she wants to be isolated."

"Well, she wants to go to Honduras." Jude filled his travel mug with coffee and turned to leave.

"You and I agree that she can't fly off to Honduras by herself. Maybe we can find a way that she can write about the orphanage or something. Everything was going so perfectly. What stunt will she pull next?"

"I've got to go. I'll talk with her tonight. Don't worry about it. Concentrate on your book for the next few hours. See you tonight." Jude gave Anna a quick hug and bolted out the door, off to his world of numbers and spreadsheets. Anna made a glass of ice water and walked toward her desk. She asked God to help her focus on her story and help her parent her wildcard child.

1851

The first full day of traveling was blessedly uneventful. The company traversed almost twenty miles on their way to Topeka, Kansas. Most of the path was cleared by previous travelers. Where there were obstacles, the men took turns with shovels and hatchets to unblock the path.

At dusk, the group made camp on a prairie clearing. Families quickly dug holes to be used as makeshift bathrooms and started fires for their evening meals. Sarah and the girls set out dishes for the household and began heating bacon in beans. They would prepare dough tomorrow morning to have fresh bread at their next meal. Fidget would appreciate that. Trenton was milking the goats and cows, and Asher was meeting with the men of the company.

"Rules of the Trail" were set while the men met. Horace Moore was elected the leader of the loose council, and the men returned to their families with the new covenants.

Asher sat beside his wife and said a blessing over the food and asked for continuing travel mercies. As he began to share the new rules, he noticed that Jeremiah was missing. "Where is Fidget?"

"He needed to run a little bit, so I let him go play with that group of boys over there," Sarah said. "I'll call him in a few minutes."

"Very well, Star. Let's go over the rules." Asher looked at each member of his family before he continued. "First, we must follow Spit's commands, even if we don't like them or don't agree with them." Sarah nodded in agreement. "We've established a rotation of the men to stay up and guard the camp. We will have two-hour posts every third day. I will take the early morning shift tomorrow morning."

"I can help, Papa!" Luke announced.

"I'm very thankful, son, but we decided that only the men of the family will take the guard duties. We will have plenty for the others to do as well. Next, we wake at dawn and leave within an hour. No swearing and no alcohol."

Luke laughed. "Spit has already broken the swearing rule."

Asher smiled. "Yes, he has. But he's not part of the company. We can't very well kick him out, can we?" The others smiled along with Luke. "Now, if anyone becomes sick, we will all help where needed. We will treat Indians as friends unless otherwise told. We will travel on Sundays if we are behind."

"So many rules," Jade announced with a sigh.

"Always watch for snakes," Asher continued. "We will continue to walk in the rain unless we see a tornado with our eyes." Trenton looked at his mother. "Women will not be alone with men who are not their husbands. And we should boil drinking water whenever we can."

After their father shared the rules, the children pummeled him with questions: "When won't the Indians be friends?" "What if Mama gets sick?" "Can I ride Remy tomorrow?" Asher answered the questions with patience, while Sarah called for their youngest to return to their camp. She made him a plate of beans and asked the girls to help her wash the rest of the dishes in the nearby stream. As she was gathering the dinnerware, Fidget walked up.

"Hey, Maw. May I eat more of that yummy rabbit stew?"

"Yes, son," Sarah answered. "Go sit by Papa. You plate is on the chair." She noticed that he wasn't wearing shoes. "Where are your shoes?"

"I lost 'em."

"What?" Sarah immediately stopped walking.

"I lost 'em to Berty Ledbetter. We was paying snickies, and I lost. I got snake eyes. He won my shoes."

Sarah turned toward her son. "You gambled your shoes? The good Lord tells us we should work hard for what we get. That means no gambling. Let's tell Papa." Surprisingly, Fidget walked toward his father with little regard.

Asher immediately noticed his son's bare feet. "Boy, you need to keep your shoes on in these prairies. Snakes are running this season." Fidget simply nodded his head.

Sarah held her son by his shoulder. "He doesn't have them. He gambled his shoes away."

To her horror, Asher began laughing. "I remember betting my shoes to Gabriel Jones when I was eight. Had to walk barefoot in the snow for two months before my parents could get another pair." Sarah didn't know how to respond. "Don't ye worry, Star. We'll try to get them back. C'mon, boy." Asher and Fidget walked toward the circle. As she watched the conversation, Sarah knew her son would not get his shoes back. He lost them fair and square. Now she could only hope they could find shoes for Fidget in Fort Kearny in two weeks. Having to walk in his bare feet would be punishment enough. Sarah shook her head and asked God to help her parent her wildcard child.

CHAPTER SIX

Saturday, May 10
2025

Graduation day! Child number two was graduating from college. The ceremony was at 1:00, so the family drove to Tuscaloosa early that morning rather than arriving the night before. Jude's parents drove separately as they wanted to get home before dark. They would skip the post-graduation meal.

Anna chose to wear pants and sensible shoes in anticipation of the walking they would be doing throughout the day. She begged Winnie to pencil in eyebrows for the graduation and subsequent family pictures, but her daughter refused. Jude finally convinced her that Winnie's eyebrows were not an end-of-the-world situation, and Anna did her best to ignore the missing features.

Jan would participate in the Arts and Sciences ceremony with nearly one thousand other graduates. The multiple ceremonies were carefully choreographed to allow time for participants and their guests to enter and exit between each observance.

Jude parked the car in a visitor's lot near the stadium, and his dad parked two spots away. The family walked through crowds of people toward Jan's dormitory. Eagerness was in the air as future alumni were walking about with black gowns flowing in the breeze. Family members and friends were following and documenting the day with plenty of photos on their phones. Anna stopped to take a candid picture of the excitement.

Jan had brought most of his clothes home on the weekend of the anniversary party. The rest of his "stuff" would fit in the back of his truck and could easily be taken home in one trip. Grandma Sylvia and Grandpa Tom were available to carry any "spillover" if needed. Anna had reserved a small moving truck to move Jan to Atlanta on Memorial Day. He would be bringing his bedroom furniture and a used couch Anna found online. That was only two weeks away. Time was moving too quickly.

The group found Jan already wearing his gown and holding his cap. Anna was the first to hug him before the picture-taking began. They joined the crowd walking to the Coliseum. To no one's surprise, the grandparents kept up with the pace easily. At the indoor stadium, Jan broke from the group and headed to the graduate staging area while the rest found seats. Anna hoped for the perfect "middle" seats but was satisfied with "slightly to the right and higher up." Before she sat, she distributed the photography assignments.

"Jude, you will video the entire time Jan is walking to, over, and away from the stage. Tom, you will capture the handshake. And Sylvia, you will make a sound recording of the speaker announcing Jan's name. Maya and Hunter can take random shots. Do you mind helping, Winnie?"

"Sure, Mom. Would you like me to hang from the rafters to get the overhead shot? Or I could pull a drone out of my pocket for a close-up." The entire family chuckled at Winnie's sarcastic response.

"Okay. Okay. I know this is a bit much. But Jan has worked very hard for this day. We took tons of pictures of you, Maya. And will for you, Miss Drone Pilot." Winnie smiled and agreed to take pictures of the family taking pictures of Jan. It was all very nonspontaneous, but the family knew that Anna would prepare a beautiful photo book of the day. It would be added to the family's growing stack of milestone photo books.

After a few minutes of chatter, the traditional *Pomp and Circumstances* tune began to play over the arena's sound system. The audience stood as the stage party and graduates marched in. Anna quickly scanned the students and narrowed down her son to two possibilities. The second one looked up at the crowd and smiled. Instantly, Anna recognized Jan. She followed him and watched his mortarboard until everyone was seated.

University officials made opening remarks, and a speaker droned on about taking the "road less traveled." Anna scoffed him in her mind. *The road less traveled doesn't pay rent on an Atlanta apartment.* When the speaker finished, a buzz lifted in the air. An official declared the students as graduates, and the crowd erupted in applause. He next asked the friends and family members to "hold their applause" as the deserving graduates were called by name.

"Places, everyone!" Anna said to the family, beaming with pride. "You know what to do."

Students receiving Fine Arts and Performing Arts degrees stood first. Anna discovered that Natural Sciences and Mathematics were the last division of the college, so Jan would be called toward the end. He would graduate in the Department of Chemistry and Biochemistry, right after the biologists and before the geographists, if that was even a word.

Regrettably, the names were read by a voiceover service that used professional recording, and for an hour the crowd listened to monotone names being listed over and over. For the most part, family and friends were respectfully quiet while the virtual readers kept their pace.

"Here we go, Mom." Maya tugged Anna's blouse. "They are almost finished with biology."

"Cameras up!" The family laughed as Anna mocked her own compulsiveness. They were ready to complete their individual assignments.

The students with Chemistry and Biochemistry degrees were passing by quickly. "Ian Rosenwald. Natalie Smith. Deja Tucker. Katelyn Wright . . ." *Toot! Toot!* Yelling and cheering exploded three rows in front of the Yearlings. Someone began blasting an airhorn. And two teenagers held up a huge sign for the blessed Wright child.

Not only could Anna not hear her son's name being called by the tireless robot, but she could not see over the hideous sign. She stood with her camera at eye level, hoping that Jan's name would be called after the commotion, but was disappointed to hear the Department of Geography introduced.

"What just happened?" Maya turned to her dad.

"I don't know, but Mom's gonna flip out," Winnie whispered quietly. "Did anyone get a shot?"

Sylvia spoke up quietly. "I recorded the air horn."

"And I got several pictures of the big sign." Gene spoke as cheerfully as possible. Everyone looked cautiously at Anna.

"We didn't get anything. I didn't hear his name. This is a tragedy."

"No, honey. This is definitely not a tragedy. Today is a blessing from God. Let's lower our voices so the geographists can be heard."

"How am I going to make a book with pictures of the back of a sign?" Anna was softly muttering to herself while resisting the urge to pummel Katelyn's family.

Jude squeezed her hand. "We'll laugh about this someday. And you will make a beautiful book with the rest of today's pictures. It will be fine." Anna knew she should let it go, but she couldn't. Jan would never have another college graduation. Sure, he might go to graduate school someday. But Jude's parents were getting older. And the family was scattering. What will she do without this book? She can't just skip this one. And Winnie's eyebrows won't look right either. It was all a disaster.

As the family watched the rest of the ceremony, Anna quietly developed a plan to use artificial intelligence to create mock images of Jan walking across the stage. She would fix Winnie's brows and make herself a size or two smaller while she was at it.

When the last physicist was introduced, the entire arena cheered. All but the Wright family had held their applause and were now permitted to demonstrate their pride. The Yearlings cheered with the rest of the audience, but Anna still mourned over the missed shots.

After the processional, the group slowly made their way to a large grassy area with convenient lettered signs to aid families in finding their graduates. Anna spotted Jan under the "U–Z" sign and rushed to greet him. Before she could give him a hug, he pulled the arm of another graduate to him.

"Everyone, this is Katelyn. We've been studying together. I wouldn't have survived metabolism without her." To everyone's horror, Jan had his arm around Katelyn Wright. Later, Anna would regret the cold stare she gave the girl. But in the moment, she basked in it. She didn't even smile when Katelyn's family rushed in and swarmed the poor girl. Instead, she gathered her brood and moved them in the direction of their vehicles.

"We need to get moving if we want to beat the crowd to Dreamland." And that was that. No pictures. No greetings. The schedule had spoken, and the family was obliged to obey.

Jan said goodbye to Katelyn and her family, who were unaware that they would be hated by Anna until her dying day.

Winnie rode with Jan while the rest traveled in their original vehicles to the restaurant. Calling Dreamland a restaurant was close to a lie. It was more of a shack than a restaurant. But it served the best barbecue ribs in the country. And going to the shack was a Yearling family tradition.

The owners set up temporary picnic tables outside to accommodate the unusually large crowd. The family ate ribs, white bread, and banana pudding—the only food items on the entire menu—and talked about Jan's future. Thankfully, Maya snapped some candid photos of the group eating and talking. When Jan asked why his mom hadn't spoken to Katelyn, Maya explained the "airhorn incident," as it would forever be called. Everyone but Anna found it amusing.

On the drive home, Maya talked with her mom about wedding plans. She was mostly trying to prevent her mother from obsessing about Jan's imperfect graduation book. But she also worried that a few of the items would not arrive on time.

"Our rings still haven't arrived. And Andersons says they cannot track them." Maya sounded truly worried.

"We can fix that," Hunter said. "We can use plastic rings for the ceremony if we must. I'm more worried about the closing. We are buying the house five days before the wedding. If anything happens, we won't have furniture or dishes or anything when we get back from the cruise."

Anna spoke up. "First of all, you will not have plastic wedding rings. That would be a disgrace. I'll call Andersons on Monday. And what could go wrong with the closing? Don't you have an appointment scheduled?"

"We do, Ms. Anna. But the lawyer said that the bank has been running a few days slow with the paperwork. He doesn't think we'll have any problems. But we are cutting it close."

Anna sighed. "You are cutting it close, but it will work out. Both families can help with the move during the honeymoon if we must. You will be married a long, long time. If you have to sleep on newspapers the first week, you will survive."

"Mom! Newspapers? Really?"

Anna was surprised that Maya was surprised. "Really, honey. Those are the fun memories. One time Dad and I ate crackers and generic root beer for dinner when we were starting out. And we didn't mind. We were just happy to be together. You will appreciate the good times even more."

"That is so weird coming from you. You demand that everything be perfect." Maya was becoming borderline rude.

"Not fair, Maya," Hunter chimed in. "Your mom is right. We don't have to have everything perfect, especially at the beginning. But we both must go back to work on the Monday we get back. It's all a little too tight for me."

Jude decided to cut the tension. "So, what was up with Katelyn? Is Jan serious about her?" A collective groan spread throughout the car.

"Too soon, Dad," Maya said. The tension was cut. The family laughed about the airhorn incident for the rest of the way home. They never saw the front of the sign and had fun speculating what was written on it.

Once everyone arrived home and Jan's boxes were stored in the garage, Maya helped her mom bake some chocolate chunk cookies. Anna kept refrigerated dough on hand for nights like these. Hunter went home, and the fab five stayed up late recounting the last four years. Jan shared that he and Katelyn had met for coffee a few times and that her parents were veterinarians. For some reason, Anna thought that was odd. She thought of her photo book and decided that she would begin looking at AI photo creators as soon as she got home from church the next day.

1851

The wagon company arrived at Fort Kearny at 10:00am. They were three days behind Spit's timeline due to a violent thunderstorm that lasted for two days. The families had to ride out the storm huddled in their wagons, and the resulting mud slowed down travel for the next day. Despite being behind in schedule, the group would spend five nights at the fort to rest the animals and allow time for necessary wagon repairs.

Fort Kearny was established as a military post as well as a supply town. Westward travelers could replenish their goods and acquire enough food to make it to the next post at the Wyoming

Territory. The fort also offered mail services for the homesick trekkers.

Asher planned to visit a cartwright immediately to see about repairing a cracked axle on the schooner. It was currently working but would snap if not dealt with. Luke would take the horses to the blacksmith to replace three thrown shoes. And Sarah would take a shopping list to the general store. The first item on her list was shoes for Fidget. She had measured his feet using her right arm and would try to find something close. To avoid any complaining, Asher took the younger boys with him to see about the axle. Sarah brought the girls with her.

As Sarah expected, Jewel and Jade went straight to the makeup display in the store. Both girls eyed the large boxes of face powder and colorful bottles of perfume. Sarah knew they would stay occupied by the powders and perfumes, so she wandered around until she found a small selection of shoes. There were no shoes for young boys at all. The only pair that would work were meant for girls. They had pink satin on the top, but sturdy leather on the bottom. She debated the purchase and finally decided that Fidget needed something to cover his bare feet, so she picked up the pink shoes. Then she chuckled to herself. *Serves him right for betting away his shoes.*

Continuing with her list, Sarah gathered three bars of soap, a small bag of buttons and thread, a sack of cornmeal, and an extra plate for the nights that Spit joined their family dinner. She was eyeing a fresh-baked apple pie near the entry door but knew that she should be careful with their money. Asher would gather some ammunition and nails later, so she could come back with him and ask about the pie. Sarah didn't want to complain, but three weeks of bacon and beans was getting boring. A pie would lift the spirits of the family, for today at least.

As they were leaving the store, the twins noticed two brightly colored women in the middle of the street. "Look, Ma!" Jewel exclaimed. "Their cheeks are red as roses." Sarah put her arms around her daughters and steered them in a different direction. She had hoped the girls would forget the "fallen women," but the conversation continued.

"I want a bright-red dress like that someday," Jade announced. "And big ear bobs."

"Why are they just standing in the middle of the square like that?" Jewel asked.

Sarah had no choice but to address the matter. "Those women have no one to take care of them, so they are trying to make money for themselves. Unfortunately, they are doing unmentionable things for the money."

Jewel spoke up. "Those are trollops?"

"Let's be kind, Jewel," Sarah added. "Jesus will judge them. It is not for us to say."

"I understand, Ma," Jade remarked. "But I still want a red dress like that. I will wear it for my wedding."

"Me too," Jewel seconded.

"There will be no such thing. Red dresses are for women of easy virtue. And enough about that. Let's get back to the camp and begin lunch." The girls continued talking to each other in their private language. Sarah sighed to herself. They would be sixteen soon and would most likely be married within a few years. She still saw them as little girls but knew that she should be preparing them to run their own households. Jade took well to cooking and sewing, but Jewel did not. She preferred talking and observing. Sarah marveled that her two daughters could be so very similar in some areas, yet very different in others. She knew that God would have a purpose for each of them, and he equipped them for that purpose. She just hoped those purposes didn't involve wearing enough rouge on their cheeks to paint one side of a barn.

Back at the camp, the girls found the boys sitting in their chairs, waiting for the women to return. Asher updated his wife on the wagon repairs and asked her how the shopping trip went. Sarah decided to save the "colorful women" story for later and instead shared about the abundant supplies in the Western general store. She took the satin shoes out of her basket and handed them to her youngest.

"Aw, Ma!" Fidget wailed. "These are for girls. I can't wear these."

Before Sarah could respond, Asher spoke up. "You will wear those, son. And you will think twice before you gamble. The Lord expects us to earn our keep through work. Thank your ma for the shoes and put them on." Fidget grumbled a thank-you and reluctantly put the shoes on. The rest of the family smiled and began sharing stories of their time at the fort.

After another lunch of bacon and beans, Asher took Luke around to the other campsites to inquire on the well-being of their fellow travelers. He spoke easily with the other men and provided advice whenever asked. Jewel and Jade were given the task of washing the dishes in a nearby creek. While she was alone with Trenton, Sarah asked him to take out the journal Amelia had given her before she left town. She had been dictating details on their travels whenever she had the time. Trenton seemed to enjoy the task of writing and would also suggest details that she'd missed.

"How are the pens?" Sarah asked. "Will they last the trip?"

"Yes, ma'am. I've not used much ink at all. We will have plenty to git to the Oregon Territory."

"Good news. I appreciate your help with the diary. It will be an important record of our family's new beginning and of God's provisions. And it may even help one of our descendants someday." Trenton smiled at that thought and returned the writing supplies to his satchel.

When the men returned to the campsite, Asher organized the children into a game of shadow tag. He watched while the person designated as "it" tried to step in another person's shadow. Sarah watched the fun while she sewed two buttons on one of Luke's shirts. God had provided her a beautiful family. She prayed that they would make it to the West without any mishaps. Keeping seven people safe was a task only the Lord could undertake, and Sarah knew it.

CHAPTER SEVEN

Sunday, May 11

2025

"Happy Mother's Day!" Anna was greeted by her three children as she came down the stairs. They shuffled her to the table where they had prepared her favorite breakfast of cinnamon rolls and strawberries. She allowed herself to indulge in the gooey rolls on special occasions, and Mother's Day was one of them.

Sunday mornings were usually chaotic as everyone got ready for church at the same time. But this morning was different. Each person carved out fifteen minutes to eat breakfast as a group. Anna knew that they were running out of mornings like this but pushed that thought out of her mind. She thanked the others for her breakfast and thanked God for her perfect life.

When Winnie came downstairs to leave for church, Anna noticed that her eyebrows were freshly shaven again. Her daughter was still trying to make a statement. The thought of her walking around like that nearly killed Anna, so she remined herself that the antics could be worse—so much worse.

Later, Pastor Ed spoke about the legacy each mother leaves to her children—intentional or not. Anna thought of her own mom, who died from a brain bleed shortly after Anna married Jude. She never got to say goodbye to the woman who taught her everything. And her children never got to meet their spirited grandmother. Anna had so many questions to ask her mom. She needed advice and recipes and everyday counseling. The advice would not come, but her mom did leave a legacy for Anna and her family. She left traditions and photo albums. She left funny sayings and jokes. But most of all, she left Anna with Jesus. Elle Minor taught her daughter about the Savior and was the one who prayed with her when she became a believer after a day at Vacation Bible School. At only eight years old, Anna knew the truth. The greatest legacy a mom can give her children is a relationship with Jesus, and Anna was thankful for her wonderful mom giving her just that.

Mother's Day meant "mom's choice" for lunch. Anna went off the beaten path and chose pizza for the family meal. Jude drove Anna and the two younger children to Pie in the Sky. Known for throwing pizza dough in the air in public view, the charming restaurant was the best pizza parlor in Alabama. Maya and Hunter drove separately and arrived ten minutes later.

"Sorry we're late." Maya rushed in ahead of Hunter. "Pastor Ed had a few questions about the ceremony. And he gave us a cool devotional that goes with the premarital counseling we did in February. We're supposed to read it together after we get married. I'm kind of excited."

"That sounds helpful. I'd be interested to see what is in it." Anna pulled out the chair next to her for Maya.

"Marriage homework. That sounds lame." Winnie rolled her eyes.

"I agree with you, Winnie. That does sound lame." Everyone at the table turned toward Jude, wide-eyed.

"Really, Jude? Do you think that working on a new marriage together is lame? Are you serious? I think there is a spiritual war attacking young marriages. All marriages. I think that anything that draws a couple closer to God strengthens their bond. That isn't lame." Anna pounded her fist on the table to emphasize her point.

"I agree that couples should get closer to God," Jude said. "But isn't going to church enough? Homework seems a little excessive. Just live and be happy. And if your marriage doesn't work out, God understands."

At Jude's last sentence, Anna choked on her sweet tea. She began gagging and coughing in her seat. Hunter stood and started slapping her on her back. The younger Yearlings stared at the spectacle in silence.

"Ms. Anna, are you okay?" Hunter was still pounding her back.

"Yes, I'm fine. I was a little shocked that Jude thinks God will *understand* when a marriage doesn't work out."

Jude was clearly annoyed. "Why do you have to tie everything up in a bow and make it perfect? Sometimes we just need to enjoy the ride. Life shouldn't be so perfectly scripted."

"I think we should change the subject." Anna wiped her shirt with her napkin. The spray of tea was still visible. "I will call Andersons about the rings tomorrow. Maya, you should check on the cake. I'm a little uneasy about their last response. Jan, have you heard from the apartment manager? We need to send that deposit before she rents it to someone else."

"No. I'll call tomorrow morning and ask if the documents are ready." As Jan was speaking, the pizza was delivered. The family ate quietly, and Anna managed to spill sauce on her shirt, adding to the tea stains. She was thankful for her family but worried about some of their attitudes. She reminded herself that this would be a stressful summer and that she should just accept it. She would carve out some writing time tomorrow and get past the dreaded creative lull. The nameless family really need to get on their way to Richmond.

After a much-needed nap, Anna, Jude, and Winnie drove to Sylvia and Tom's house. Jude handed his mother a dozen red roses as he entered. Winnie and Anna followed him in, and hugs were shared by all.

"These are beautiful!" Sylvia exclaimed. "Let me find a vase." As she went into the kitchen, the others sat in the living room.

"The graduation ceremony was nice," Tom added cautiously. "How was Dreamland? Did you get any good photos?" Jude admitted that the photo book would be lacking some important shots, but there were enough to remember the special day.

As the two men were talking, Anna stood. She looked around the room and decided that the coffee table was not centered, and the fake Ficus tree did not look right in the room. So she moved both. She slid the table closer to the loveseat and then walked toward the tree. Without asking, she lifted it and carried it to the back door. Sylvia entered the living room just as Anna sat the tree down.

"Oh my!" Sylvia declared. "Was there a problem with the tree."

"No," Anna replied. "Well, yes. It just doesn't look right in this space. You have all of those pictures on the wall, and the tree is blocking half of them. I think it would look better on the back porch. Jude, would you take the tree out?"

Jude stood in horror. "You can't go rearranging other peoples' houses, Anna. That is just rude." He returned the tree to its original location. "I'm sorry, Mom. She is getting out of control."

Anna held back the tears and would never forget the way Jude had spoken about her. And the way the others did not defend her. Her efforts were not even appreciated by her own family. *Why do I even try?*

Later that night, Jude began to tell Anna how embarrassed he was by her actions earlier, but he stopped in the middle of the first sentence. "Never mind," Jude muttered as he walked into the kitchen. "It's not worth it."

1851

"Happy Mother's Day!" Fidget walked up to Sarah as she was tending to the campfire and preparing coffee for the family's breakfast. He was holding three wilting wildflowers and presented them to his mother with pride. Thankfully, his shoes had become so dusty that they were no longer shiny or pink.

"Thank you, son. These are beautiful. Go get the others and tell them that breakfast is ready." Sarah pulled out six hard biscuits from a bag near the fire and placed them on a metal plate. With the schooner at the wainwright's shop, the entire family slept outside on bedrolls. Normally, one or two people would sleep in the wagon each night. But last night, for the first time, the seven slept together outside. Fidget and the girls kept the group entertained with funny stories and a few songs until Asher finally ordered silence. When the talking stopped, the family could hear the rushing North Platte River.

"Is that the river we'll cross, Pa?" Fidget asked.

"No, boy. We will cross the South Platte in two weeks. We haven't had much rain, so it could be muddy. Spit will give us good instructions for crossing it."

The family ate breakfast together and talked about the exciting things they saw at Fort Kearny. Sarah smiled at Asher when the girls began talking about the "colorful women." Luke shook his head and smiled too.

The rest of the morning involved Bible reading by the campfire and family games. Afterward, Trenton wrote in the journal while Luke checked on the precious seeds. The girls picked flowers in a nearby field and made colorful necklaces for everyone in the family—even their husky father.

That night, the entire company gathered together for a formal group meeting. Horace Moore led the proceedings and scared several of the women by talking about the recent scalpings of travelers by local Indians. Jewel looked at her mother with obvious dread.

Spit quickly quelled the growing fears. "Hogwash! We are sharing the dusty paths with friendly foes. So long as we don't start a war, they won't harm us. I ask you kindly, Mr. Moore, to stop spreading rumors, or your family could get hurt."

As Horace was being admonished, he walked away from the gathering. Asher stepped up and continued the meeting. He asked for the group to share any needs and concerns. The families then worked together to solve the issues that were mentioned. Asher then visited each camp to ensure that any pressing problems were being handled.

The moon was unusually bright later that night. Luke asked if he could sleep out on his own in a neighboring field. Sarah didn't feel comfortable about his distance apart from the family but could not deny his request. The boy was getting restless. In reality, he was a man, not a boy. And he was becoming more and more restless about his future in Oregon City. Sarah prayed once again for the future family he would lead. She knew he would lead it well.

CHAPTER EIGHT

Monday, May 12

2025

Anna woke with a feeling of dread in her heart. Something was wrong. Something was going to happen. She reminded herself that she gets the "dreads" frequently these days and shouldn't worry. But she still worried. She asked God to protect her family and take away her fears, and she felt a little lighter as she got ready for the morning.

Maya and Hunter were taking the afternoon off from their jobs today. They were going to get their marriage license after lunch and meet with a representative from the band to pick out the wedding reception songs. Anna also suggested that they stop by Andersons to check on the rings. The couple would come over for supper, so Anna started a roast in the slow cooker. She would make the sides and two pans of cornbread later.

Anna decided that she would chain herself to her desk and write at least two chapters before lunch. She would try to get another one done before she finished cooking supper. Jude would be at his office all day, and Jan was working at the pharmacy until two o'clock.

Since the summer before his senior year of high school, Jan had worked at Manning's Pharmacy. The owners worked with the youth at church and offered him a part-time position unsolicited. Jan jumped at the opportunity and loved the job. It worked well with his interest in biochemistry. The Mannings gave him the flexibility to work around his high school and college schedules. Carbolytic

Pharmaceuticals mentioned that Jan's work experience was a boost in his application for the internship.

Anna made a cup of hot tea with sugar and too much milk. She walked the steaming mug into her office and looked at the ceiling. "All right, God. Give me Your words." The office was really an oversize desk placed in the master bedroom. The desk was pointed toward a window so Anna could look out at her back yard. When seated, she couldn't see the bedroom furniture and envisioned that she was in a real office. When Jan and Maya moved out next month, she would move the desk and create a genuine writing office. The plan was to turn Maya's room into her writing room and Jan's room into a guest bedroom. Anna hoped that Jan would continue to come back on weekends and figured that a comfortable room would entice him to visit more.

Before she started writing, Anna checked her email messages and completed the daily Wordle puzzle. Three attempts. "Impressive!" She sipped her tea as she watched a robin searching for worms. *What would it be like to move my family across the country two hundred years ago? What would I pack? What would we all eat?* The words came, and Anna spent two solid hours writing about the busy family before she took a break. She texted Jude to ask how his day was going, and he didn't immediately reply. That meant he was either meeting with a client or focusing on a big project.

Anna took a break and started some laundry. She grabbed a handful of nuts as a snack and went back to her bedroom cubicle. After another hour of writing, which was mostly research on early American vehicles, Anna broke for lunch. She had written one chapter and the beginning of another. Not bad for a Monday morning. But she would have to pick up the pace if she had any hope of meeting her deadline.

Around four o'clock, Anna went to the kitchen to start supper. Jan had come home and immediately left to meet a friend at the gym. He promised to be back around five thirty. She heard the front door open as she was tossing some vegetables on a roasting pan.

"We're official! We have a license." Maya came waltzing in and twirled with the marriage license over her head.

"Let me see. Did they spell everything correctly?" Anna inspected their license.

"Yes. We double-checked. Pastor Ed has to sign it. Then we'll be married forever and ever." Only Anna noticed the microscopic grimace that Hunter made. Normal cold feet, of course. Every groom gets cold feet, right?

"How did the song selection go?" Anna took a break from cooking and sat down at the kitchen table.

"Great! The guy is so cool. And he knows a bunch of songs. We're going to have our first dance to 'Chosen' by Sidewalk Prophets. You know that was playing on our first date to the Oyster Roast on campus. Don't tell Dad, but I went with 'You've Got a Friend in Me' for our father-daughter dance. We've watched *Toy Story* so many times, and he would sing it in the car on the way to school."

Anna beamed. "He will love that. Your dad doesn't get emotional, but I think he will be 'leaky' on your wedding day. It's going to be amazing. And you only do this once, so make sure you get it right." There it was again, that mini shudder. Hunter had a lot on his mind. Anna would make a point to reach out to his mom in the next day or two.

"He'll be fine. And if he isn't, please step in. I will lose it if Dad starts losing it."

Hunter finally spoke up. "Nobody will lose it. We're paying too much money for anyone to lose it." He laughed, but Maya didn't think what he said was funny.

"We'll be fine. Our biggest problem will be Winnie's eyebrows. I know she is shaving them every morning just to annoy me." Anna said, rolling her eyes. "What about the wedding party introductions? Did you pick out something for those?"

"Yes, Grunge. His name is Grunge, but he's all right, Mom. You'll like him." Anna put her hand to her forehead in a mock faint. "Seriously, Mom. He's great. He suggested 'Crazy Little Thing Called Love' by Queen. We're gonna practice our intros at the Jack and Jill bachelor party. Each couple will do something different, but we're gonna keep the one song going the whole time. I can't wait to see Michele-One-L and Sam. They've been texting, and I just know they would be perfect for each other."

Anna went back to the stove to put the vegetables in the oven. "Tell me again how they are paired up. I thought you were going by height."

"We were, but I want Sam to escort 'One L.' Of course, Winnie and Hunter's dad will be together since they are maid of honor and best man," Maya explained.

"Is Mr. Gene okay with this intro thing?"

Hunter chuckled. "Oh, he is, Ms. Anna. He was practicing the Charleston with my mom last week. I think they made it up, but it seems like something Winnie would like."

"Yep, Winnie would probably love to walk in doing the Charleston," Anna agreed. "It's not made up."

Maya thought for a minute. "Jan will escort Michelle-Two-L. They are close in height. Devin will escort Carlee. And, of course, Sam will escort Michele-One-L. It's gonna be great. Oh, should we do a cake-cutting song? I've never heard of that, but it might be cool."

"I don't think so. Isn't it usually quiet when the bride and groom cut the cake? I don't remember?"

"I don't either," Maya said. "Do you and Dad want to have a special dance? We can arrange that?"

"I don't want to take away from you guys, so no. But it would be nice if the band played 'I Will Always Love You' at some point during the night. I may be able to convince your dad to dance to that," Anna said.

"I'll text Grunge now." Maya pulled out her phone and started typing.

The couple went to the living room and talked about wedding plans while Anna made the cornbread batter. She wasn't going to visit Maya and Hunter in the first year, but there was no rule about inviting them over for dinner. That would be fun. She started making plans for the Fourth of July holiday. It was a three-day weekend, so Jan could come back from Atlanta. A big family cookout would be a great idea.

"Delivery!" Jan walked in with a huge Amazon box.

Anna rushed to him. "How did we miss this being dropped off at the front porch?"

Maya stood. "What is it?"

"These are your shoes," Anna declared. "I ordered every pair of three-inch heels they had. Not really. But sort of." Jan started laughing and asked what Maya would do with dozens of shoes. "We can pick the best pair and ship the rest back. We'll only be charged for the ones we keep. If they are exactly three inches, they will work with your dress. When are you picking it up again?"

Hunter cut the tape on the box as the rest watched. "Saturday," Maya said. "It will be ready by then. I thought we were getting the clear acrylic ones. They look like Cinderella's shoes."

"Those are tacky," Anna announced, "but are in here somewhere. You can try them. How about a fashion show after dinner? We can vote on the best pair." Anna clapped her hands as Hunter and Jan looked at each other. "This is part of being married. Get used to it." With that, Anna set the Wedding Shoe Runway event for that evening.

Dinner was relaxed as the six family members discussed their days. Jan pleased his parents by declaring that he had paid the deposit for his Atlanta apartment, plus the first and last month's rent.

"Are you okay with that?" Anna asked.

"Yeah. It cut my savings deep, but I'm okay. I start work in two weeks, so I should be getting a full-time paycheck soon. Dr. Manning said I can work at the pharmacy until next Friday."

Jude patted his son on the back. "Good going, Jan. I'm proud of you for doing so much on your own. I never had my own apartment. Do you need a roommate? I'm available."

For the second time in two days, Anna choked on her sweet tea. This time Winnie whacked her back.

"Just joking, Anna. Sheesh. You've got a serious drinking problem." Jude lightened the mood. But Anna wasn't laughing. Did Jude really want to live in a bachelor pad without her? He would probably eat chicken wings every night, and his cholesterol would skyrocket. That's not something to joke about.

"No thanks, Dad. I'm looking forward to having the place to

myself. I'm thinking of getting a huge saltwater aquarium for the front room."

"Well, I'm available as a bachelor if your change your mind," Hunter joked.

Spit-take number three! Anna spit cornbread onto Jude's shirt. The family was quiet for a full minute before Winnie started laughing. "We can use this to our advantage. Just talk about moving out, and Mom will spit her food. I'm going to have fun at the wedding reception."

"Now, now. That's enough," Anna choked out her plea. "Let's finish up so we can start the wedding fashion show. I think I'm having some sort of acid reflux. I just need an antacid. Bank on someone else for pranks, Winnie."

"Sure thing, Mom. And did you know that Honduras was the first country to ban smoking in one's own home? And they don't feed prisoners. If their family doesn't bring them food, they starve."

"Cool!" Jan was the only one to respond. Thankfully, Anna stopped choking.

The group finished eating. Anna had refused to make dessert until after the wedding so that she and Maya would fit into their carefully tailored wedding day dresses. She knew that the rest of the crew were sneaking cookies and ice cream at night, but she didn't put up much of a fuss. They weren't wearing a dress one size too small in thirty-three days.

The shoe show was a lot of fun. Hunter stayed occupied with his phone the entire time, but the rest of the family cheered and jeered as Maya marched through the living room in twenty-two pairs of three-inch heels. Of course, opinions were mixed. And, of course, Maya went with the tacky clear shoes.

"We'll make these work," Anna said as she and Winnie packed the rest of the shoes into the large box to return.

"Thanks, Mom. Hunter, should we show them?" Hunter looked up from his phone and shook his head slightly. "They will see them eventually."

"What?" Jan asked. "Show us what?"

"We ordered custom socks for the groomsmen to wear. They have dog poop on them. You know that Devin always calls Hunter "party pooper." I don't even know what that's about, but the socks are so funny. Go get them out of your car, Hunter."

Thankfully, Anna didn't have tea in her mouth, or she would have spit it all over the living room. "Dog poop? Really? This is a ceremony before God. We can't have groomsmen running around in feces socks. You may give them to the men, but they must not wear them at the ceremony."

Everyone in the room looked at Maya. "It's not a big deal, Mom. No one will see them. Hunter just wants to get one picture with everyone in the socks. We even got some for Dad."

"Maya, I must forbid this. It feels sacrilegious."

Maya walked over to Hunter. "We are grown adults, Mom. You can't tell us what to do."

Jude stood and put his arm around Maya. Anna knew right away that he would side with their daughter. "It's not a big deal, Ann. Our groomsmen wore pink bow ties. They were horrified but did it to please you. I say we wear the poop socks. Will you get them, Hunter? I can't wait to see them." Hunter froze. He knew better than to defy his future mother-in-law. The room went quiet.

"I'll get them." Maya opened her hand for Hunter to give her his keys. He slowly removed them from his pocket and handed them to his fiancé. Anna stared daggers through him, then walked to the kitchen. Winnie and Jan finished packing the unwanted shoe boxes. A few minutes later, Anna heard the family laughing about the socks. Winnie asked if she could have a pair. The sound of her people laughing together was the best sound in the world. But the thought of her friends seeing the disrespectful socks troubled her. She would employ Pastor Ed's help in the matter. He would be on God's side. It was his job.

When Jude finally came to bed, he didn't say a word. He fell asleep quickly, and Anna replayed the evening over and over in her mind. How could he side with Hunter? It didn't make sense. Anna couldn't let it go. She would do whatever it took to get her way. There would be no dog excrement in Maya's perfect wedding photo book. Anna was certain of that.

1851

Three days until they would be traveling again. Sarah was enjoying the stationary days in Fort Kearny more than she had expected. She washed clothes and prepared extra biscuits for the next leg of the trip. Asher and Luke were carefully restocking the wagon, which now sported a reinforced axle. The family had been traveling for three weeks, and spirits were still high. Everyone knew that times would get harder. The heat in the Kansas Territory would be tough. The winds and subsequent dust in the Nebraska Territory would be tougher. And the possible snow and freezing temperatures in the Rocky Mountains would be the toughest. In his best attempt to avoid the snow, Spit kept the company on a tight schedule. Three more nights until they would leave for Ash Hollow.

"You okay, Star?" Asher finished tying the bedrolls to the schooner and was about to feed the oxen.

"I'm blessed, Pa." The children were cooling off in the stream. Fidget was using a broken stick as a pretend rifle, and Sarah could only smile. That child would wear her out, but she had a feeling God would use his energy in a big way.

"Eugene Franklin asked if you would check on his wife. She is having some pains and is becoming concerned."

"Of course," Sarah said. "I'll bring over some biscuits. They might settle her down." Asher looked into his wife's eyes. Without saying anything, his eyes told her how much he loved her. He didn't use a lot of words but always made sure Sarah knew she was appreciated. They made a great team, and Sarah still could not believe that she almost rejected this precious man's interest. She did not like that the congregation assumed they would be married only hours after the picnic where they met. But they were right.

Sarah needed a man to care for not only her, but also her sisters. Asher was quiet and unassuming, and Sarah had always pictured her husband as an outspoken leader, not a quiet servant. A Paul, not a Joshua.

But Asher won her over. He immediately began bringing food to the girls and the pastor. He did small repairs to the parsonage and talked about the future. Sarah was filled with hope and readily agreed to marry Asher eighteen years ago. Five children later, they were more in love than Sarah ever imagined possible. The *eros* love had faded, but the *agape* love was stronger than ever. Asher was kind and patient and everything else listed in 1 Corinthians. He was a wonderful father and a hard worker. But his work for John Morgan was not enough to keep their growing children fed. The hope for a better life in the Oregon Territory was all he needed to secure his family's future. Sarah would follow him anywhere. He was "her person."

Later, when Sarah approached the Franklin camp, she found Susan sitting on the ground sweating. Eugene was telling her from a distance that everything would be okay, which was not necessarily true. Sarah told him that he could go about his chores while she sat with Susan. He seemed more than relieved.

"Where is the pain?" Sarah asked.

"Thank you for coming. This is my first pregnancy, and I'm not sure how it's supposed to feel. I have a migraine, and I feel plump all over." *Plump?* That was a strange way to describe birth pains. Sarah noticed that Susan's feet were severely swollen. Her shoes were off her feet and laying beside her. Not being a midwife, Sarah wasn't sure what to do, but she knew that eclampsia was a dangerous complication for pregnant women. She had heard stories of women "plumping up" and dying before the babies could be delivered.

"Let's get you up and walking," Sarah encouraged.

"Oh, I don't think I can move. I just feel so swollen and tight."

"You will feel better if you move your body around. Let's get you something to drink. Can you make it to the creek? We can sit in the water together, and I will send one of my girls to get you some coffee." Susan reluctantly agreed to move to the water. Once moving, she claimed that she felt slightly better. The baby hadn't moved all morning, and Sarah hoped the coffee would help it stir a little.

While they were sitting upright in the cool creek, Jade brought the expectant mother a cup of cold coffee. The homemade elixir seemed to help, as Susan began to gain some vigor. Her swollen feet decreased in size slightly, and her headache eased some. Sarah suggested that the women remain in the water for a while longer.

While cooling in the creek, Sarah discovered that Susan was Eugene's second wife. His first had died during childbirth, and her mother insisted on raising the baby. He knew that he could not care for his son, so he reluctantly agreed to let his in-laws raise the boy. Susan was excited to give him another child and was praying that it would be a boy.

"Oh, happy Mother's Day, plus a day," Susan added.

"Thank you, dear. And next year you will be celebrating your own Mother's Day, God willing." Susan smiled at the thought and drank the remainder of the coffee. She thanked her friend for her help and offered to wash clothes for the family.

"Nonsense! You will do no such thing. In fact, I will send my girls over to help you with supper tonight. You need to rest as much as possible. Send for me if your feet begin to swell again. You mustn't let them become too plump." Susan laughed at the last word and promised to take it slowly. Sarah knew that she wouldn't rest. She couldn't. But she felt comfort in the fact that time in the creek helped the pains. Before she went back to her camp, she prayed with Sarah for a safe delivery of a healthy baby boy.

Later in the day, Asher reported to Sarah that Horace Moore's family would be returning to Missouri. Their children were not traveling well. The youngest was plagued with daily diarrhea and needed to be carried by either a parent or an animal. Horace's wife, Kitty, refused to travel any farther. She sat on the ground and declared that she would not move until her husband turned their wagons around. He finally yielded. The Moore family would retrace their steps alone.

Sarah suggested that their family join the Moores for supper, but Asher warned that was a bad idea. Kitty was not speaking yet, and Horace was subsequently breaking the alcohol and swearing rules.

"Are we making a mistake, Pa?" Sarah asked. "This trip is so strenuous on us. Poor Luke looks lost."

"He does, but he will be fine. And Fidget is having the best time of his life."

Sarah laughed. "He is. I hope he doesn't become a wagon master when he's grown. We'll never see him."

"He very well may do that. I hope he doesn't hear about the gold in California. He may be inspired to leave us at the Parting of the Ways."

It felt good to laugh. And to talk about the future. The daily rigors of travel consumed the minds of all the travelers. There was precious little time to think of normal life, whatever that was anymore. Sarah thought she would miss her sisters more that she did, but her mind was so busy that she couldn't even mourn her old life yet. Managing her emotions would have to be on hold for the next few months. Sarah prayed for the delicate minds of her children and husband and for her fellow travelers.

CHAPTER NINE

Saturday, May 17

2025

Four weeks until the big day. Maya and Anna sat on the living room floor reviewing the wedding portfolio. License. *Check*. Band. *Check*. Shoes. *Check*. The extended list of tasks was steadily being reduced.

Today, the girls were working on the wedding favors. Each guest attending the ceremony would be given a packet of wildflower seeds. They would be asked to plant them "as soon as convenient" and send pictures of the resulting flowers to the couple. Maya and Anna were adding hand-printed messages with Maya's email address to each packet. Winnie was then wrapping each in lavender-colored twine. The twine would match Maya's chosen colors of pale lavender and mint green.

"Will you plant some seeds, Mom? I want to dry some when they bloom and make an arrangement for our house."

"I can do that, My," Winnie boasted. "I can make a special section of the garden for the wedding seeds." Winnie seemed eager to help her sister memorialize the day.

"Thanks, Win. I would love that. Maybe we can do seeds for your wedding and have matching arrangements."

Winnie smiled, and Anna saw it. Her youngest did think about the future—just not out loud.

After placing the finished seed packets into an ornate basket, Anna whisked the favors away to safety. Maya went to the foyer table and picked up the RSVP cards piled in a wooden tray. The pile was getting larger.

"Mom, are these all of the RSVPs?"

Anna appeared at the top of the stairs and walked down. "Yep, that's all of them. How many are there?"

"We have forty-two cards. Probably around seventy people total. Does that seem right?" The Yearlings had invited over one hundred fifty people but expected only about half of them to make the wedding.

"Yes. The bulk of them came in right after we sent the invitations. We may receive a few more, but that's about it. Don't forget that we will also have the family and the wedding party. It will be a good turnout." Maya smiled and sat near Winnie. They rifled through the RSVP cards and noted any potential drama among the guests.

Winnie held up two cards. "We should sit the Weavers and the Joneses together. Mr. Lanny bleeds orange and blue. I'm sure he will get Mr. Phil riled up." Fans of rival football teams in Alabama were relegated as lifetime enemies.

Maya snatched the cards from her sister. "Ha! We aren't having assigned seats. But that would be kind of funny. We could assign seats according to tension levels. Nikki from work is coming. She just broke up with her boyfriend. He works in HR and is still planning to come. We might have to keep an eye on those two."

"I should write a screenplay called *The Reception*," Winnie said. "The entire movie could be about the different people at a wedding reception. Their cross-linked pasts and their interwoven futures. The big finale would be on the dance floor with certain people making eye contact with others." With that thought, Winnie rushed to her bedroom and began writing in her idea journal. She was a writer like her mom but didn't like to acknowledge it to her family.

Thirty minutes later, Hunter picked Maya up to retrieve the wedding dress from the seamstress. He promised to not peek at the mysterious attire and would never admit to Maya that spending so much money on a one-time outfit was too lavish for his tastes. He would be fine with saying "I do" in blue jeans and a flannel shirt. But the Yearling women would never go for that. Never ever.

When Hunter and Maya left, Jude came in from the garage. "I'll be back."

"Where are you going?" Anna was restacking the RSVP cards on the foyer table.

"Just out. Do I have your permission?" He stood with his keys in his hand, waiting for an overly dramatic response.

"You know you don't need my permission. We usually tell each other those details. And I may need you to pick something up."

"What do you need?" Jude asked quickly.

"Nothing. Should I plan supper?"

"Whatever is fine," Jude said indifferently, then left.

The "dreads" returned to Anna. She knew that Jude wasn't a child. He didn't have a curfew. But he was being secretive. Married couples shouldn't have secrets. Anna hoped that Jude was doing something special for the wedding—either for her or for Maya. But deep down she knew that he was doing something he didn't want her to know about. Despite her heart telling her to call him and try to figure out what he was doing, her mind forced her to divert her thinking. She wasn't in the mood to write, so she made a sandwich and watched a few episodes of *The Golden Girls*. The adventures of four senior ladies in Miami always cheered Anna up.

When Hunter and Maya returned, Maya rushed her dress to her bedroom. Hunter visited for an hour before going home. He would be back the next day to take Maya to church. As soon as he left, Anna and Maya ran up the stairs to see the dress.

"I tried it on when we were there," Maya assured. "It fits perfectly."

"Let's try it with the shoes. And Grandma's pearls. My mom would be so thrilled to know you were wearing the same pearls she wore when she married my dad." Maya quickly changed and walked into her parents' bedroom where she would have more room to move. She twirled twice in front of the full-length mirror. Winnie walked in and whistled her approval of the fitted dress covered in delicate lace. The seamstress had to raise the neckline, as the original design was much too revealing for Anna's taste.

"I love it, Mom. Thank you."

Anna gave her daughter a hug. "You are beautiful. The dress is perfect."

"Yeah, sis. Hunter's gonna flip out." Winnie sat on the bed and watched Maya sashay back and forth across the room.

The dress was finally put away, and Anna had a crazy thought. "Let's get ice cream."

"What? We haven't done that in years. The Miller Creamery closed," Maya said.

"I know. But the Freezer is still open. Or we could even drive through the Sonic. We don't have many more days left as a family. It will be fun." Anna gathered the two girls in her arms.

"As a family? Mom, I'm not going away. I'll be in the next town. We can still get ice cream on Saturdays."

"You'll see, Maya. Once you move out, it won't be the same. And that is right and proper. You will be starting your own family. It really won't be the same. Plus, Jan will be living in Atlanta. It will be a fight for me to get him to come back here."

"You'll always have me, Mom. I'm not going anywhere." Winnie smiled and walked away from the group hug. "I may live here forever and become a hermit."

Anna knew that her daughter was joking, but she did not like the content. "Nonsense, Win. You'll probably be the first one in our family to live on Mars." The three put on shoes and met in Anna's car. Ice cream it was.

On the way to the Freezer, the ladies talked nonstop about the wedding. Maya reminded Winnie of her duties as maid of honor. "The ceremony will be easy. You just have to hold my bouquet during the vows. Two L and Carlee are planning the Jack and Jill shower, so you must be there and be approachable."

"Approachable?" Winnie asked. "What do you mean by that?"

"All of our friends will be there. You are the maid of honor. You should be fluttering around, socializing."

Winnie snickered. "I do not flutter. You know that, Maya."

"I know. I just want the party to go well. It's stressful mixing our friends, coworkers, and family."

Anna finally spoke up. "All right, girls. First, it's a shower not a party. And second, Winnie is your sister. She won't embarrass you. Although I do think you should wear that green dress, Win. It looks so good on you."

"Ugh! I don't think I can make it four more weeks. I'll agree to the Wizard of Oz dress, but I get full rights to my speech at the rehearsal dinner. No parental editing."

"Nope!" Anna and Maya responded in unison.

"Then I won't give a speech," Winnie avowed.

"C'mon, Win. Why does everything have to be a battle with you? Mom can write the speech for you, and you can read it off index cards. Super simple."

Winnie folded her arms akimbo. "Fine. I wrote something special for you months ago. But I'm deleting it as soon as we get home. I'll read Mom's gold-plated speech like a robot. Would you like me to read it with a British accent? Would that be classy enough for you?"

Winnie had officially pushed past Anna's limits. "Okay, girls. Let's put the wedding on the back burner for now. Your speech will be perfect, Winnie. I can't wait to hear it. Let's focus on ice cream. I'm getting rocky road. Anyone else?" The car was silent. "Okay, what else can we talk about?" More silence. "Are Michele and Sam still texting?"

"No."

On the way home after ice cream, Anna was talking about shoes and the best way to walk down the stairs in a wedding dress. As she was talking, Jude's car passed in the opposite lane.

"There's Dad," Winnie noted.

"Are you sure? Why would he be on this side of town? On this street?" Anna got the "dreads" again. Jude was being suspicious and had no reason to be in this particular neighborhood.

"Maybe he's lost." Winnie laughed, and Maya joined her.

"You both know that Dad wouldn't get lost in Wonder. Surely he was visiting someone."

"Sheesh, Mom!" Maya was clearly unhappy with Anna's mild accusation. "He's not a spy trying to hide something from the family. I'm sure he has a good reason. This has been a long day. I'm going for a walk when we get home. Getting married shouldn't be this exhausting."

The rest of the ride was quiet. No one spoke. Anna's mind turned in a thousand directions, trying to figure out what Jude was keeping from her. She knew there was a simple and logical explanation. But it still didn't sit well.

When he got home twenty minutes after the girls, Jude went straight to his recliner and turned on a golf program. Maya had gone on her walk in the neighborhood, and Winnie was in her room. Anna started to ask about Jude's whereabouts but decided against it. She didn't want to seem petty and didn't want him to know she saw him.

That night when she was brushing her teeth, Anna rearranged Jude's bathroom sink. His side of the counter was too messy. Two bottles of cologne. Toothpaste. Hairbrush. All of it was too much clutter. She had placed a nice basket in the cabinet under the sink, but Jude refused to use it. Anna placed everything in the basket for him and hid it nicely in the cabinet. The counter looked much neater, so Anna chose to straighten Jude's shoes in their walk-in closet next. Feeling better about taming the chaos, she went to bed and fell asleep, thinking of the *Wizard of Oz*.

1851

The company had been on the trail for two days since leaving Fort Kearny. The weather was comfortable, and the trip was uneventful. The Montgomery family had a scare on the first night back on the trail. Betsy discovered three scorpions in the back of their schooner and was stung by one as she was sweeping them out. Spit applied a poultice, which Sarah figured was nothing but tobacco, and Brother Barton said a prayer. After four hours riding in her wagon, Betsy had no signs of nettles in her arms and legs. The entire company thanked God for His mercy and continued their travels.

Shortly before lunch, the first few families in the caravan spotted two dozen Indians traveling in the same direction but on the northern side of the Platte River. Spit traveled from family to family informing the wide-eyed travelers that they had seen Pawnee people and shouldn't be alarmed. The Pawnee lived in villages along the river and were known for their advanced farming practices. Luke joked that he would like to learn their planting methods, and Fidget bragged that he would fight the "Paw-knees" with a stick if they came across the river. Asher scolded the boy for suggesting violence when not provoked. Sarah noticed that Trenton had taken the journal out and was writing furiously. She also noticed that he had sketched a man's head with one black-tipped feather sticking up in the back.

After another hour of traveling, the group "nooned" near a thick meadow. Asher verbally thanked God for the abundant grass and began walking the mules to the center of the field. Sarah and Jewel began preparing beans and bacon for lunch as Jade set out plates and spoons. Luke was helping his father with the animals, and Trenton was starting a small fire to heat the food and water for coffee.

Twenty minutes later, the entire Wilkes family was sitting in a circle beside the fire. Asher started the conversation by asking the group what the most interesting thing they had seen that day was. He immediately regretted the query when Fidget spoke up.

"The *Paw-knees*!" the boy exclaimed. "They was watching us to attack us later."

"No, son," Asher reassured. "They watched us to make sure that we didn't attack. They are peaceful people. Now, what else did you see?"

"I saw a silver fox sleeping in the grass!" Luke declared. "He didn't move at all."

"Good eyes, boy. I never saw him. What else?"

"I saw a woodpecker fly overhead," Trenton shared. "It was as big as Pa's arm."

"Goodness, Trenton," Sarah added. "I wish I had seen that.

Just as the group was finishing their meal, Jewel spoke. "I saw Brother Barton talking to Jade when she was washing the breakfast dishes. They were whispering."

The entire family became silent and turned to Jade, who stared back with wide eyes. "He was asking me about Susan Franklin. And Jewel said a swear word in front of little Annie Montgomery."

"All right, enough sharing," Asher declared. "I'll have no more tattling unless someone is in danger." He made a mental note to keep an eye on both of his daughters. And he felt slightly guilty for admittedly giving the boys more attention than the girls. He was busy every day tending to the animals and the supplies. Sarah spent more time with Jewel and Jade. But that didn't excuse him from fathering them. He walked toward his wife to apologize for his short-sightedness when he heard one of the Montgomery children calling for her.

"Mrs. Sarah! Mrs. Sarah! Come quick! Mrs. Susan is bleeding real bad."

Sarah grabbed her bonnet and ran toward the Franklin wagon. Inside, Sarah found Susan lying on a mattress with Eugene sitting nearby. He was muttering "It's all right" over and over. Sarah excused him and asked the gawking child who ran with her to fetch Brother Barton's sister. She removed the blood-stained quilt that was covering Susan and was horrified to see that her feet and ankles were so swollen that they didn't even look like feet and ankles. The baby must come now for Susan to survive.

Sarah yelled for Eugene to bring some water. She found a clean cloth and waited for help to arrive. Susan was moaning about her head hurting terribly. Her hands were planted on each side of her face. Sarah noticed that her fingers looked like little sausages.

When Eugene presented Sarah with a large bucket of cold water, he walked away toward the oxen pulling the schooner. Sarah began cleaning Susan and asked her about the frequency of her pains. Susan could not elaborate on their timing and reported that they were constant. Sarah made the decision to have Susan begin to push.

"Just push as hard as you can, Susan. The baby is ready." Brother Barton's sister, Violet, arrived shortly after Susan began to push. "Find a clean cloth and cool Susan's forehead with the water. Her head is splitting." Violet did as she was asked.

After fifteen minutes of pushing, Susan begged to stop. She was too tired to continue. But Sarah pleaded with her to continue. The baby would not survive if it weren't delivered soon. As Susan resumed her pushing, Sarah felt the schooner jerk and begin to move. Not even a risky birth would alter Spit's travel schedule. The would-be mother groaned with each bump, and Sarah began to worry. Part of the baby's head was now visible. She asked Violet to fetch her brother. Petitions to the Almighty were needed now.

As Sarah was waiting for Brother Barton, Susan let out a scream as blood began rushing from her mouth. She had bitten her tongue. Sarah found the cloth and dipped it in the water bucket, which was now sloshing back and forth with the movement of the wagon. As Sarah was wiping the blood from Susan's mouth, she noticed the mother become still.

Please, God. Don't take this woman. Help me, please!

Susan's heart was still beating, but she was not moving. She was having a spell, and there was nothing Sarah could do but pull the baby out. She rushed back to the head and heard Brother Barton running toward her.

"She's having a spell. We must take the baby out now." The pastor understood and put his hands around the baby's head. He gently pulled the head out. To their horror, the three helpers saw that the baby was blue and not moving. Brother Barton delivered the rest of the baby and wept as he saw that it was lifeless.

A boy. Susan Montgomery had given her husband a son, but the boy would not live to meet his parents. The pastor wrapped the baby in the soiled blanket and jumped out of the wagon. Sarah did not know where he was taking the child, but she knew it didn't matter. She rushed back to Susan's head and continued wiping the blood from her face.

Within ten minutes the exhausted woman began moaning. Her eyes fluttered open, and she tried to sit up. "The baby? Where is my baby?" Sarah shared the heartbreaking details and cried with her friend for over an hour.

That night before supper, Eugene Montgomery buried his second son in a wooden breadbox on the south side of the trail. A makeshift cross was crafted out of one of their running boards. Susan stood beside her husband as Brother Barton read the Twenty-third Psalm. Her eyes were not focused on the casket. They were looking past it to her failure to give her husband a son. Two families provided dinner for the Montgomerys so that Susan could rest. But she would be expected to resume her daily chores with breakfast the next day.

Sarah hugged her children a few extra times that day. All five of them were somber for the rest of the evening and went to bed early, even Fidget. To provide some comfort, Asher read from the Psalms by the campfire before everyone retired. Sarah noticed Jade crying as he read.

CHAPTER TEN

Sunday, May 18

2025

Sunday morning involved the usual rush for the family to get ready for church. Jude seemed strangely annoyed when there was no "soft butter" for his toast. Somehow, Anna had missed the need to reorder it when she had scheduled the grocery delivery that week.

When Winnie came downstairs, Anna noticed that her eyebrows were growing back. She knew better than to say anything about them but was secretly grateful that the issue was resolving itself. Now, about the poop socks.

Hunter was running late and would meet everyone at church, so Maya rode with the family. Anna thanked God for one more time as the fab five, even it was only for fifteen minutes. On the drive, Jude was quiet. But Anna was getting used to his icy posture. It occurred to her that he must be stressed by the new software his company began using this month. Changes, especially with technology, always made him tense. He usually shared that with her. But with the upcoming wedding, he was probably keeping it to himself. Anna made a mental note to ask him about the conversion later that evening.

Pastor Ed's sermon today was about giving God complete control of their lives. He shared the story of Samuel, the last judge of the Israelites. Because Eli's two sons were greedy and wicked, the people demanded a king, and Samuel helped guide them to Saul. Samuel was the first prophet after Moses, and he was called by God to serve the people. Eli's two sons had been appointed as leaders due to their family line, not by their willingness nor God's desire. They were ultimately rejected by God. Samuel trusted God and obeyed.

Anna nodded in agreement with the pastor's three main points. *Yes, God places an individual call on each person. Yes, God works through generations of families. And yes, God is always sovereign. But God doesn't speak to us today as clearly as he did to Samuel, does He?* Sometimes, Anna believed, we must "move things along." If we are following godly principles and not hurting anyone, we can trust our thoughts and actions. Right? When God started texting Anna His wishes directly, she would follow them to the letter. Until then, she would attend church regularly, read her Bible at least once each week, and pray for wisdom. Then she would continue driving her car through life. She silently thanked God for her perfect life.

Lunch at Say Cheese was light and merry. The bride and groom gushed over the upcoming Jack and Jill shower, and Winnie joined in with the excitement. Jan shared that he was looking forward to moving to Atlanta in a week. His apartment had a resort-style pool and an extensive fitness center. It even had a co-working space with desks and computers for anyone working remotely. Anna dreaded leaving her son four hours away but knew that the internship was too good to pass up. She would ensure that he visited regularly and wasn't staying out too late with friends.

Out of nowhere, Hunter suggested something radical. "Why don't we rent an apartment, Maya?" Ten wide eyes stared back at him.

"What do you mean?" Maya asked.

"Well, we could rent an apartment for a year or two before we buy a house. One with a pool and a fitness center. Wouldn't that be better? A mortgage is such a huge commitment."

Before Maya could speak, Anna took control. "You are closing on your house in two weeks. The paperwork is nearly finished. And the house is in such a cute neighborhood. You can't just change your mind at the last minute."

"But . . ." Hunter stammered.

"And you have locked in a good interest rate. Tell him, Jude. They can't rent an apartment. It wouldn't be wise." Anna stood mid-sentence and was leaning toward Hunter. She meant business.

Jude rolled his eyes enough for everyone in the restaurant to see. "Don't bring me into this, Anna. It's their decision, not ours. An apartment with a pool sounds fun to me. I don't see the problem."

Anna sat down with a thud. Why did her family constantly test her? Renting for a year or two was not a good idea. She shut down that topic quickly. "I still don't like the poop socks. Have we decided about those?"

The groans from her family were a clear indication that she had pushed too far. Anna moved her pizza crusts into parallel lines on her plate and remained quiet. Jan broke the silence. "If you don't get an apartment, you can come visit me anytime. I won't be coming back here much, so you can stay for weekends if you like." Anna grabbed another slice of pizza. She needed carbohydrate fortification.

"Me too?" Winnie piped in.

"Of course! You can sleep on the couch." Jan seemed proud of his peacemaking skills, but Anna was slowly considering him a rival. She now had to develop a plan to keep the kids from spending too much time in Atlanta.

The rest of the day was uneventful. Anna took a nap and worked in her garden. Jude slept in his recliner with YouTube videos running nonstop. And Jan spent three hours detailing his truck.

Anna noticed Winnie sitting on the deck with her idea journal. She walked over to her youngest, who was peacefully writing her thoughts.

"What are you working on?" Anna asked.

"My maid-of-honor speech. I wrote something in January, but it doesn't seem right now. I was looking forward to being an only child in the house, but now I'm not so sure. The days will be so quiet. And I can't just walk over to Maya's house. She and Jan will both be a drive away. I don't think I realized how quiet it will be in a few weeks."

Anna thought before she spoke. "You're right. It will be different. But we can call Maya and Jan. And I will make sure they come back to visit. We'll have holidays and birthdays to get the family back together. Plus, you'll be so busy with your senior year that you won't miss them as much as you think you will."

"I know, Mom. But it changes my speech a little. I'm the last bird left in the cage, while the others managed to break free. I want to tell Maya to fly as high as she can without looking back."

"Goodness, Win. Do you have to be so dramatic? Your cage has air conditioning and unlimited Pop-Tarts. You're not exactly suffering." Winnie didn't laugh and added that her mom would never understand. Not everyone has their dream man vomiting on them in love. Anna agreed that she didn't fully relate and added that she was available to help with a "proper" speech.

"I've got it, Mom. Thanks for the offer."

Anna dusted her hands and folded her gardening gloves in half. This, she hoped, would keep spiders from climbing inside. She took a quick shower and went to set out sandwich fixings for supper. Maya and Hunter were sitting at the kitchen table discussing the upcoming shower.

"Don't push Sam," Hunter warned. "He likes texting Michele, but I don't think he's serious about her." Hunter's arms were folded tightly, and he was leaning back in his chair.

"Of course they aren't serious. They haven't had a real date yet. Get him to ask her out for coffee or something. They can't move into the 'love stage' by texting." Maya's elbows were on the table, and she was leaning forward. "What do you think, Mom?"

Anna stood behind an empty chair. "They do seem perfect together. Maybe we could invite them to our cookout on the Fourth of July. I'll make sure they sit next to each other."

"Oooh!" Maya exclaimed. "I like that plan."

"Aren't we going to Atlanta to visit Jan that weekend?" Hunter interrupted. "What about the fireworks on Stone Mountain?" Anna straightened and looked toward Maya. Neither woman spoke. "Sorry, Ms. Anna. We made plans with Jan this year. We'll try to be here next July."

"But we always have a cookout here," Anna said dejectedly. "It's a tradition. I'll just tell Jan to come home that weekend. Then we can invite Michele-One-L and Sam."

"Sure thing, Mom." Maya agreed quickly.

"No, Maya. She can't tell you what to do after we are married. We are grown adults. We will be married. We can do whatever we want."

Maya was caught between her mother and her fiancé. "It *is* a tradition, Hunter. We can visit Jan another weekend."

Hunter stood to leave. "No. I'm going to Atlanta for the Fourth of July. With or without you. I've got a busy day tomorrow. I better go. Thank you for lunch, Ms. Anna and Mr. Jude." As Hunter walked toward the front door, he locked eyes with Jude. Neither Anna nor

Maya noticed, but the two men were thinking the same thing. Anna was frozen by Hunter's exit. Her perfect plans were starting to unravel. She would have to fix them before they loosened any more.

1851

The trek continued west shortly after sunrise. The travelers behaved as if a child hadn't been lost hours earlier. Sarah knew that life must go on, but she didn't understand how a soul could be seemingly forgotten so easily. She thanked God for the health of her children and that she was able to help Susan during the worst time of her young life.

Today was the twins' birthday. They turned sixteen and were now considered to be women by most of society. Sarah planned to use four extra eggs and some baking soda to prepare a cake to be enjoyed by the family after supper. Sugar was scarce, but she would use a fourth of a cup to sweeten their dessert. Sarah decided to include the Franklin family in their birthday dinner. They might be resentful of the Wilkes' healthy children, but Sarah didn't want to risk alienating them during their time of grief.

Shortly before their lunch stop, the wagon train passed seven graves on the north side of the trail. Fresh graves were common, but Sarah hadn't seen so many in one place. Each earthen mound bore a small cross created out of two sticks and twine. *Did one family lose seven members? How did they all die three days outside of Fort Kearny?* Sarah tried not to think about the dangers they would be facing while traveling with the company. Most likely the seven souls were lost to cholera. Asher had heard stories of the rapid spread of the disease while back at the fort. Many would die from the bacteria in less than a day after contacting it. Spit promised that their group would be safe if they would boil their drinking water and water their animals away from camp.

After lunch, clouds began to build in the sky. Trenton was terribly afraid of lightning, and Sarah feared he would come running at the first drops of rain. She knew that rain would help cool the animals and fill water barrels, but spending time calming Trenton would interfere with her chores. She decided to send him into the schooner to work on the journal.

"What should I write, Ma?" Trenton asked.

"I'll sit with you a while. Let's record details about our days since you last wrote in Fort Kearny." Sarah and Trenton climbed into the schooner and sat on a large wooden chest. "Where did we stop?"

"We was telling about the supplies Pa and Luke were loading into the wagon," Trenton added as he read the last entry.

"That is a great place to start. We can tell about the first day back. And the scorpions."

"And Mrs. Montgomery's baby?"

Sarah felt his reservation but wanted to include everything they had encountered on the trail. "Yes, son. We will write about the baby." As she was responding, rain drops began to fall. Trenton looked up at the roof of the wagon and then at his mother. "We are safe, son. Papa is just outside, and I am here with you. Let's start our writing.

After thirty minutes of writing, lightning and thunder begin rolling in. The light in the wagon had dimmed, and water was spraying into the back of the wagon, so Sarah reluctantly asked Trenton to put the journal away. "We will write more tomorrow. You can record about Jewel and Jade's birthday cake. And Fidget's will be next. We have a lot to look forward to."

But Sarah's attempt at distracting her son did not work. He put the journal into the leather satchel and began wringing his hands. She put an arm around him and began humming "Amazing Grace." The tune seemed to calm the boy slightly. But the rain came down harder, and the lightning continued. Sarah felt the wagon stop, and the rest of her family climbed inside. They were dripping wet and huddled together amongst the chest and assorted furniture.

From the front of the schooner, Asher yelled over the rain. "We are risking the wagons and animals getting stuck in mud! But the lightning is too close!" Trenton squeaked. Asher spoke directly to his middle son. "We are fine, boy. The lightning is aiming at those trees north of us. I don't think the storm will last much longer. Those winds will blow it out. As soon as the lightning moves past, we will start moving again."

As Asher predicted, the lighting moved away from the trail, and the rain stopped shortly after it started. Men rushed to get their animals pulling again. Fortunately, the ground was rocky enough for every wagon to begin rolling and continue the march along the trail. The travelers' clothes dried quickly in the windy air. Sarah watched as Fidget stomped his pink shoes into every puddle of water he found. She didn't stop him. Careless fun was hard to find on the trail.

To make up time for the rain stop, the caravan traveled an extra hour before stopping for the night. Sarah rushed to start a fire as the boys watered the animals. Jewel and Jade started a pot of beans and sat out the dinnerware. Sarah combined the ingredients for a birthday cake. She used her recipe for Johnny cakes but replaced the cornmeal with dried apple pieces. The result was not as lovely as the popular queen cakes from back home but was indeed a sweet treat that the family savored after endless meals of beans and bacon.

As Sarah was serving pieces of cake to each member of her family, Brother Barton walked up. "Good evening, folks."

Everyone noticed Jade's eyes light up. She smiled and walked over to the pastor.

"Good evening," Sarah responded. "Please join us for some cake. We are celebrating the girls' birthday."

Jade giggled. "He knows, Mama. Look at the beautiful ribbon Dewayne gave me." Jade promptly pulled a pale-blue ribbon from her pocket. Sarah looked at Asher, and Asher looked at Brother Barton.

"Uh, I got that when we were at Fort Kearny," Brother Barton stuttered. "I thought it would look nice in Jade's golden hair."

The conversation was awkward, but Sarah managed to thank the man for his kind gesture. He joined the family in eating the cake but did not speak. Thankfully, Fidget droned on about his "splashing shoes" and kept the family laughing. When he finished his cake, Brother Barton excused himself back to his wagon. Sarah presented the girls with the white satin ribbons she had brought for the occasion.

"Which one will you wear first?" Jewel teased.

"Hush!" Jade said, pretending to be annoyed. She then began scolding her sister in their private language.

Asher declared the day over and sent the children to set out their bedrolls. He walked with his wife, carrying the dishes she was about to wash. "Dewayne?"

"Oh, Asher. Does he have a fancy on Jade?"

Asher laughed softly. "I think he does, Star. He's a fine man. And Jade seems to be smitten."

"But he is ten years older than she is." Sarah didn't know Brother Barton's age but figured that he was close to twenty-six. "And he has been married before."

"Now, don't get the cart ahead of the mule, dear. They aren't getting married anytime soon. They are just enjoying company while on the trail. I see nothing wrong with that . . . yet."

Sarah sighed. "You are right. We have enough to worry about without adding the kind preacher. How's Luke? He was quiet tonight."

Asher rinsed the dishes in the cool stream, and Sarah stacked them in her skirt to make carrying easier. "He is missing the Campbell girl. Apparently, they were fonder of each other than we realized. Luke asked me today if he would be able to move back to Missouri once the family gets settled in Oregon."

Sarah dropped the dishes. "No! He can't leave us. I won't have it."

"He's a grown man, Star. We can't live his life for him," Asher warned as he piled the dishes on a flat rock. "It's only been a few weeks. By the time we get to our new home, he might have forgotten about her. He's a wise young man. Don't add this to your frettin'. Give him to God and let him make his own way."

Sarah knew that her husband's advice was sound, but she couldn't imagine her oldest child living so far away from the family. *Who would help him feed his family? Or work his fields? What if he got sick?* Parenting older children was just as worrying as parenting babies.

PART TWO

Stormy Seas

When you pass through the waters,
I will be with you;
and when you pass through the rivers,
they will not sweep over you.
When you walk through the fire,
you will not be burned;
the flames will not set you ablaze.
—Isaiah 43:2

CHAPTER ELEVEN

Saturday, May 24

2025

The wedding was in three weeks. To steal some extra time with her daughters, Anna took them to their favorite coffee shop while Jude and Jan worked on a home repair. An oversize woodpecker had recently turned the rail on their front porch into Swiss cheese. Jan had to work at the pharmacy from noon until five o'clock, so the men started early on the porch.

As Anna sat down with a banana-nut muffin and a cup of hot cocoa, Winnie asked Maya about their honeymoon. "Did you see that woman who found the treasure on *Plunder* last week? She claimed that she used AI to find it. Now people are complaining that she shouldn't have won."

"I saw that," Maya said. "She set up the parameters herself so she shouldn't be disqualified. Hunter and I agreed that we don't want to waste too much time on our honeymoon trying to solve clues. Of course, fifty thousand dollars would be nice to have."

Anna peeled half of the wrapper from her muffin. "Explain it to me again. They just hide gold somewhere random? For anyone to win?"

"Sort of." Thinking of her fitted dress, Maya had opted for a fruit cup and hot tea. "The cruise line hides fifty thousand dollars' worth of gold coins each week in a real treasure chest. Any passenger can find the prize. And there are clues leading to the hiding place."

"I would spend all of my time searching for the treasure!" Winnie said excitedly.

"But they only get one honeymoon," Anna added.

"Yeah. The treasure is exciting, but we've never been on a cruise. The ship has a huge pool, an ice-skating rink, and a gym. Plus, it's got all the pizza we can eat. I can't wait!" Maya pulled up some pictures from her phone. "Look at the theater. It's amazing! And we'll be going to three private islands. I just love coconut palm trees."

Anna sighed. "It sounds amazing. You will have so much fun. Remember everything so you can tell us when you get back. With your dad's motion sickness, I will never step foot on a cruise ship. So I need you to tell me all about it."

"I will, Mom. I plan to take a million pictures. You may have to make two photo books for my honeymoon."

"I'm happy to do it. Just don't go overboard." Anna laughed nervously.

"Like those people did last year. Didn't they fall off the ship trying to find the treasure?" Winnie's eyes were wide.

"No," Maya said. "They fell from *Golden Fortune*, our sister ship. A teenager was daring another to stand on the rail. We won't be doing anything like that. Hunter would never dare me to do something that dangerous."

Anna acted overly relieved. "He better not. So, tell me how the clues work."

"I'm not sure. Hunter's uncle said that the first clue will be in our cabin. We go from there. There's a website with a list of all the past clues, but I haven't looked at it. I read that they are all different, so past clues won't help. We aren't supposed to call or write people for help, but I'm sure people do that."

"I saw that some cruise lines go to Honduras," Winnie said quietly.

"Goodness, Winnie!" Anna said. "That doesn't seem safe."

"I know. But I was thinking that maybe we could go next summer for a senior trip or something. We could help at the orphanage for a day, and you could judge if it's safe or not. I'm just asking for you to check it out."

"No, sweetheart. I won't let you be that far from home in a third-world country. I do like the idea of the two of us taking a cruise together, but it wouldn't be safe for two women to travel alone. And I would prefer to go to the private islands with Jewel Cruise Line. Just walking around Honduras is out of the question." Winnie looked crushed. "Look. Maybe we can go on a trip with Maya and Hunter in a few years. That's not a bad idea. But not to Honduras. I'm scared just thinking about it."

"Sure, Mom. Whatever you say." Winnie stood up to throw her cup away.

Maya tried to help. "Those cruises are safe, Mom. You could go with a tour group. Maybe you could just let Winnie see Honduras without going to the orphanage. It's the only thing she seems interested in besides that idea journal."

"Don't gang up on me, Maya. I'm sure that God doesn't want my baby in Honduras. I don't even know where it is. It's not part of my plan. Not gonna happen." With Anna's final declaration, the girls headed back home. The excitement about the cruise vanished. Anna tried to cheer up the group with talk of wedding cake mishaps, but neither daughter felt like participating.

Anna spent the afternoon in front of her laptop trying to make progress on her book. She knew that Laney would call on Monday to ask about her page count and to pressure her to finish "a smidge" before the deadline. The stress of the wedding and Jan's move to Atlanta was stifling Anna's creative juices. Plus, Winnie was just about determined enough to run away to Honduras during the night. Maybe she should try to write in the middle of the night to keep an eye on the front door.

After cleaning up and eating leftover pizza for lunch, Jan drove to Manning's Pharmacy. He loved his job and would miss the customers when he moved to Atlanta. The older ladies were his favorite. They always dressed nicely for their trips to the pharmacy and often brought treats for the staff.

Today was Jan's last day. He would spend time with his family tomorrow and drive to his new apartment—and new life—on Monday. Memorial Day traffic would be a nightmare in the city, so he planned to get an extra-early start. He hadn't told his mom this yet, but he would be back home in three weeks for the wedding, so she shouldn't put up too much of a fuss.

The Mannings surprised Jan with a goodbye cake, and employees not scheduled to work came by at five o'clock to wish him well. For a moment, he wished he were staying to work at the pharmacy full time. But the opportunity at Carbolytic was too good to pass up. A permanent position with a major pharmaceutical company was his dream job—after NFL quarterback, of course.

Two of Jan's friends, Caleb and Manny, surprised him by showing up as he was leaving. One of the cashiers had clued them in that there would be cake. After hugs and goodbyes, Jan drove his friends to Bamburgers, a popular fast-food diner in town. Greasy food was served inside the restaurant, at outdoor picnic tables, and in vehicles using old-fashioned trays attached to open windows. Jan parked the truck, and the boys found a picnic table.

Caleb's sister immediately bounded to their table. She worked weekends at Bamburgers and pestered her brother whenever he was there. "The usual, fellas?"

"Yes, Avi, the usual. But give us a minute. Don't bring the food too quick." Caleb was patient with her. She was the oldest of his three sisters and the least annoying.

"Sure thing. I'll bring the Cokes and wait on the burgers." Avi twirled on her toes and marched toward the building.

"I can't believe you are really moving to the A-T-L," Manny said. "It seems so much farther than Tuscaloosa."

"Well, it is in another state," Caleb joked. "Hey, you're not gonna start pulling for the Bulldogs, are you?"

"Never!" Jan was appalled. "I will always bleed crimson. Roll Tide!" All three of the men put a hand on their heart and repeated, "Roll Tide!"

After a few minutes, steamy burgers and crispy fries arrived. Avi gave her brother a side hug for no reason. The boys started salting and ketchupping everything.

"You know, something is weird," Caleb began.

"What?" Jan asked.

"Your phone isn't buzzing every ten seconds. Is your long-distance *acquaintance* mad at you?" Caleb asked.

"No. We're still texting." Jan looked around and realized that he didn't have his phone. "I left my phone in the truck. No worries."

"Dude," Manny said with pretend concern, "go get your phone. You won't be able to eat without it."

"I'm fine."

"No, you aren't," Manny and Caleb said in unison.

"Okay. Okay. If it will make you happy, I'll get my phone."

As Jan walked to his truck, Caleb yelled, "Don't answer the four hundred messages until we eat! That could take all night."

"Ha!" Jan opened his truck and was surprised that he couldn't find his phone. *Where could it be?* He walked back to the table. "I must have left it at work. The last time I remember having it was when I was unloading the afternoon shipment."

Caleb looked up. "The pharmacy isn't open tomorrow. Are they closed on Memorial Day?"

"Yes, they are," Jan groaned. "I can run in and get it when I drop you off at your car. I still have my key and know the code to the storage room. I'll text Dr. Manning when I get my phone and tell him what happened."

The group finished eating and spent a little time talking to some friends from their youth group also eating at a picnic table. Most were excited about summer plans and upcoming beach trips. Talk turned to work, and Caleb joked that he was already looking forward to retirement.

After eating, Jan drove Caleb and Manny back to the pharmacy to retrieve Caleb's car. He disabled the alarm and used his key to enter the building through the back door, and his friends followed.

"It's kind of creepy at night," Caleb whispered.

Jan agreed. "It is, but you don't have to whisper. We aren't hiding from anyone." Manny found that funny. Jan punched in the code to the back storage room and walked in.

"Whoa! Look at all these drugs. Someone could get rich selling all of this. Let me get a picture," Caleb said, in awe of the shelves full of prescription drugs.

"No. Let's find my phone and get out of here. There are cameras everywhere, so don't do anything stupid." Jan walked between two rows of shelves.

"Found it!" Manny was holding Jan's phone. "You left it near these boxes. How many messages from Katelyn do you have?"

"Thanks. And let's get out of here. I'll let Dr. Manning know that we were in here."

Manny walked out first. "How many messages?"

Jan gave in. "Okay, twelve. Twelve messages. It's not that big of a deal." He waited for Caleb to leave the storage room. As Caleb was walking out, he took a selfie of himself in front of dozens of bottles of oxycodone.

"That's enough," Jan declared. "Let's go." He led his friends out of the building, locked the door, and set the alarm. "I think I'm gonna call it a night. Are you two doing anything?"

"Let's ride to Josh's house, Manny. He's lighting the firepit tonight." Caleb got into the car and leaned out the window. "We'll see you at the wedding. Have fun in the big city."

"And tell Katelyn we said hi," Manny added.

"Will do!" Jan laughed. He drove home and found his mom alone in the living room.

"Where's Dad?"

"I'm not sure," Anna replied. "He said he had to run an errand but didn't tell me what it was. Do you know anything about it? Is he planning a surprise for the wedding?"

"No. I haven't heard anything. I bet it is a surprise. That sounds like something Dad would do."

Anna didn't seem relieved. "I'm sure it's fine. How was work?"

"It was fine. The Mannings got me a cake. I'll miss working there."

"You will," Anna agreed. "But Carbolytic is such a better job for your degree. You will be helping develop new drugs that pharmacists can sell. That is exciting."

"It is. Are you okay by yourself? I'm gonna go to my room."

"Sure, honey. Don't forget to set your alarm."

Jan walked upstairs but couldn't help wondering where his dad was. His parents rarely went out at night, especially without the other. As he was thinking, his phone buzzed. Katelyn was getting worried. He sat on the side of the bed and responded to her now fifteen messages. She would be going to pharmacy school at Auburn University, which was two hours from Atlanta. He planned to visit her more than his family but would never tell his mom that.

An hour later, Jan heard his dad's car drive into the garage. Strangely, he didn't hear his parents talking after his dad came inside. His mom must have gotten tired waiting for him and gone to bed.

Jan went downstairs and found his father sleeping on the recliner. He must have crashed before he even turned on the TV. Walking quietly, Jan went into the kitchen and found some cookies in the pantry. He ate them at the kitchen table. Tomorrow would be his last night living at home. But tonight was just weird. Everyone was asleep, and the house was eerily quiet.

The company arrived at the California Crossing shortly before the nooning hour. The wagon train would stay on the east side for the rest of the day before crossing the South Platte River early the next morning. The crossing was treacherous, so travelers took the day to rest and stock up on supplies.

Asher left before lunch to purchase a load of firewood. He took the three boys with him. Wood could usually be found on the trail, but occasionally it was scarce or too wet to burn. He liked to keep a week's worth in a dry box in the front part of the wagon.

While Asher was gone, the girls began the preparations for lunch. They started a small fire and set out six chairs. Sarah noticed that Jade was unusually quiet.

"A penny for your thoughts, Jade?" Sarah offered.

"Not much to say, Mama. Do you think we will make it all the way to the Oregon Territory? It feels like we will be traveling forever."

Sarah sat in the closest chair and looked at her daughters. "God has sent us west, and our family must obey. I know the trail is tough. But our lives will be so much better for this sacrifice. You young ladies will start your families in the Oregon Territory and build your roots. We will be happy out there."

"What if something happens to us?" Jewel asked softly. The family had passed the "cholera cemetery" as they approached Ash Hollow. Dozens of lives had been lost to the horrible disease. The children had seen more death in the past four weeks than they had in their entire lives previously, and Sarah feared they would lose their innocent zest for life.

"I don't think anything will happen, Jewel," Sarah reassured. "God will be watching over us all the way to Oregon City."

"But others have died, Mama." A tear fell down Jewel's face. "It could be me."

Sarah stood and walked to her daughter. "This is a fallen world, dear. Bad things will happen. But we mustn't stop living because a bad thing might happen. In fact, we must live even more fully knowing that something like that could happen. We must enjoy every day. And love as much as we can."

Jewel looked up and smiled. "Thank you, Mama."

"Of course, my loves. Let's get the beans ready. We will have time to rest this afternoon. We can pick wildflowers or write letters to your aunts. There is a post office in town. I will ask Papa to take us there before dinner."

The tone was lighter until Jade spoke. "May I have dinner with Dewayne and his family tonight?"

Sarah's heart dropped. Jade was getting too close to Brother Barton. Asher had insisted that the man would be forgotten when they finished their trek. But Sarah now feared that the opposite would come to pass. She decided to postpone her answer. "We will ask Papa when he gets back."

Despite Sarah wagging her eyes at him, Asher quickly offered his permission for Jade to eat dinner with Brother Barton when he returned from town. She asked him as soon as he returned to the campsite.

"I think we should eat as a family tonight," Sarah pled privately. "It's our only night at the crossing."

"It will be fine, Star. Don't get too far ahead of God's plans. Let's put the kids to bed early and sit by the stream tonight." Sarah knew that Asher was trying to ease her concern about Jade, but she did like the idea of spending alone time with him. They hadn't had much time to talk over the past few weeks.

"I would like that. Thank you."

After lunch, Sarah took the girls to pick wildflowers as she had suggested earlier. Afterwards, the trio went to an old trapper's cabin that served as a makeshift post office. They purchased the supplies to write letters. Each wrote a different aunt back home. Sarah spent much of her time spelling words for the girls. They had attended a town school until they turned fifteen, but both enjoyed socializing more than academics.

"I want to ask Aunt Mae about her wedding night," Jade declared. "Is that okay with you?"

Sarah's eyes grew large, and Jewel snickered. "Gracious, Jade. Let's not pry. Why don't you ask her about her chickens. I'm sure they are missing you by now." Slightly disappointed, Jade went back to her writing. Sarah could only hope she was writing about the birds.

On their way back to the camp, Sarah led the girls through the cholera cemetery. She was struck by how fresh the graves were. The cemetery was vast, but all the deaths had occurred within the past two years. Sarah prayed aloud that God would protect her family from the dreadful disease.

That evening, Sarah enjoyed dinner more than she had expected. Jewel didn't have her sister to chat with, so she spent most of the meal talking with her mother. Sarah discovered that Jewel was interested in becoming a midwife or a nurse. Surprisingly, the tragedy of Susan Franklin's loss led her to consider the health care field. In 1851, few women had careers outside of the home. But the numbers were slowly increasing. Since she was moving to a new territory, Jewel would have no prospects for a mate in the near future. The idea of meaningful work for her daughter seemed quite promising to Sarah.

While Jewel was washing the dishes in the stream, Jade returned. She rushed to her sister and began talking in their shared language. Sarah watched the girls for a full minute. Life had been changing so rapidly this summer. But so many things were still the same. The mysterious "twin speak" was one constant Sarah appreciated.

When the dishes were cleaned and the bedrolls were spread around the fire, Asher ordered the children to settle down for the evening. "Ma and I are having a date over by the canyon. Stay here and don't cause any trouble. Luke is in charge and will report back to me." Fidget giggled first, then the rest. And in a moment that Sarah would never forget, Asher scooped her up in his arms and carried her to a bluff overlooking the rushing stream. They sat behind three trees so they would have a moderate amount of privacy.

Once seated side by side, Asher tucked Sarah's stray hair behind her ears. "You look beautiful, Star."

"And you are quite handsome, Pa." Sarah leaned her shoulder into Asher's and didn't move. He put his arm around her, and the two watched the flow of the water for a few minutes.

Asher spoke first. "You are doing very well, Ma. This is hard work, but you are doing very well. I'm proud to have you as my wife." Sarah smiled. She loved that Asher was considerate enough to give her praise and encouragement when she needed them. "Our next stop is Fort Laramie, then Independence Rock. That is almost halfway to the Territory. Spit says that we are on time and should beat some of the snows in the Rockies. The children will enjoy spying Chimney Rock."

"What about crossing the Platte?" Sarah asked quietly.

"It will be fine. Spit says that the waters are high enough for us to ferry like we did in Independence. When the waters are low, the bottom becomes like quicksand, and animals can get stuck. But that won't happen tomorrow. We just have to watch the current. Luke and Trenton are good with the horses. The winds are calm tonight, so we shouldn't have any trouble. Our wagon will be fifth, and we'll head out like normal after breakfast."

"It sounds so scary. Are you sure our boys can make it?" Sarah picked up a twig and began breaking it into tiny pieces.

"Yes, they can make it. Our rig isn't as heavy as many of the others. We didn't bring the table and the sewing machine. We'll be fine. You'll see."

"I trust you, Pa."

Asher chuckled. "It's not me you need to trust. It's God. We need to put the lives of our entire family into His hands."

"Let's pray. We need the Father's blessings now more than ever."

Asher agreed. He took one of Sarah's hands and asked God for travel mercies. He thanked Him for his family and their safety thus far. Then he thanked God for his precious wife and her obedient spirit. When he finished, he asked Sarah to pour out her fears to him. Taking advantage of this time alone with her husband, Sarah shared her heart with him for nearly an hour.

They talked about Luke and his recent melancholy. And Jade's budding attraction to Brother Barton. Sarah informed Asher about Jewel's recent interest in nursing and Trenton's growing writing ability. And they wondered together how God would use their youngest child's curiosity and vigor to serve the kingdom. Finally, the couple shared that they were both looking forward to "real" privacy in a "real" home.

Sarah's spirits soared high as she and Asher walked back to the camp together. She slept peacefully that night—better than any other night on the trail—unaware of the tragedy that would overtake her family the next day.

CHAPTER TWELVE

Sunday, May 25

2025

Maya rode with the family to church on Sunday. Hunter wasn't feeling well. Anna suspected it had something to do with the new Mexican restaurant they ate at the night before. She had warned Anna and Hunter about visiting a new establishment this close to the wedding. One shouldn't be so risky this close to a formal event.

Anna gathered the group before they walked into the building. "If anyone gets a chance to talk to Pastor Ed this morning, be sure to remind him that we are moving the rehearsal up thirty minutes. I will email him, but it's always good to remind someone in person."

Pastor Ed began a new series on the Parable of the Sower from the fourth chapter of Mark. Jesus shared that the condition of our hearts determines how well we hear God and act upon His messages. Those with "hard" hearts do not allow the words to penetrate their heart before Satan snatches them away. Those with "rocky" hearts are excited by God's words at first, but quickly forget them. Those with "thorny" hearts are distracted by the cares of the world. But those with "good" hearts have a strong faith and godly lifestyle. They produce fruit for the kingdom of God. Anna felt sorry for the people in the congregation with barren hearts.

After church, the family went to the "old" Mexican restaurant. Anna walked in with her planner and two ink pens.

"Can't we just enjoy our lunch?" Jude was clearly frustrated with the wedding planning.

"No. The wedding is in twenty days, Jude. We must discuss everything." Anna saw Jude roll his eyes but ignored him.

After everyone ordered, Anna opened her planner. "First up, the Jack and Jill shower. How is that going?"

Maya was also annoyed. "Fine, Mom. We've got everything covered."

"That's great," Anna said with a smile. "I know we are all getting weary from the planning, but we can't slow down now. We are hosting a major event. It must be perfect."

"Sure, Mom." Maya tried to show some enthusiasm. "What's next?"

"The rehearsal. Did anyone remind Pastor Ed this morning?" No one responded to Anna's question. "Fine. I will call him on Tuesday. I don't think he will be in the office tomorrow. Do you think that Grace and Gene will be able to get everything set up at the Potter House?"

Maya tried to hide her frustration. "I'm sure it will be fine, Mom. They are hosting the rehearsal dinner. That's not even on us."

"I know," Anna agreed. "But we want everything to be perfect." Jude interrupted when the food arrived and asked if it was okay for the family to eat. Anna agreed but started talking after only three bites of her quesadilla. "About the socks . . ."

"Enough!" Jude answered loud enough for the entire restaurant to hear. "You are squeezing the fun out of this entire wedding. Just let it go, Anna. It's not your wedding."

Anna was shocked. She was the mother of the bride, the MOB. She was on the executive committee of the whole affair. And it didn't look like anyone else even cared. "I'll drop the socks for now. But I plan to speak to Grace about this. I'm sure she can talk Hunter into changing his mind."

Without thinking, Winnie spoke up. "He ordered a pair of socks for me too. I'm wearing them at the reception—with my dress."

Anna's eyes began to tear up. *Why did things always have to be so hard? Can't everyone see how distasteful the socks would be?* She pivoted to a new subject before the tears fell down her face. "Can we talk about the honeymoon? Or will that upset everyone also?"

By now, the family was weary from the wedding talk, but Jan attempted to lighten the mood. "Aye aye, Captain Maya. Tell us about the treasure." His terrible pirate accent got laughs from everyone.

"I'm getting excited," Maya admitted. "We aren't even sure what to pack, but I'm focusing on swimsuits and fancy dresses. I hope the treasure hunt isn't too messy. Jan, are you sure you don't mind driving us to Birmingham? We can't be late for our flight."

"Of course. Caleb and Manny want to come along." Anna gasped but kept her comments to herself. She would give in on this one point to keep the peace.

Maya smiled. "I'm fine with that. Dad, can we drive your car? It will give us enough room for the five of us. I'll make sure that Devin and Sam don't write crude messages all over it."

"Absolutely," Jude added. "It will be late when Jan drives home, and I'd rather he not be alone." Anna hadn't thought about the safety issue. Jude was right about friends coming along, and she was relieved that she hadn't opposed the idea aloud.

After lunch, Anna decided to take a real nap in her room while Jude watched a golf tournament. Maya went to check on Hunter, and Jan went to Manny's house to play basketball with some friends.

Winnie watched a few minutes of golf before settling on the back porch with a sketch pad and charcoal pencil.

When Anna awoke, she was shocked to see that she had slept for over two hours. That's what wedding stress will do to a MOB. She passed Jude, who was still watching golf, on her way to the kitchen. A quick pot of white chili sounded good for dinner, so she started gathering the ingredients. As she was searching for a can of northern beans, she heard the front door fling open.

"Mom! Mom! Where are you?" Maya slammed the door and rushed past Jude.

Anna looked up as Maya rushed toward her. Her daughter's eyes were red and filled with tears. "What in the world has happened? Sit down." Maya wouldn't sit. She was pacing back and forth in front of the refrigerator. Jude quietly stood in the doorway.

"He called it off! How could he do this?" Maya was talking to herself more than her parents.

"What do you mean?" Anna asked. But she knew the answer. Hunter had been acting odd ever since he suggested they rent an apartment over buying a house.

"Hunter doesn't want to get married." As Maya blurted out the news, Winnie opened the back door.

Anna's mind went into level-ten control mode. "Everyone, sit down. There must be a mistake. Tell us everything, and I will sort it out." Anna noticed a slight flinch by Jude. His approach of wait-and-see never worked, and she knew that was going to be his suggestion. She would just ramp up her response to level eleven.

"I went to Hunter's house. He wasn't sick. He just didn't want to go to church. We were talking about the house when he just said that he wanted to wait. He doesn't want to sign for a huge mortgage.

And he doesn't want to be 'tied down.'" Maya's breathing slowed down a bit. "A few weeks ago, he was talking about some opportunity with his job in Nevada. I told him that I could never move that far from my family. Apparently, he doesn't understand and wants to move to Nevada. He said I could come with him but not as his wife. He wants an apartment with a huge pool and free gym." Maya looked up with wide eyes. "He wants Jan's life."

Before anyone had a chance to think, Anna took control. "He can't cancel now. We've paid deposits and bought dresses. It's too late. Jude, call him and ask him to come over. He just has cold feet."

Jude held his hands up. "Don't order me around. I don't blame him from running from this family. He can't even think on his own." Winnie snickered at her dad's comment but quickly quieted at her mom's subsequent fiery gaze.

"So you're just giving up, Jude? Without a fight?" Anna was crying now. "He was just venting. I'm sure of it. I'll call Grace and sort everything out."

"No, Mom." Maya placed her hand on her mother's shoulder. "There isn't anything to sort out. He doesn't want to get married. He already told his boss that he would take the job in Nevada. We'll lose the earnest money, and my adorable kitchen." Maya broke out into sobs. "I love that kitchen."

"Maybe we should pray." Winnie interrupted the crying women. "Isn't that what we are supposed to do?"

"We don't have time to pray. We have to fix this." Anna knew how foolish she sounded, but God would understand. There are times when people must attack a problem first.

"I would feel better if we prayed," Maya whimpered.

"I would too," Jude added. "Let's hold hands." Anna agreed, and the four formed a circle as Jude gave their problem to God. She would have liked for Jude to steer God toward a wedding, but did feel lighter when Jude was finished.

"Thanks, Dad," Maya said tearfully.

"Sure, Duckie. This isn't the end of the world." Jude was speaking calmly. "Let's eat supper and give Hunter some time. You can call him or text him or whatever tomorrow, and we'll go from there."

"Don't cancel anything," Anna added. "We'll work all of this out."

"Work what out?" Jan asked. He had walked in through the front door without the family hearing.

Anna spoke first. "Hunter is having a little bit of cold feet. Not to worry. The wedding is still on."

"That's Mom's take on it," Maya explained. "Hunter called off the wedding and is moving to Nevada."

"That's brutal. I have news too." Anna suddenly noticed that Jan looked pale. "Carbolytic called me thirty minutes ago to withdraw my internship. I didn't know they could do that, but they did."

"What?" Anna froze.

"Caleb posted a picture on Instagram and tagged me. Apparently, the company checks social media regularly and caught the picture this morning. I'm not in it, but my name is on the post."

Jude pulled out a chair. "Let's sit down again. Start from the beginning." Jan explained that he had left his phone at the pharmacy the night before and went back to get it with Caleb and Manny. He didn't think anything about Caleb taking a selfie in front of the bottles.

Carbolytic Pharmaceuticals now saw him as a "character risk." They cancelled his internship and wished him well.

"I'll call your supervisor first thing in the morning," Anna declared. "They can't fire you before you even start. You put a deposit down on an apartment."

"Um, yes, they can, Anna. They can do whatever they want," Jude said.

"No! I will not allow it! Let me finish the chili, and we will figure out a plan to get everything back to normal." Everyone at the table looked up in silence.

Jude stood. "I've had it, Anna. You are squeezing the life out of everyone around you. I'm done!" He found his keys and wallet and walked out the front door, slamming it behind him.

Involuntarily, tears began to flood down Anna's face. She felt like vomiting but knew that she should finish the chili. So she got the can opener out of the drawer.

Winnie walked toward her mom. "I don't think anyone feels like eating. Why don't you come into the living room with me. You need to sit down."

Anna put the can opener down and followed her daughter to the couch. She sat down and faced her children. "Someone say something."

"There's not much to say, Mom." Jan tried to be comforting but didn't ease Anna's emotions. "Things change."

Once again, Anna's emotions took over, but this time she began to laugh. "Things change? Really? So we just move to Plan G? La dee da! Everything has changed. Flip the entire game board over and start the game again? Is that what we do?"

"Yeah, something like that," Jan mumbled. Maya started crying, and Winnie moved near her. The room was quiet for a full three minutes.

"What next?" Jan put his hands on his knees and looked at the women. "Isn't that what Mr. Marco told us in youth group? When bad things happen, we don't ask why. We ask, 'What next?'" Winnie and Maya nodded.

"Okay," Anna interrupted. "That sounds great. But we haven't even tried to fix things. I can make some calls."

Maya looked hopeful. "Mom, Dad is your problem. Not the wedding. Not the internship. You can't control everything. God may be trying to finally get you to let go of the wheel and let Him drive."

"Yeah, Mom." Winnie smiled. "These aren't your battles. These are God's."

Anna shook her head. "You don't understand, kids. I am responsible for your lives. I must make things right. It's what I do."

In unexpected wisdom from a sixteen-year-old, Winnie amazed her mother. "The world is too big, Mom. You can't fix everything. You aren't some sort of superhero. But God is. He knows what is going on. He can fix it. Let's pray again." Anna's tears stopped, and she held Winnie's hand. The family formed another circle of four.

Winnie started. "God, we're back. Things got worse, but I guess you know that already. Please show us what to do next. Bring Dad back home. Fix Jan's internship. And help Maya undo the wedding."

"Help Hunter come back to Maya," Anna interrupted. "We want the wedding to go on."

"Help us deal with what is going on. And help Mom accept it. In Jesus' name, Amen." Winnie had single-handedly brought calm to the living room by inviting God in.

Anna remained quiet. She wasn't ready to give up yet. Winnie reached for her mom's hand. "He's not coming back, Mom. I heard him on the phone renting an apartment."

"In Nevada?" Anna asked with surprise.

"No, here. I'm talking about Dad."

1851

Breakfast consisted of Johnny cakes and fresh goat milk. The children talked nonstop about the upcoming crossing and the new fur hats Asher surprised them with shortly before they ate. He had purchased them from a trapper the day before and delighted the family when he promised they would need the warm hats before the summer was over.

Sarah gathered the hats while the girls washed the breakfast dishes. She placed them in the wooden chest in the wagon and checked on the bedrolls Trenton and Fidget were tying to the side of the wagon. "Tie them tightly, boys. The winds will be swift."

"Yes, ma'am," Fidget replied.

Asher and Luke found Spit and listened to his final instructions. The older boys would swim the horses, and Asher would take the mules like they had at the beginning of the journey. The current on the South Platte River changed by the hour, so Spit advised that the men should let the animals dictate the pace while they were in the water.

Back at the schooner, Asher went over the instructions with his family. "Luke and Trenton will swim with Remy and Red. I'll take the mules. The rest of you hold tight to the schooner and listen for instructions. Don't let go until we are way past the water. The mud is thick, and you could get run over if you get stuck in it." Jewel walked closer to her mother and anxiously listened to her father's commands. "No need to worry, children. Just do as you're told. Let's pray." Asher asked Luke to pray for the crossing, and Sarah was comforted to hear her son's authentic conversation with Jesus.

"Star, take my watch." Asher handed his grandfather's pocket watch to Sarah. She placed it in the front pocket of her dress and squeezed her husband's hand. Today was the last crossing until Independence Rock in the Nebraska Territory. A few weeks of "normal" traveling, if anything on the Trail could be normal, would be welcomed after today.

The family walked beside the schooner as it fell into line behind the Montgomery party. Asher was checking the saddle straps on the horses and mules, and Luke was calming the oxen. Sarah could hear the roaring water and became fearful when she saw how wide the Platte was. After two and a half hours of waiting, the time came for the Wilkes family to cross.

Luke coaxed the oxen onto the platform, and the wagon followed easily. He smiled at Fidget, who was holding tightly to the front wagon wheel when it stopped. Sarah and the girls fell behind Fidget and found secure places to hold onto the wagon. Luke jumped off the ferry into the shallow water and found his horse. When everyone was at their stations, the ferry master began the crossing.

Sarah tried to watch the boys swimming the animals but was unable to get a clear view. Water was spraying into her eyes, and she could not let go of the wagon to shield them. The crossing appeared to be uneventful, until Sarah heard someone shouting.

"Luke! Luke! Don't let go!"

Through blurry eyes, Sarah could see three figures fade into two. Luke was in trouble, and there was nothing she could. So she prayed. *Please protect Luke, Father. Protect us all.*

Sarah continued to pray even when she heard Asher shout again. Even when the shouting stopped. Even when Jewel began calling for her. "Hold on, children. Wait till we get to the other side."

But Sarah knew. She knew there was a problem with Luke. And she knew she was helpless standing beside the schooner. She closed her eyes and listened for any sounds of hope.

When the ferry stopped, no one came to lead the oxen off it. Fidget looked at his mother with big eyes. "I can do it, Mama." Sarah had no strength to reply, and the boy began coaxing the animals forward.

Time had stopped. Sarah had no idea how long it took for the wagon to leave the ferry, but at some assigned point in the past, time had stopped. She collapsed beside the schooner and waited. The younger children did not speak. Each person was looking toward the river—and hoping. After what seemed like an hour but was probably only ten minutes, Trenton rode up on Red. When he saw his mother, he fell off the horse and ran to her.

"They're gone! They went under the water." Sarah wanted to run, but at that time all she could do was gather her four children in her arms and weep. The crying didn't last long. Tyler Montgomery, from the previous wagon in line, came running toward them. He was followed by his brother Gomer. They had heard the yelling and unfortunately saw Luke's struggle.

Apparently, Remy became spooked by a log and began swimming back to shore. Luke tried to stay on the animal but was thrown off when she made the sharp turn. Asher tried to pull him onto one of the mules but was swept away also.

"They could be miles away by now, but there's a bend just ahead with some fallen trees. My pa is going to look for them now." Sarah smiled at the boy, but she knew. She just knew that she would never see Asher and Luke again. Her mind raced forward with the lonely nights she would endure and the wedding Luke would never have and the sudden predicament her family must face without their leader.

Tyler helped Fidget and Trenton move the wagon to the campsite a half mile west of the river. Sarah and the girls stood watch by the water, waiting for a miracle.

But a miracle was not granted.

Tyler and Gomer walked solemnly toward the women. "We's sorry. Pa found their bodies stuck in two crossing trees. They didn't make it." Jade and Jewel hugged each other and began to wail. Sarah sat down slowly and put her arms around herself. She rocked back and forth for a while before Betsy Montgomery tapped her on the shoulder.

"Sarah. Sarah," Betsy called out with compassion. "Let's get all of you to the wagon. We'll start a fire and get dried off." Sarah did as she was told. Thinking for herself was too painful. At their wagon, she saw the boys standing silently.

Betsy and her boys helped the family set their chairs around the fire. Sarah couldn't sit but encouraged her children to take a chair. She finally sat and stared at the flames in the fire. Through the fog in her mind, she heard Brother Barton run up. He rushed to Jade and hugged her so tightly that her feet lifted off the ground.

"I'm so sorry, Sarah. This is an unbearable tragedy, but I will be here for you. I will help however I can." Sarah looked at his eyes and saw the sincerity of an honest man. She felt an instant peace that she could not later explain. And she found courage. The Holy Spirit granted her courage in the moments after her loss.

"Thank you. We will need help with the bodies and the burial." Jewel cried out in sorrow, but Sarah continued. "And I don't rightly know where to go from here. Please pray for wisdom and for our provision." The pastor promised to help their family. After a heartfelt prayer, he went to find the Montgomerys and see about the bodies of Asher and Luke.

That night, most of the families comforted the mourning Wilkes with food and prayer. Trenton wrote furiously in the journal, carefully recording everything he could remember. Sarah appreciated the care from the others but worried about what to do next.

Don't worry about tomorrow. I am already there.

Without questioning, Sarah understood that God was speaking to her. Tomorrow would be a chance to demonstrate the faith that she and Asher had shared. The faith that they were teaching to their children. She prayed for wisdom and courage to lead her hurting family. And then she helped set out the bedrolls. Life went on.

CHAPTER THIRTEEN

Monday, May 26
2025

Anna woke to dark skies and rain showers. It was fitting for Memorial Day and the day after Armageddon. She didn't fall asleep until after three thirty this morning and woke up every twenty minutes after that. Her perfect life had fallen apart in less than an hour. How was that even possible?

The sound of pots and pans in the kitchen floated up to her room. How could life go on after the total disaster of yesterday? Jude never came home. For some reason, Anna wasn't surprised by that. He had been acting distant ever since their anniversary party. The children probably hadn't noticed, but Anna had. She decided in the middle of the night that she would let him do what he wanted to do. She knew that he felt confined, so she would give him space to get it out of his system. Surely Winnie had misunderstood his conversation about renting an apartment. Jude was probably sleeping on Justin's couch. He would have to come back tonight, at least to get clothes for work tomorrow.

The problems with Maya and Hunter were a little more challenging.

Anna dressed quickly and went downstairs to help with breakfast. Her shattered heart swelled when she saw her three children cooking eggs, bacon, and biscuits together. They were smiling. It was as if the weight of the wedding and move to Atlanta were lifted from their souls. Also, Jude's pessimistic attitude was missing. The mood was eerily light.

"Watch those eggs, Win. They need to be flipped." Maya was setting plates and napkins on the table.

"I'll get them," Anna said.

"How are you doing, Mom? Did you get any sleep at all?" Maya asked.

"Not much sleep. But watching you three fluttering around the kitchen gives me peace." Anna gathered utensils and two jelly jars.

"Have you talked to Dad?" Jan sounded concerned.

"No. He just needs some space." All three of her children looked skeptical. Was there something they weren't telling her. She didn't want to know. "Any word from Hunter?"

"We texted a little last night." Maya looked so grown up today Anna thought. "He really wants to move to Nevada. And he does not want to be tied down with a wife and a mortgage. I think I'm in shock. Everything was planned. I can't buy the house on my own. What about the wedding? I don't know what to do. But I don't think he will change his mind. And I don't want him if he doesn't want me."

Anna knew that her family was balancing on the edge of a huge cliff. Any wrong move could send them all crashing over the edge. Did that mean they should just stay still? Never in her life had she ever waited on life to happen. She always moved it herself. Maybe God was telling her to take her hands off the wheel for a little while. He would fix everything without her help. It seemed unnatural, but Anna decided to wait on taking any actions until God could work first. She silently asked Him to restore Jan's internship, repair Maya's relationship with Hunter, and return her husband. That's all she wanted. Her perfect life rebuilt.

The family was quiet as they ate their food. Each tried to make small talk, but the looming crises blanketed any conversation. Jan resigned that he would not be moving to Atlanta today. He decided that he would call Dr. Manning and ask if he could still work at the pharmacy while he sorted things with his internship. In the meantime, he would set up an appointment with Carbolytic to explain his part in Caleb's Instagram post. He had no idea what would happen with his apartment lease. He had paid the first and last month's rent, so June was covered. He wouldn't move any furniture yet. But he could sleep there when he met with the supervisor.

Maya's problem was more complicated. She wanted to give Hunter some "leg room," as he called it. But the rest agreed that there wasn't time for that. She needed to talk with him again in person—and soon. Anna wanted to join their discussion, but Winnie talked her out of interfering. It took more willpower than she thought she had for Anna to stay out of the situation. But she had confidence in God's ability to put their lives back in order.

Maya made plans to meet Hunter at Say Cheese for lunch. She admitted to her family that she didn't plan to beg but did hope that he would change his mind. Her entire future was linked to his. What would happen to her if he just removed himself from their team? Canceling the wedding was not an option.

"What are you going to say to him?" Winnie asked.

"I really don't know. I guess I will know what to say when I get there. I'm kind of numb right now."

"I think you should give him some space," Jan advised. "He loves you. He's just not ready to be tied down."

"'Tied down?' Marrying your sister is a blessing, not a curse." Anna was over the give-him-space answers. "Just tell him that everything will be fine. He can go fishing or golfing on the weekends to get away." Jan started laughing, but quickly realized that his mom was serious.

"I don't want to move to Nevada," Maya added softly.

Anna nodded sharply. "You can't move to Nevada. We are here. Your job is here. That cute house is here. Hunter will come to his senses. Men always do. When you get back, we can look at nail polish colors online. You need to be prepared before your appointment at the salon. Kenny Arnold's daughter panicked and picked bright blue for her nails last year. That color absolutely ruined the pictures."

"So, what about Dad?" Winnie surprised everyone by bringing up the oversize elephant stalking the room.

"He'll come back too. Just like Hunter." Anna wasn't so sure but could not imagine the alternative. "I'm giving him his space."

"We didn't want to tell you, but he sent us his new address this morning. He has a new apartment near the park." Anna could hear Winnie speaking, but the words sounded like they were coming through ten feet of water. Acid churned in her stomach, and her knees became soft.

Maya walked over to her mother. "Sit down, Mom. You don't look good."

Did Jude really move into an apartment. Does it have a resort pool and a gym? Is there another woman there with him? What is going on? Her axis was tilting. Her perfect sandcastle was being washed away before her eyes. Someone pulled her perfect life right out of her hands.

Not knowing what to do, Anna sat down and looked at her children. Surprisingly, tears did not fall on her face. "What do I do?"

"Let me talk to him, Mom," Jan said. "I can go over there and find out what he's thinking."

"That's sweet, but you have to deal with Carbolytic. And Maya has to deal with Hunter. I should go over there."

"No!" All three children stopped Anna before she could speak any further.

"It's okay, Mom. Let me go. I'll call Dr. Manning on the way and see if I can pick up a few hours this week. I can't call Carbolytic until tomorrow, so there's nothing else I can do. Oh, Caleb just texted that he took the post down. Maybe that will help."

"I'm not sure that is a good idea. But I'm not sure if what I'm experiencing is reality either. Someone please wake me if this is a dream." Anna sounded scared. "We have a great life. Why would Dad just want to leave like this? Do you think his blood pressure medicine is affecting his brain, Jan? Ask Dr. Manning." Anna would never forget the looks on her children's faces. They felt sorry for her. There was no fight in their actions. This was really happening.

Anna and Winnie cleaned up the breakfast dishes as Maya and Jan got ready to meet their respective defectors. Or were they fugitives? Either way, the conversations taking place today would affect the Yearlings forever. Anna knew in her heart that she should pray. She should get on her knees and pray until Jude came home. But she couldn't. She couldn't hand over her future to God. Of course, He could do "all things." But she wasn't a quitter. She would come up with a plan. So Anna asked God to help her design the best plan to put her sandcastle back together.

When Maya and Jan left, Anna and Winnie moved to the back deck. Anna didn't feel like sitting but didn't feel like pacing either. She clicked a pen and started writing on a notepad. The first task was to talk some sense back into Jude. Did he want a pool and gym like Jan in Atlanta? Is that it? Maybe they could join the country club. Or the new fitness center in town. That was easy.

And there couldn't possibly be another woman. Anna would know. Of course, Jude was spending a lot of time with that Brandee woman from the office. He claimed that he oversees her training. But she cleans the building at night. What training does she need? Could Anna be losing her husband to a girl with two *E*s at the end of her name?

Winnie sensed her mom's emotional spiral. "It's gonna be okay, Mom."

"I know. He'll come back."

"No. He might not. Whatever happens, it will be okay. Lou's parents still get together for Christmas. She gets to see her dad nearly every day."

Anna's heart skipped two or three beats. Divorce? That was never in the cards. That *is* not in the cards. She needed to talk with Jude. Now. As she leaned over to get her phone from the side table, Winnie warned her. "Don't call him, Mom. He doesn't want you telling him what to do."

Ouch! "I wouldn't tell him what to do."

"Yes, you would. You always tell us what to do. It's okay. We know you love us. But Dad is getting tired of it. Calling him to tell him what to do will only make it worse."

Anna dropped her shoulders. "Am I a monster, Win? Am I?"

"No, you aren't a monster."

"But Dad is acting like I am. I have given my whole life to this family."

"Mom—" Winnie put her sketch pad down and looked straight at her mother. "Let it go. You can't fix everything. Just let it go. Trying to control Dad will backfire on you."

Anna was proud of her daughter's wisdom, but she didn't like what she had to say. "What does that even look like? Do I just frolic around the house like nothing is wrong?"

"Yes. That is exactly what you should do. Let's go get ice cream. Or walk around the lake. That would be fun."

With her life in utter shambles, Anna never considered having fun. That seemed backwards. "I don't want to leave the house. I want to be here when your brother and sister get back. How about ordering pizza later? We can eat it out here."

"That sounds good. Wanna look at some of my sketches?"

Shame draped over Anna. She had never asked to look at Winnie's drawings. She always assumed they were just doodles. "Sure. Let me see." Winnie turned to the front page of her book and started flipping through the pages. Anna was stunned to see her daughter's unique style of drawing. Most of the drawings were of members of their family. Winnie drew with great detail in the center of the faces, and the shading increased toward the outer edges. Her technique was spectacular.

"Is this what you do while you are sitting out here? How do you remember the details of our faces?"

"I look at pictures on my phone. It's relaxing to create new drawings. You should get a hobby to calm you down too."

"I am calm."

"Ha! You are the least calm person I know."

That smarted. Did everyone see her as some high-strung control freak? "I write. That's a great hobby."

"Does it calm you down?" Winnie had a smirk on her face.

"No, it doesn't. I'm behind schedule on my current book. It's actually very stressful."

"What do you like? What calms you down?" Winnie closed her sketch pad and sat facing Anna.

"I don't really know. I do like working in the garden."

"Well, that's a start. You could control the plants instead of us." Winnie immediately regretted her comment. "Seriously, I like the garden idea. But there's also journaling or exercising or baking. What sounds good to you? I personally hope you choose baking. Brownies, cookies, cinnamon rolls—that sort of thing."

"I bet you would. Our lives are too crazy right now for me to start a new hobby," Anna remarked. "I need to get everyone back on track before I add something else."

"No, Mom. Now is the best time to start something. Sitting around and worrying isn't good for you. It isn't good for us either. Hold on . . ." Winnie jumped up and dashed into the house. A minute later, she came out with a pen and hard-bound journal. The book was light gray with an embossed rose on the front. It had about two hundred blank pages inside. "Grandma and Grandpa gave this to me for Christmas. I haven't finished my current one, so I haven't used it. It's yours."

"First of all, I can't take a gift from you. And second, I write for a living. I do that all the time." Anna knew that was a little bit of a lie. She *should* be writing all the time. Right now, she was only *thinking* about writing.

"Take the journal. And buy me one to replace it. Will that make you happy?"

"I guess."

"And this is different. Your books are fiction. They aren't exactly about you."

Anna thought about that. She usually put part of her personality into each story. But the characters were entirely fiction. Entirely from her imagination. "Okay, I'll try. What do I do?"

"There are lots of ways to journal. No one way is right. And you can change as much as you want. I like to think that God will be reading my words, so I tell Him what's going on. But you can write whatever you want. Why don't you start out by writing to Dad. Tell him what you are thinking. I know you want to call him. Write down what you would say."

"Good idea, Win. I'll try. It feels silly, but it's better than sitting here doing nothing." Anna opened the journal and wrote the date on the second page. The first page might be needed for a table of contents or dedication. Or was that just an author thing? She sat quietly for a moment. Winnie was sketching something in her pad. She decided to start by describing her surroundings.

I don't hear any birds right now. They are usually quite vocal in the late mornings. The humidity is coming back. It's not quite summer but slowly getting there. I may need an extra cup of coffee today. No, I may need ten. What are you doing? You can't just up and leave our family. We have a life together. We were going to grill chicken tonight. It's Memorial Day. We always grill chicken.

Winnie was right. This felt good. Anna poured out her thoughts without anyone countering her points. She told Jude that she was worried, and she laid out a plan for everyone to get back on track. At some point, Winnie went inside. But Anna kept writing. She had to get everything down before she forgot it. When she had said, or written, her final thoughts to Jude, she closed the journal and looked around. Her sandcastle was still in ruins. But she was looking past that now, to the waves and their shades of blues and greens. The journaling helped her see past her immediate crisis—a little bit. A very little bit. But it was something.

Anna went inside and decided that a late cup of coffee wouldn't kill her. She wasn't one hundred percent sure it wouldn't kill her but was up for finding out.

Jan returned first. He had spent two hours with his dad. "He's not coming back anytime soon, Mom."

"What? That can't be true. I need to call him." Jan sat at the kitchen table and motioned for Anna to sit. Winnie stood in the doorway.

"Don't call. Not yet. He's already expecting you to call and order him to come back. That's kind of the point."

"Point? What do you mean?"

Winnie sat next to Jan. "That's why he left. You order us around too much."

Anna was getting tired of hearing the endless loop of unchecked oppression. If she really had control, things would be different. They would have planted more flowers and less vegetables in the garden. They would eat at the cute diner near the courthouse more. And she wouldn't have mauve towels in the hall bathroom. Jude insisted they remain, since his parents gave them as a gift. But they were hideous. And Anna let Jude have his way on that. Why was the entire family ganging up on her? "How is he?"

"I hate to say this, but he's fine. He ordered hot wings for us and bottles of root beer. Not cans and not diet—bottles. We talked about some of our family vacations. But he also talked about the future. He wants to live his life how he wants it from now on. He's been thinking about it for over a year and made the deposit on his apartment the very same day I did on mine. All Dad has are some beach chairs and a blow-up mattress, but I don't think he cares." Winnie looked to Anna to speak first.

"Did he ask about me?" Anna asked defeatedly.

"Not really. He said he would call you tonight. I think he wants to get some stuff out of the attic. Like pots and pans and pillows."

"Brutal," Winnie responded. "This is officially weird now."

Jan nodded his head. "I thought so, too, until I saw Dad. He's happy. I had a lot of fun hanging with him. He said I could stay with him if I can't get the internship back."

Cue the tears. The last comment was too much. Anna covered her face and started ugly crying. Everything in her soul wanted to sit up and fix the situation. But she knew that she couldn't. Jude was in control right now. "Does he have a girlfriend?" Anna managed to utter between sobs.

"Oh, no. He doesn't have a girlfriend. Well, I don't think so. He didn't say. Do you think he does?"

"Jan, don't make it worse!" Winnie put her arm around her mom. "It's going to be okay, Mom. You'll see. He doesn't have a girlfriend. He's just acting stupid right now. We'll laugh at this someday."

Anna had no words. She dried her eyes and stood to make lunch. That was something she could control. She asked Winnie and Jan to talk about something pleasant while she made some grilled cheese sandwiches. As she was pulling out her large frying pan, she heard Maya's car drive up. Without even seeing her daughter, she knew that the wedding was off. Hunter was going to flee the family just like his no-longer future father-in-law. She went to the pantry for bread.

"I'm back, and it isn't good." Maya tossed her keys on the foyer table. "I don't care anymore. If he thinks Nevada will be better, let him go."

"Way to go, sis! I like your fire." Winnie had both fists in the air. Anna mindlessly walked over and moved Winnie's hands to the table.

"What happened?" Anna asked.

"The more we talked, the madder he got. He's going to Nevada, and I don't think he wants me to go. I spit out a list of things we will have to do to undo the wedding, but he didn't care. He just said to text him half of the list and that he would take care of it. Will you help me make a list, Mom?"

"Wait!" Anna blurted. "The wedding can't be off. We've made all the plans. The Jack and Jill shower is in two weeks. The seed packets. The dress. He can't just cancel now. It's too late."

"Apparently not," Maya countered. "It's over." The three children looked at Anna. She didn't speak as she continued cooking the sandwiches.

Nobody spoke until Jan's phone buzzed a few minutes later. "Dr. Manning said I could come in after lunch tomorrow."

Anna rolled her eyes. She would take the small win though. As she finished lunch, she thought to herself that this couldn't be happening. Life couldn't take an abrupt turn like this, could it? Of course it could. But knowing that it could didn't make it any easier to accept.

Later that evening, Jude called. He planned to come over later to get some clothes and asked Anna to set out both suitcases. She held her emotions deep inside and agreed to whatever he asked. Thankfully, she wrote his demands down, because she didn't remember any of them when they hung up.

Anna went to the upstairs hall closet and found the suitcases. Both still had airline tags from their trip to Dallas in October. Jude hated flying but made the trip to help a client looking to purchase a strip mall in a suburb of the area. Anna came along and called her time in the hotel a "writing retreat." Jude took a Dramamine when the plane took off and slept through the flight.

Next, Anna removed Jude's toiletries from the tidy basket and put them into his travel bag. She threw in extra soap and toothpaste. Jan helped his mother line the suitcases and toiletries in the foyer. Jude would have to pack his clothes on his own. As a last-minute thought, she placed some cans of soup and a manual can opener in a grocery bag. She didn't add crackers. He should suffer a little.

When Jude arrived around nine thirty, Anna went to the back deck and sat on the swing. She did her best to hold her emotions in check. The others were clearly talking in cheerful tones. That didn't seem right, but Anna let it go.

After a few minutes, Jude opened the back door and leaned out. "I'll be back on Wednesday to look in the attic. You don't have to help." After that distant comment, he was off. No goodbye. No hug. No conversation. Just gone. Anna sat on the swing for another twenty minutes. The crickets and tree frogs were unusually loud tonight. She knew in her gut that she should give all of this to God, but she just couldn't. Not yet. She needed to try to fix everything first. That was what her brain was saying, and that was what she would do.

Sarah managed to get an hour of sleep and considered that a blessing. The children were quiet and claimed to not want breakfast. But Sarah insisted that they continue their normal routine by heating up beans and bacon. She added biscuits this time. Thankfully, no one complained.

Shortly before the family finished eating, Brother Barton arrived. He had Spit with him. The two of them sat with Sarah and discussed her future.

"We kin bring you along, Miss," Spit volunteered. "But without a man your animals won't git very far."

"I can help them," Brother Barton responded. But everyone recognized that the Wilkes family could not make the rest of the journey without Asher and Luke—and the horse and mules that were also gone.

"We leave in two days," Spit responded as he walked away. "Got four more wagons to cross tomorrow."

Sarah sighed. "What should we do, Brother Barton?"

"First of all, call me Dewayne."

"Okay, Dewayne. What should we do?" Sarah began crying.

"Let's get the others and have a family meeting. This decision affects them too." Sarah liked having something to do so she called the children to the chairs. And she wasn't bothered when Jade stood right next Dewayne.

"All right, we have a decision to make," Dewayne started. "I am here to help this family. You have lost your pa and Luke, plus a horse and the mules. I don't think you can make it to the Oregon Territory. But this is your decision. I would like to hear from each of you."

Jade spoke quickly. "I want to go where you are going, Dewayne." The rest of the family groaned at her response.

Trenton was next. "I can lead the family now. I say we keep going."

"We need Papa," Jewel whimpered. "I don't want to ever do another crossing again." With that comment the decision was made. None of the others wanted to cross another river either.

"That means that we cannot go back to Missouri," Dewayne added. "We would have to cross two rivers to get back. We can go forward with the company and stop at the next town. That would be Ash Hollow. What do you think? It's not very far."

Sarah marveled at how well her family worked together during this horrible time. They hastily agreed that they would travel to Ash Hollow on Wednesday, which was less than a day's travel from the Crossing. They would spend the next day resting and mourning their loss before the short journey.

"What about Papa and Luke?" Fidget asked.

"We haven't forgotten about them, sweet boy," Sarah added. "The Montgomerys buried them by those trees last night. Brother Barton will lead a funeral service for us before we leave."

Dewayne smiled and was amazed at Sarah's strength. It could only come from the Holy Spirit.

The funeral was short. Everyone from the company came, plus a few ferry workers. But life was cruel. As soon as the memorial was over, the Wilkes family made plans for the trip to Ash Hollow. Sarah wanted to live by the graves of her men forever. She never wanted to leave. But life under the trees was not possible. She had to keep moving forward.

Shortly before sunset, Sarah returned alone to the graves of her husband and son. She wanted to bid them goodbye one more time. Ash Hollow was close enough that she could travel back to visit, but she knew that such traveling would be difficult, and she wasn't sure how long she would stay in the nearby town.

"I don't know how I will go on without you both. I am only living by the Spirit. But I will see you again someday, and we will rejoice like never before. I'm glad you have each other to share glory." She wanted to say more but could not make the words come out of her mouth.

As she reached down to touch the fresh dirt on Asher's grave, Sarah felt his pocket watch in her pocket. "Your watch. You forgot your watch. I guess you don't need it anymore." She took out the watch and turned it over. The hands were not moving. Time had stopped at 10:17—the exact time that Asher fell in the river. Sarah held the watch to her chest and thanked God for the reminder of her hardworking husband.

Back at the wagon, Sarah asked Dewayne to read Psalm 10:17–18 to the family. The Psalms had been Asher's favorite book. And the time on the watch seemed appropriate. The pastor opened the Bible he kept with him and read. "You, LORD, hear the desire of the afflicted; you encourage them, and you listen to their cry, defending the fatherless and the oppressed, so that mere earthly mortals will never again strike terror."

CHAPTER FOURTEEN

Tuesday, May 27
2025

"Operation Wedding Undo." Where were the helpful books for a situation like this? Jan should be starting his internship today, and Maya should be packing for her new house. Jude should have eaten breakfast at their house, not in some trashy bachelor pad on the other side of town. Anna thought of her friends. What would they think if they saw Jude? She would come up with an explanation until he came back home. Maybe he could be allergic to something in the house. That would work.

"You ready, Mom?" Maya walked up to Anna at the kitchen table with a notepad and funny-looking pen. She had taken the day off work to "deal with personal stuff," as she told her boss.

"Where did you get that pen?"

"Dr. Shultz, the dentist, gives these out now with our cleanings. They have different teeth on the top and look like toothpaste on the sides." Both laughed at the ridiculousness of their conversation given the gravity of what they were about to do.

"Okay, then you write and I'll talk." Anna sounded resigned. "First, we need to tell everyone. We need to go through the RSVPs and let those who replied yes know that the wedding is off." Anna stumbled at the word *off* but managed. "Some have reserved hotel rooms."

Maya drew a line down the middle of the page. She wrote her name at the top left and "Mom" at the top right. "Will you call the RSVP yes list if I call the wedding party?"

"Sure. Have you told Grace and Gene yet?"

"No, they are Hunter's parents. He should tell them. What about Grandma Sylvia and Grandpa Tom?"

Anna thought for a moment. "That's tricky. I think Dad should tell them. It's weird right now while he's going through this 'spell.' Things will be back to normal soon."

"Are you sure, Mom? Both of our lives blew up on Sunday. I'm not sure it will ever be normal again." With that thought, Maya broke down crying. Anna was surprisingly calm through the meltdown and got a cool cloth for Maya's face.

"It's okay. If these men need some space, we'll just wait them out. You'll see. It will be okay. Let's get back to the list. That is something we can control."

Maya clicked the pen several times and made a determined effort to move forward. "What's next?"

"We need to call the vendors. List them out loud, and we'll divide the work."

"Cake."

Anna responded quickly. "That was a small deposit. I'll call tomorrow and cancel."

"Flowers."

"I think those should be easy. I'll call Brittany. She'll understand. I don't think she's ordered anything this soon. We can cancel the candle holders too. Won't need to rent those now."

"Tuxes."

"Hunter."

Maya started a list for Hunter on a new sheet of paper. "What about the photographer? Will they understand?"

"I will call them. They gave us a great deal. Maybe I can schedule some family pictures to make it up to them."

Maya looked up. "Without Dad?"

A tear ran down the corner of Anna's eye, but she didn't respond.

"I can cancel my hair and makeup appointment. But I will probably keep my nail appointment. Why not?"

"Sounds good. We're tackling this well, I think."

"What about the caterers? That's a biggie."

Anna sighed. "I will drive over there in the morning. We paid for half of the food up front. If we can't get out of that, I will see if we can get some of the food and just freeze it for our next family get-together."

"Once again, Mom. Without Dad?"

"Don't worry about Dad. This is just a phase."

"I guess I'll keep my dress. Do we let the bridesmaids keep theirs? You and Dad paid for them."

"Yes, they've been fitted. We can't return those. Maybe the photographers can take some pictures of the girls in their dresses." Anna straightened the salt and pepper shakers in the middle of the table.

"That would be weird. I'm thinking that we all go out in our dresses for fun. Like for pizza."

"Now *that* would be weird." Anna cracked a smile. "What's next? Did we ever book a videographer?"

"No, Uncle Carl was going to set something up with a tripod."

"Well, that one is easy. And I'm so glad you went with the church as your venue. That was on a 'donation basis,' so we didn't lose a bundle there. Oh, goodness. The DJ. Your songs. They were so perfect." It was Anna's turn to cry. She stood and walked into the living room. Maya didn't move.

After a few minutes, Anna returned to the kitchen. "This feels like grief. That just hit me. Dad was going to dance with you. I couldn't wait for that."

"I know. It hasn't really sunk in yet for me either. June fourteenth is going to be so sad."

"We'll plan something fun to take our minds off the day. Is that all the vendors?"

"Will you call Pastor Ed? Hunter is handling the house closing and furniture. I told him he had to deal with that."

"Sure. I'll tell Pastor Ed that you're waiting till after the job in Nevada."

"That's not exactly true, Mom. Please don't lie to our pastor."

"I'll come up with something. We don't want the truth to get all over the church." Anna realized what she had said. "Okay, I won't lie."

"Thanks. I think that's all the vendors. Wanna take a break?"

"No. Let's get this finished. I would like to see my assignments."

As Anna was talking, Jan walked into the kitchen. "What are you two doing?"

"We're *undoing*," Maya said.

"Ah, that's grim." Jan dug an apple and a sports drink out of the refrigerator. "I'm going to the pharmacy. I left a message with Carbolytic. When they call back, I'll make a plan to meet with my supervisor tomorrow or Thursday. Hopefully, I can start next week."

Anna clasped her hands together. "Oh, that sounds great. Be careful."

"Will do."

After Jan left, the undoing continued. "What about the gifts, Mom? They've been coming in for months. And the shower gifts? What do we do?"

"I'm not sure. Let me look that up." Anna got her laptop from her desk and brought it to the kitchen. She scanned a few websites. "It looks like the proper thing is to return everything. Even that personalized cutting board. Have you sent out thank-you notes yet?"

"No. We were going to do those after the wedding."

"Let's use the notes to tell people that we will be returning the gifts. You'll need to make another list of everything you received. Then we'll figure out if we can hand deliver them or mail them. That can be our project for this weekend. How about Saturday? Then we can 'deliver' them the next week. What a mess!"

"It is. I could kick Hunter in both knees for doing this." Maya quickly turned to the anger stage of grief.

"So could I. This was terrible timing."

"Or maybe it was great timing. What if he moved to Nevada after we got married. That would be worse."

"I'm not so sure . . . The ring! What about your ring?" Maya held out her hand, and Anna looked at her ring. She started to remove it, but Anna stopped her. "Don't take it off yet. People will talk. Let's wait until everyone knows before you take the ring off. Oh, it's so pretty. Hunter did a great job picking that out."

"I hate it! And I hate him!" Maya drew a large sad face on the notepad. "I hope he thirsts to death in the desert."

The last comment got a chuckle out of Anna. "Okay. Let's not go that far. I'm feeling pretty good about this. Is there anything else?"

"The cruise."

"Oh, I forgot about the honeymoon. Grace and Gene paid for it. And the flight to Miami. Maybe they can take the cruise instead."

"They can't. One person must stay on the itinerary. Cruise lines will only let you change one name and only once. Hunter said that his parents want us to go. But he doesn't want to go. I don't want to go by myself. But I do have that week off from work."

"No. I don't want you to go by yourself." Anna couldn't imagine her daughter sailing in the Bahamas alone.

"What about you? Yes. That is a great idea! We could go together. You've never had a chance to go on a cruise because Dad gets motion sick. This would be perfect!"

"Oh, I don't know about that. I can't just leave Winnie. And Dad will probably be back by then."

"Mom, Dad has an apartment. He signed a lease. He's not coming back in eighteen days."

Anna turned instantly pale. She hadn't thought about a lease. Was this permanent? No. It couldn't be. Jude would come home. Jan would get his internship back. And Hunter would regret his decision. He and Maya would throw together a quick backyard wedding, and everything would be perfect. That's how it had to be.

"Mom. Are you okay?"

"I'm fine. Ask one of the Micheles about the cruise. I need to be here for Dad." Just as Anna finished speaking, her ringtone sounded. She dashed into the living room and spun around a few times before she could find her phone. "Hello . . . What? . . . When? . . . I'll be there."

Anna ran upstairs to put on some shoes. Maya hurried to the bottom of the stairs. "What's wrong?"

"Winnie got hurt at school?"

"At school? Aren't they out?" Maya helped her mom gather her keys and phone.

"The yearbook club was working today. Something about moving the unsold yearbooks. Apparently, a shelf collapsed, and some boxes of books fell onto Winnie and Marjorie. They both got hit in the head. Since school is technically out, Mr. Jones is driving them to the ER."

"I'll drive." Maya opened the front door.

On the way to the hospital, Anna prayed out loud. "I can't take any more, God. You promised not to give us more than we could handle. This is too much. Please let Winnie be okay. And fix my *perfect* life."

Maya stopped for a red light and looked over at her mother. "God never promised that He wouldn't give us more than we could handle. That's kind of the point. We can't handle this life *on our own.*"

"I know we need God. But He wants us to be happy, doesn't He? What if Winnie has a serious head injury? Or a broken neck? This is too much." Anna softly wept, and Maya kept driving. She made it to the hospital as quickly as she could without breaking any speeding laws. Or not too many of them.

In the emergency room, Anna spotted Mr. Jones. He was holding two clipboards and passed one to her. "You need to fill this out. Marjorie's parents aren't here yet."

"How is she?"

"She seems okay, but she said that sounds were muffled. Like she was underwater."

"Oh, my goodness. Where is she?" Anna looked around for a door leading to her baby.

"Once you fill out those papers, you can go back to see her. Only one person." Anna realized that the papers must be completed, so she sat in a nearby chair and filled them out quickly. She knew every piece of information by heart.

As she stood to return the papers, she thought of Jude. "Will you call Dad, Maya? He needs to know."

"Sure. I'll call him right now. And I will wait here for you. Please text me if you find out anything. I'll call Jan after Dad."

"Thanks."

As Anna was standing at the nurses' station with the clipboard, she heard Maya in the distance. *Hey, Brandee. Can I talk to my dad.* The sandcastle was officially gone. A tsunami had wiped out her perfect life in less than forty-eight hours. This had to be some sort of cruel spiritual joke. How can something be completely obliterated so quickly? Like wildfire. Her life had been wiped out by a wildfire. But how does a person fight a wildfire after it has burned everything down? Anna looked down at her feet. She had house slippers on. Just great. It got worse.

A beautiful nursed named Rosa led Anna to her daughter. Winnie was in a holding bay by herself. She had a blood pressure cuff on her left arm and looked to be sleeping. Anna felt a sudden surge of strength and reached for her daughter's hand. Winnie's eyes opened but were droopy. Anna smiled at her and decided to remain quiet. In what seemed like an eternity, a doctor finally came into the bay.

"You must be Winter's mother. I'm Dr. Ross. She took quite a hit to the head. Her vitals and reflexes look good though. I'd like to get a CT scan of her head to be sure. If that comes back clean, you can take her home. But we will have a protocol for you to follow for twenty-four hours. Were her eyebrows like that before the accident?"

"Yes. Thank you, Doctor."

Anna knew she should say more, but her strength had disappeared as quickly as it had arrived. She held on to Winnie's hand until a nurse came to wheel her daughter to the imaging area. While she waited in the sterile bay, she silently thanked God that Winnie hadn't been hurt worse. Her mind was numb. All she could do was thank God.

"Anna? How is she?" Jude appeared out of nowhere. So much for the one-person rule.

"They just took her back for a CT scan. She could have a serious brain injury. If you hadn't moved out, this never would have happened."

"How did me moving out affect her accident? Really, Anna?" Jude was clearly frustrated. But Anna was more frustrated.

"She would have talked with you and left for school later. She wouldn't have been near the shelf when it collapsed."

"This is exactly why I left. You have to control everything. Even the narrative. I can't take it anymore. I *won't* take it anymore."

"Does a covenant with God mean anything to you?" Anna was fighting dirty now.

"It does. But it must be a three-way covenant. You've taken over all the roles. I can't be part of a one-way covenant-with you in charge."

"What about the kids? Winnie was nearly killed. Jan is getting his position back by himself. No thanks to you. And Maya and I spent the morning undoing the wedding. Are you too busy being in control of your life to help our children?"

"I'm in touch with the children. We've been texting. I just gave Jan some suggestions on how to approach his supervisor." Anna hadn't realized that Jude was texting the kids. That hurt as much as him not texting her.

"Why don't you just get over this and come home. You don't belong in an apartment."

Just as Anna completed the last sentence, Pastor Ed walked into the bay. "Anna. Jude. How's Winnie? And what is this about an apartment?"

An involuntary shiver ran down Anna's spine. How could this day continue to get worse? She had to take control and fix this mess. "Oh, it's nothing. Jude is having an allergic reaction to something in our house. He's staying in an apartment until we figure out what it is. And Winnie is getting a CT scan right now. We'll know more in a little bit. Thank you for coming to see us." Jude rolled his eyes about the apartment lie but didn't expose Anna's fib.

"Of course. I was here visiting two of our members, and I saw Maya in the waiting room. She told me that Winnie and a friend were hurt with boxes of yearbooks. That sounds frightening."

Anna hadn't thought about the emotional effect of Winnie's injury. She hadn't thought about the emotional effects of the past two days on her entire family. What a huge mess!

"She seems to be okay," Anna answered. "But we'll know more soon."

"I'd like to pray for her and for Jude's allergy. Where is the new apartment?" Pastor Ed looked straight at Anna. She froze because she had no idea where Jude was staying. Just that it was across town. She was about to respond when Jude spoke up.

"The Lodges. I'm at the Lodges for a little while. Would you also pray for Jan? He may have lost his internship with Carbolytic. And Hunter called off the wedding. So please pray for Maya. She's going through a lot right now."

Pastor Ed's eyes doubled in size. "When did all of this happen?"

"This past weekend," Jude said matter-of-factly. "Can you believe it?"

"Yes, I can believe it," Pastor Ed said. "This is spiritual warfare. I'm glad I'm here. I will pray for your family now and later. Could I come by the house later today to meet with the children?"

"No!" Anna blurted. "We're fine."

Jude shook his head. "No, we're not fine, Anna. We're sailing through a storm right now. I think it would be a good idea for Ed to meet with the kids. Could you give us a few days, Pastor? Everything is a little raw right now."

"Sure. That sounds like a good idea. Anna, I will call you in a few days. But please know that you can reach out to me anytime. I will continue to pray. And please keep me posted on Winnie's condition."

"Thank you, Ed. I will let you know when we get home." The pastor put his hands on Anna and Jude's shoulders and lifted their family up in prayer. Anna felt better when he finished. A little bit of her burden had been shifted to God. She felt a little lighter. Not much lighter, but enough to notice.

When the pastor left, Anna and Jude remained quiet. Neither had anything to say to the other. After a few minutes, Winnie was rolled back and cleared to go home. She should be closely monitored over the next twenty-four hours, including waking her throughout the night. Anna could handle that. She didn't expect to get much sleep over the next few days. On the way out of the emergency bays, Anna's phone buzzed. Laney Oates, her editor, was calling. Anna ignored the call. Once again, her writing would have to wait.

When the girls were seated in Maya's car, Jude leaned into the passenger window. "I'd like to come over tonight to get a few things out of the attic. I think we have some old pots and pans I can use. And those wooden end tables."

"That would be fine," Anna responded coldly. "I know where the pots are. I can show you." Then she rolled the passenger window up and waited for Maya to drive off. She remembered Winnie in the back seat and reminded Maya to drive slowly and to avoid any bumps.

Back home, she settled her daughter on the couch with a blanket and two throw pillows. Winnie insisted that she was fine but a little tired. Anna convinced her to rest for the day by promising takeout from the "old" Mexican restaurant. Maya went to her room to call her bridesmaids.

When she sat down, Anna remembered Pastor Ed and sent him a text telling him that Winnie was home. Ten seconds later, her phone buzzed. Ed was calling. "Hello," Anna whispered.

"Hi, Anna. Thank you for the update. I'm concerned for you and your family. How are you doing? You've had a lot come at you recently. Is the wedding officially off?"

Anna moved to the back porch. "We are fine. Really. Maya and Hunter are taking some time off."

"It sounds more serious than that. Let me ask. Does Jude really have a mysterious allergy?"

For the third time that day, Anna started sobbing. The lack of control over her emotions was unsettling. "No. He doesn't. He moved out for a little while. It's not a big deal."

"Anna, moving into an apartment *is* a big deal. But not too big for God. I will be praying for your marriage and for all your children."

Anna cried tears of appreciation. She had no words. Pastor Ed listened patiently and finally asked if there was anything he could do to help.

"Would you please help us cancel the church? We obviously don't need it for June fourteenth anymore."

"Of course. Consider it done."

"And would you answer one question? Why does God cause bad things to happen? Why all at once like this?"

"God doesn't cause anything bad to happen," Pastor Ed spoke slowly. "Ever! He doesn't make plans for accidents or heartaches. But He isn't surprised by them either. Why He allows things to happen we will never fully know. But we live in a fallen world. We make bad choices. People around us make bad choices. Suffering is a part of this world."

"That's difficult for me to believe right now."

"I know," the pastor said kindly. "You've been dealt a lot right now. But your response should be to trust God. Tell Him how you are feeling, and listen for His promptings. The greatest Man who ever lived faced pain. He did not blame God but glorified Him. When you are on the other side of this, remember to tell others of how God helped you. I suggest you keep a journal. Then you will remember exactly how God was with you."

Anna was skeptical but felt a peace about Pastor Ed's words. "Thank you for your time. It means a lot to me. I will try to listen for God's voice. I really will."

"That sounds great. And don't worry what others will think at church. I hope your entire family will be in your usual pew on Sunday.

I'm preaching about the Christian perspective of comfort and compassion. You may find extra meaning in the message."

When she hung up, she gathered her journal and a pen. Winnie was sleeping, but Anna wanted to keep an eye on her, so she sat on the loveseat nearby. The words flowed today, and it felt good to write them down. She told God of her fears for her marriage and each child. Surprisingly, she mentioned others' opinions of her family more than once. Why did she care so much what people thought of her? She drew lines through those parts. God was the important One for now.

Anna ordered street tacos for supper, and Jan picked them up on his way home from the pharmacy. The family ate in the living room so that Winnie didn't have to move. She picked at her food but ate enough to satisfy her mother.

Jan looked sad when he got home and eventually revealed that the supervisor was serious. The internship was gone. It had already been offered to someone else. "I'm stuck here with no job and no future."

Maya tried to cheer him up. "No. You are just getting started. You just have to pivot to plan B. What would that be?"

"I don't even know. What about you, sis? Do you have a plan B?"

"Not really. I have a job and will stay here until I figure something out. What else can I do?"

"Pray." The short response came from Anna. "We should all pray and listen for God to tell us what to do. That's what Pastor Ed said today. And we know that is what Mr. Marco told you in youth group. That's the *what next* part."

"Wow, Mom. You don't sound like yourself," Winnie spoke up.

"Ha! I don't feel like myself. I feel like a huge sinkhole opened, and I fell into it. But God had His hands under the dirt and caught me. Now I'm hoping He shows me how get out of this dark hole."

The three children smiled. "Don't hope, Mom. Expect. Let's *expect* God to show us the way out. He will," Jan said confidently.

"Okay," Anna agreed. "We will *expect*. Winnie, will you make us a nice sign tomorrow with the word *expect* on it? I want to stick in on the refrigerator. That will help all of us remember that God will work things out for our good. You know, I feel better when I'm talking about God. When I start thinking about the 'new' future, I get anxious. This is new territory for me, but I'm trying."

Just as Anna admitted her weakness, Jude came through the front door. He looked at the tacos the family was eating but didn't ask for any. Instead, he asked Winnie how she was feeling. Anna walked into the kitchen to give Jude some time with the kids. She felt as if she were living someone else's life while she straightened the drinking glasses into neater rows.

After a few minutes, Jude came to the kitchen and asked Anna if she had time to help him in the attic. Anna appreciated his respect of her time but thought the entire situation was selfish. She led him as they walked to the pull-down staircase in the garage, and he brought the heavy ladder down.

The storage space above the garage was large and well-organized. When they had moved into the house, Jude added plywood flooring and wooden shelves at each end of the attic. Most of the contents were cardboard boxes labeled with their contents. Jude quickly found the end tables and brought them down the ladder one by one. When he returned a second time, he found Anna sorting through a box of Maya's childhood mementos. She had collected artwork, medals, photos, and uniforms for each child. "Look at her tiny dance shoes. It doesn't seem that long ago." Anna passed tiny pink ballet slippers to Jude.

"No, it doesn't. I remember how excited she was for her first recital. But she stood behind the curtain and peeked out twice. We paid for two outfits and never saw the second one on stage."

"She doesn't like to do things first. That's strange for an older child." Anna placed the shoes back in the box and pulled out a graduation tassel.

"Is she okay?" Jude had a serious tone in his voice.

"She's fine."

"No, Anna. Is she really okay?"

"I think so. Hunter is moving to Nevada, so there's not much she can do. We have been undoing the wedding. I'm praying that he will come to his senses and we can do this again next year."

Jude's tone got softer. "Be careful about that. Their breakup may be a blessing in disguise."

Anna put the tassel back in the box and closed the flaps. "Nonsense! I'll get them back together. It will work out."

"That's the problem I have with you. You think you are God. You don't control the universe, Anna. You only control your response to it." The last words stung. Jude had verbally underrated her ability as a mother. He just said that she was a bad mother.

"Well, you have your opinions. I will keep this family together while you go play house." Anna wanted to add "with Brandee" but held back. She didn't want to give him any ideas. "Let's find the pots. Is there anything else you need?"

"Any kind of kitchen stuff would be good. I'm using paper plates right now." Anna stifled a snort. The whole situation was ridiculous.

But she would let Jude go. If he didn't want to be with her, he was free to live in his juvenile apartment.

Anna moved some boxes and found one labeled "G-G-G-Grandma Lilly." She had moved several boxes from her parents' house when her father died, and they had been stored in the attic for over two decades. From her memory, the box in front of her held worn blankets and some journals. Anna was about to maneuver over to where Jude was rearranging boxes when she felt a pull to open the box. She really needed to pare down the clutter in the attic, but now was not the time. Yet the urge to open the box remained. So she sat on a nearby red wagon and pulled back the flaps of the box.

As expected, several blankets were on top of the contents. Anna held them up and marveled that they were handmade quilts. Thirty years ago they were simply blankets to her. But today, she recognized the skill needed to make such delicate stitches. She moved the blankets to see what was below them.

Directly under the quilts were four bound leather journals. The top one had "Diary" carved on the front cover. Anna remembered something about her great-great-great-great-grandmother keeping detailed diaries. It was a family treasure that she had completely forgotten about. One of the grandmothers had painstakingly typed out the words in the diary, leaving a written legacy over one hundred years old. But Anna had no idea where the electronic version was now. She took the top journal out of the box and vowed to find the whereabouts of the typed version sometime over the summer. She carried the diary down the ladder.

Two minutes later, Jude came down with a box of kitchen items. "This should get me started. I'm going to buy a coffee maker and some cheap eating utensils to get by. And I may come back to look up there again. This should be enough for now."

Everything inside of Anna begged to ask Jude to stay and talk. But she just couldn't do it. He was acting foolishly and had to learn the hard way. Besides, she needed to take care of the children first. Their issues were more important now.

When Jude left, Anna moved the diary to her dresser. Maybe the journal would give her ideas for her novel. As she came downstairs, she discovered that the kids had cleaned up dinner and were watching *The Sound of Music* on TV. Once again, her life seemed surreal. She was going through the motions, and she knew it. But there wasn't much else to do right now. Anna pulled a bag of chocolate chunk cookies out of the freezer and brought them to the living room. No need to worry about the too-small mother-of-the-bride dress now.

1851

I can't go on.

CHAPTER FIFTEEN

Anna woke and was briefly confused to see that she was in the living room. She quickly remembered that she and Winnie had slept downstairs so she could check on her daughter every hour. Thankfully, Winnie slept well and did not have any ill effects from the accident. Anna let her daughter sleep a little longer and went to the kitchen to start some hot tea.

Maya was at the table eating a yogurt cup. "Morning, Mom."

"Hi, sweetie. Are you okay to go to work?"

"Yeah. It will be good to see everyone. I have a big project to finish before the wedd— before the cruise, so I need to get back to it."

"That sounds good. I will work on my *undo* list today. We can do this. I'm sure of it." Anna took her favorite mug out of the sink drainer. The one that declared her to be the world's greatest mom. Ha!

"Well, we don't have a choice. Thank you for all your help. I'm serious about the cruise. I don't want to go alone."

"You don't have any friends who want to go?" Anna allowed herself to briefly consider taking the fabulous cruise. What would Jude think about that?

"Nope. Everyone has plans. Please, Mom. Please consider it." Maya stood to throw her yogurt container away. She squeezed her mother's shoulder on the way to the garbage can. "We would have so much fun. And you would have lots of time to write. We don't have to do the treasure hunt."

"We can't just leave Winnie alone. Jan will be in Atlanta trying to get his internship back."

"No. Accept that Carbolytic is over. Jan will be working at the pharmacy this summer. He and Winnie will be fine. They could even stay with Dad some if you would like that."

The thought of Jude having to see his children's suffering made Anna consider the cruise even more. This would be a once-in-a-lifetime chance to sail on the wide-open sea. And Maya was practically begging. "I will think about it."

"Please, Mom. I already bought new swimsuits and three new dresses. Please don't make me miss out."

"Whoa, I'm not the one causing your predicament. But a week vacation on the sea does sound heavenly. Let me think about it. We can talk with Jan and Winnie tonight."

"Sounds great. I need to go. Have a great day."

"You too, sweetie. Don't work too hard."

Anna brought her tea into the living room. She watched Winnie sleep and heard Jan rummaging around in his room getting ready.

Thank you, God, that my family is safe. Please put us back to the way we were.

An hour later, Jan was at work and Winnie was up and texting on her phone. "I'm thinking about working part-time with Dad. He said they still need help with the filing. What do you think?"

"I think that's a great idea," Anna responded quickly. "You will get to see your Dad and get a little spending money." *Plus, she could keep an eye on hovering Brandee.* "When would you start?"

"I'm not sure. I'll ask."

Anna went to her office to begin calling vendors for Operation Wedding Undo. First up was the bakery. After a quick call, she was only out her deposit. Not bad.

Next was the photographer. This call was a little longer but, in the end, Anna arranged a deal for senior portraits for Winnie. Her daughter would resist, but the woman on the phone suggested some clever backgrounds. Winnie would probably like one of them.

The call to the florist would be a little tricky. Brittany was a friend from Anna's small group in church. She was trying to keep her business afloat and counted on wedding business in June. After ten minutes of catching up, Anna revealed that the wedding was "postponed." She would not yet declare it to be cancelled. Fortunately, Brittany understood. She had plenty of business for that weekend to keep her busy and simply asked Anna to remember her when the wedding was rescheduled.

Three calls in thirty minutes. Pretty good work. Anna would have to visit the caterer to work out the canceling, since she and Jan had paid for half of the food up front. After she found the right shoes to wear with her white shorts and lime-colored T-shirt, she went downstairs. Winnie was drawing on her sketchpad. "I have to go to the caterers downtown. Want to come with me?"

"No, thank you. I'm gonna hang out here today. I don't have a lot of energy."

Anna became somewhat concerned. "Do you have a headache? Nausea?"

"I'm fine. None of that. I just feel like taking it easy today. I'm going to start at Dad's office on Monday, so I'm going to work on a few sketches while I have the time."

"That sounds like a good idea. We'll figure out lunch when I get back." Anna drove to the caterer and was proud of herself for nearly perfect parallel parking in front of the storefront. The manager found the contract for Maya's wedding, which stated that the entire balance had to be paid if the wedding was cancelled within thirty days. Anna was sick about it and asked if they could still have the food.

"That's a little unusual, Mrs. Yearling. But yes, we will provide the food if you pay the balance. I will look over our requests to see if we have any for the fourteenth. If we can find another party for that day, we will only keep your deposit. Otherwise, we must collect the second half of the balance as spelled out in the contract."

There was hope. "Thank you for working with us. Please let me know if you find another request. And we would like to work with you again when the wedding is rescheduled." Her postponement of the wedding was starting to feel like a lie. But Anna was not ready to declare the marriage of Maya and Hunter permanently over.

The Yearlings did not have freezer space for fifty fried ravioli dinners and one hundred sesame chicken bites. What would they do with the salad? And the chocolate fountain? Anna laughed to herself. Maya wanted a fountain. Could they set it up on the back deck and drown their sorrows in warm chocolate fondue? That might be a good idea. Maya could invite her bridesmaids over for a Death by Chocolate party. She would be flying to Miami that evening, so it would have to be an afternoon affair. But it could be fun.

Anna thought about the cruise on the drive home. She couldn't send Maya on her own. That wasn't even a possibility. If none of her friends could go, they had few remaining options. Jan could go, but he didn't need to disappear for a week. Carbolytic may try to call him.

Plus, Maya and Jan would not be able to peaceably share a cabin for a week. Anna knew that wouldn't work. Should she go?

Anna never expected to go on a cruise in her life. With Jude's severe motion sickness, her vacations were limited to land-based trips. Jude didn't even like the It's a Small World ride at Disney World. He never actually rode it but worried that the boats would suddenly begin to rock out of control. A week on the ocean would be nice. And a once-in-a-lifetime opportunity to spend time with Maya. Maybe this could work. She would talk with Maya after dinner. Winnie would be at youth group tonight, so they could discuss logistics in detail. Anna walked to her bedroom and pulled out her newest bathing suit. A trip to the Bahamas might be just what she needed.

1851

The Wilkes family traveled with the wagon company until early afternoon where they stopped in the small town of Ash Hollow. Known for its abundant ash trees, the canyon area provided fresh water and plentiful grasses for the animals to graze. Sarah courageously found the strength to continue, and the family made camp near a grouping of trees. Trenton cared for the animals while Fidget began to unpack chairs and firewood.

Dewayne announced that he would stay with the Wilkes in Ash Hollow and said goodbye to his sister's family. The rest of the camp offered their well-wishes as they continued on their journey. Sarah was too tired to be suspicious of Dewayne's motives. Regardless, she was thankful for his presence at this time. As they were settling down, Dewayne left to walk toward the small town in search of a church. Jade begged him to return before sundown.

During the down time, the children began asking questions and sharing their fears. Sarah was utterly overwhelmed and had no idea how to answer them. She finally began singing through her tears. The others joined in and sang alongside their mother. There was nothing else to do and nothing else to say but give praise to the Father and pleas to His Son.

Fidget was the first to notice Dewayne hurrying back to their wagon. The man was smiling, and Sarah hoped that meant good news for her family. The group then noticed another man following Dewayne about fifty feet behind him. They rushed toward the pastor.

"I have good news to share," Dewayne said while breathing rapidly. "There are several farms up ahead and a town square. I even found a church. The pastor is right behind me." When the man caught up, Dewayne made the introduction. "This is Pastor David Miller. His wife's name is Mary. They have no children. I explained to them our situation, and they have offered your family the use of their barn for the near future."

Brother Miller explained that he and his wife lived in the parsonage of their church. And an empty barn sat on the same property. The church used the barn for social events but would be happy to extend hospitality to the grieving family.

Sarah's head was spinning. How could her life had changed so drastically? She and Asher were leading their family out West together. Now they were no longer traveling. She would be leading them alone. At that thought, she shivered. She would never be alone. God promised that to her.

"What do you think, Dewayne?" Sarah asked.

"I think the barn is divine providence. Let's go look at it. It should be an adequate shelter for now. I can stay in the wagon on the other side of the barn to avoid any impropriety."

"Nonsense, son," Brother Miller declared. "You can stay in the guest room of the parsonage. Mary would insist."

"This is awfully kind of you, Brother Miller," Sarah said gratefully. "I don't believe we have another choice."

"Wonderful. Let's go. And please, call me Davey."

Trenton and Dewayne hitched the oxen back up to the wagon and led the family to town. Sarah knew that the temporary shelter and the kindness of strangers came straight from God. But she didn't want them. She wanted her old life back. Even the long days of walking in the sun. She would do anything to get Asher and Luke back. But that was not possible. Her heart was shattered, and all she would do was to keep moving forward.

Please give me strength. I have none of my own.

Saturday, May 31

2025

A seven-day cruise to the Bahamas! Anna had never dreamt of such an adventure. But it was official now. She and Maya would fly to Miami—the place with the palm trees—in two weeks. She had so much to plan. Her old swimsuits would do, but she really needed one or two more. Plus coverups and two formal dresses and matching shoes. The dresses would be easy. Maya said that she could use her rehearsal dinner and mother-of-the-bride dresses. That just left the swimwear. Anna made mental plans to go shopping in town next week. She wasn't sure of her financial situation with Jude living in an apartment, but decided that a little wardrobe update wouldn't hurt.

As Anna wiped crumbs off the kitchen counter, she recalled a phone call from her editor. Laney had reminded her of the August first deadline. *We cannot move the deadline, Anna. Tom said that we could take a shorter book, but it has to be set in the nineteenth century. That is what we are marketing now.* Anna was in a serious crunch. The unexpected crises in her family had put a halt on her writing. She would get serious on Monday morning and work a few late nights before the cruise. She would write as much as possible on the cruise and work nonstop when she returned. The plan could work—if there were no more surprises.

The dreaded task of writing every guest who had RSVPed to inform them that the wedding was postponed was the task of the morning. Anna had volunteered to "undo" the guests, while Maya would "undo" the bridal party. When she reached for the basket of RSVP cards, Anna smelled a disgusting smell. Had something died in the foyer? The entire area smelled like rotten chicken. Or was that rotten fish? She quickly opened the front door to let in fresh air and called for the kids.

Jan arrived first and covered his nose with his shirt. "What is that awful smell?"

"I don't know. But it's right here. I couldn't smell it in the kitchen." Maya and Winnie arrived and began screeching about the stench near the front door. Anna moved the basket of RSVP cards to the kitchen table and looked in a cabinet for some sort of air freshener. She found a potpourri spray labeled "Blueberry Crumble" and brought it to the foyer. As soon as Anna sprayed the blueberry spray, the odor became worse.

"Stop, Mom!" Jan pleaded. "You're making it worse."

"Great," Winnie said, "now it smells like a dead Smurf." At that ridiculous comment, all four of the Yearlings sat down, laughing. The situation was grim, but the response was not. After a week of gloom, the family broke into uncontrollable giggling. Maya even snorted twice. The release was needed and felt great to Anna.

"A dead Smurf?" Maya put an arm around her sister. "Where did you come up with that?"

"Ha! I don't know. That's what it smells like to me."

Anna stood. "All right. Everyone, get dressed. We're going out for brunch. How about the Yolk Factory? That will be fun. We can sit outside on the porch. I'll figure out the smell before we go."

Winnie stood beside her mother. "I'll call Dad. He can take care of it."

"No!" Anna responded quickly. "I want to do this myself. He is being selfish and isn't around to help. Get dressed, and I will take care of the dead Smurf."

"No more blueberry spray, Mom. That stuff is horrible," Maya said as she walked upstairs.

Jan helped his mom search for the source of the deadly smell. They moved the hall table and looked under the throw rug. Nothing was found. Anna decided to open the two screened windows in the living room and let the house air out while they were gone.

At the restaurant, the family sat outside as Anna suggested. They laughed about the mysterious smell and enjoyed a late breakfast. Jan asked Maya about the cruise. "Will you really be searching for treasure?"

"We might," Maya answered. "Mom needs to write, but we can keep up with the clues. It will be fun. I'm excited about getting away from everything."

"What islands do you visit again?" Winnie was interested in the cruise for the first time. "Are any of them near Honduras?"

"No. Jewel Cruise Line only visits their own private islands. That's part of the treasure hunt. The islands are all in the Bahamas. I think it's Cutter Cay, Mermaid Cove, and Treasure Island. They all have beautiful beaches and open-air restaurants. I can't wait to eat with my feet in the sand."

"Oh, the food. Can you eat as much as you want?" Jan asked.

"Yep. Mom and I can eat all day. They have a fancy restaurant and a buffet. Plus unlimited pizza until late at night. You should see this cute soda shop they have." Maya took out her phone and searched for a picture of the soda shop on *Plunder*. She showed the group the first photo and several others of various spots around the ship.

"That looks so fun! I can't believe all of that is on a ship."
Winnie perked up even more.

"I can't believe I'm going on one of the famous Jewel ships,"
Anna declared excitedly. "And I haven't planned a thing. You know
that is not like me."

Maya put her hand on her mother's shoulder. "I'm proud of
you, Mom. Everything is planned for you. You can just take it easy. We
can look at the activity calendar when we get on the ship and make a
schedule then. You just need to pack a suitcase. Did Dad take your—?"

"He did, but I can use Jan or Winnie's. Gosh, I need to start
packing." Anna took out her phone. "Do you think I can find a list on
the internet telling me what to pack?"

Maya sighed. "There you go, Mom. For once, don't worry about
it. Just pack what you got out."

"What about medications? Extension cords? Sweaters?"

"Let her find a list, Maya," Winnie added. "She can't let go of
being a control freak cold turkey." The group agreed that Anna could
start planning what to pack. But that was it. Nothing else.

After brunch, Anna drove the children to a local nursery. They
chose a few colorful annuals to plant in the front yard flower boxes.
Maya spotted a friend from high school and walked over to her. Anna
cringed and hoped the postponed wedding did not come up, but she
hear Maya say "cancel" and "Nevada." I guess the word was out now.
She got a knot in her stomach but decided to ignore it the best she
could. The new normal was slowly taking shape, and Hunter's place in
it was slowly fading.

When Anna pulled the car into the driveway, Jan yelled out,
"No way!"

"What?" Maya asked.

"Look at that swarm of flies." To Anna's horror, the entire front door and both window screens were covered with flies. Hundreds of them. How could so many insects find their house in less than two hours?

Anna parked in the garage, and the foursome entered the house through the interior kitchen door. They were immediately surrounded by the sound of intense buzzing.

"This is crazy." Winnie started filming the flies on a screen with her phone. "No one would believe this if I didn't show them."

Anna wanted to cry, but she wouldn't let the children see her give up. She would not call Jude. Where was he anyway? What could he be doing all day in his unfurnished apartment? "Let's close the windows."

Jan walked toward the windows. "Looks like they are attracted to the dead Smurf. It still smells terrible. Mom, we need to find the smell. I'm calling Dad."

Anna felt defeated and sat on the couch. "Please, let me do this. I don't want to call Dad every time I have a problem."

Maya sat beside her. "I get it, Mom. Let's figure this out." Jan and Winnie took everything out of the foyer and looked around. There was nothing to cause the smell.

"Could it be in the attic, Mom?" Jan was looking up.

"I guess that's possible. Dad and I were up there on Tuesday. Will you and Maya check it out?"

All three of the children ran to the garage to ascend the attic ladder. Anna could hear yelling and howling and figured that the smelly culprit was indeed in the attic. She let Jan take charge. He would have to do more of that while Jude was away.

After a few more minutes, Winnie rushed into the living room. "We found the cause of the smell: a rotten chicken taco. There are flies everywhere. Do you have any gloves and a bag for Jan?" She was smiling. The kids were having fun removing the spoiled food. Anna enjoyed listening to their excited conversation.

"Sure. Let me get them. Do you want the blueberry spray too?"

"Seriously, Mom. No! Do we have bug spray?"

Anna gathered some supplies and sent Winnie back to the garage. The crazy mishap gave her an unexpected bit of peace. They were still a family. She could handle things around the house. And she was learning how to pivot. Anna still prayed for God to return her family the way it was merely one week ago. But she was also learning to accept change—a little at a time.

After the stinky culprit was thrown into the outdoor trash, the three children fell into the living room, laughing about their escapade. Apparently, tacos turn bad quickly. And hundreds of flies were camped out in their neighborhood just waiting for rotten food to appear. The dead Smurf was handled without Jude.

The flies slowly left the front of the house, and most of the horrid smell went away by evening. The family ate sloppy Joe's on the deck and were surprised that they weren't attacked by hordes of flies while eating. Anna started messaging the RSVPs. She would finish them tomorrow and check in with Maya on the rest of Operation Wedding Undo. That night, Anna continued to ask God to return her old life. But for the first time, she added a request for guidance if He did not.

The barn was a blessing from God. That was all Sarah could think. As soon as the family walked in, Fidget climbed the ladder to the loft. Even Dewayne's warning about rattlers didn't slow him down. He and Trenton claimed the entire area as their new bedroom.

The girls would live and sleep downstairs. Dewayne and Davey added a thin wall partition to create a modest sleeping area, and Sarah organized their cooking supplies into a makeshift kitchen. The barn did not have running water, but an outhouse and cool spring were nearby, making normal life possible.

The family had enough money to survive the summer and fall but would run out before winter. Thankfully, Luke's seeds had survived the crossing, so a fall planting would be possible. To make ends meet, Sarah and the girls would look into washing clothes for money. They could also sell loaves of bread and homemade blackberry jam.

Dewayne was also a blessing. He helped with chores and modified the barn to make it more like a home. Sarah couldn't deny that he and Jade were falling in love. She could see the signs. But she hoped they didn't rush into anything. Sarah wasn't sure if they would be staying in Ash Hollow permanently and did not want to think of the possibility of her daughter moving away.

That night, Trenton and Fidget returned from playing in the orchard. Pastor Miller allowed the children to collect apples that had fallen on the ground for the family to eat. The boys found the chore to be more fun than work.

"What is that smell?" Jewel was holding her nose and pointing at the boys. Anna soon smelled the rotten odor following Trenton and Fidget. Flies were buzzing above them.

"He messed with a skunk!" Trenton announced.

"Eww!" Jewel and Jade cried out, then stepped back twenty feet.

"You know better than that, Fidget," Sarah said while also holding her nose.

"I just touched him with a stick, Ma," Fidget cried. "Honest."

Sarah stepped into parent mode. Single-parent mode. "Trenton, get his nightshirt. Jeremiah, take your clothes off and leave them behind the barn. Go wash off in the spring, and your brother will bring your bed clothes." Sarah sighed. Fidget's behavior hadn't changed since the accident, and Sarah was grateful. Normal was good for now.

Sunday, June 1

2025

Anna had second thoughts about going to church this morning. She really didn't want to have to explain anything. Not about Jude. Not about Maya. Not about Jan. And not about Winnie's accident. But the children were up and getting ready as if their lives were normal. *Normal. Is this our normal now?* It can't be normal without Jude.

After everyone dressed and ate, the crew left for church in Jan's truck. On the way, Anna wondered if Jude would be there. If so, would he sit beside the family in their usual pew? Would he tell his side of the story? Would Brandee be with him? Could she back out now?

It was too late. Jan parked and the kids piled out as if nothing disastrous could possibly happen. Winnie stopped to talk to three youth friends while the rest found their seats in their usual pew. Anna was thankful that no one came up to ask her about their "situations." The morning felt surprisingly normal.

Winnie settled in next to her mother just as the worship band began. Anna was quiet at first but soon began singing along with the congregation. And if felt great. Her soul felt lighter just by singing words of praise to Jesus.

Pastor Ed came up to the stage wearing a colorful pool float around his waist. He asked if anyone had ever been shipwrecked. His question got chuckles from the crowd until ninety-year-old Ken Wallace slowly raised his hand. Anna knew that he was on a Navy vessel that struck a drifting mine during the Korean War only days after surviving a major typhoon. He had shared his testimony with the church many times over the years. Four men on the ship were killed instantly, and the survivors spent a dark night in the Pacific Ocean before rescue ships arrived. He told anyone who would listen about how he felt the arms of God hugging him throughout the night. He was completely out of control but knew without a doubt that God was in command of everything.

Anna could not image the helpless conditions the sailors must have endured. Lately, she had been enjoying the comfort and safety of her perfect life. Sure, things were a little off right now, but they would go back to normal soon. She would trust God to work His plan for her and her family.

As Pastor Ed began speaking, Anna sat enthralled. The world around her disappeared. She listened as if he were speaking directly to her. "We have all heard about the sinking of the *Titanic*. And many of us have heard about dear Mr. Wallace's harrowing experience during the Korean War. You may be familiar with the tragic sinking of the *USS Indianapolis*."

The pastor took off the float and looked at the congregation. "Have any of you heard the story of Violet Jessop?" A picture of the young woman appeared on the video screen above him. "Believe it or not, Violet was shipwrecked three times in her life. In her early twenties, she was working as a stewardess on *RMS Olympic* when it collided with *HMS Hawke.* This was on September twentieth, 1911. She was twenty-three years old at the time. Amazingly, *Olympic* made it back to port with no fatalities.

"In 1912, Violet was moved to a sister ship, the *RMS Titanic.* On her fourth day aboard the *Titanic*, it hit an iceberg and began to sink. Violet survived only because she was ordered into lifeboat number sixteen as a model of how to safely enter the boats. As a servant, she shouldn't have been in one of the lifeboats. But she was.

"Four and a half years after the sinking of the *Titanic*, Violet Jessop was working as a stewardess on board the *HMHS Britannic*—another sister ship of the *Olympic*. The ship hit an underwater mine and sank in less than an hour. Thirty passengers died. Violet made it safely to a lifeboat but was struck in the head by one of the ships propellers. As she jumped out of the boat, she suffered a fractured skull by colliding with the spinning propeller.

"Amazingly, Violet continued working for the White Star Line. She went back to the *Olympic* two months after the *Titanic* sank and sailed for thirty more years. She died at the age of eighty-three.

"We read in Acts that Paul was shipwrecked off the coast of modern-day Malta. In fact, Paul shares in Second Corinthians that he had been shipwrecked three other times in his life. And one time he 'spent a day and night in the sea,' likely clinging to wreckage from the ship.

"I want you to understand how Violet survived the sinking of the *Titanic* and the *Britannic*. It wasn't because she was rich. It wasn't because she was well-behaved. It was because she found a lifeboat. She found safety. In Acts, we see that Paul encouraged the sailors to stay on the boat rather than jumping out of it.

"At times our lives will become shipwrecked. It will happen. Being a Christian does not mean that we will always sail in smooth seas."

Anna listened intently and got chills when Pastor Ed mentioned shipwrecked lives. That was exactly how she felt. Her perfect life was sinking. The preacher was speaking directly to her.

"Jesus tells us that we will have trouble in this world. The Bible is full of stories of people with shipwrecked lives. My challenge for your today is to analyze your response to the problems of this world. Are you trying to control your problems? Or have you given them to God?"

Anna felt a slight conviction. She knew that she was trying to control the futures of her entire family. But she couldn't just sit back and watch everyone sink. Pastor Ed continued by offering three questions to ask when a crisis hits: First, what part of your life are you clinging to the most? Second, is it something you should control? Or should you give it to God? For example, "I should replace the old tires on my car. But I shouldn't try to change people around me." Third, do you truly want God's will, or do you want your own? He shared that Paul continued to sail the Mediterranean because he was willing to do God's will, and he trusted God's plan.

The thought of giving God complete control of her life sounded "churchy" to Anna. Sure, God knows best. But He couldn't expect her to just sit on the sidelines and watch people she loved suffer. Surely, God expected mothers to get their hands dirty. They were responsible for the well-being of their families. In the back of her mind, Anna knew that she was aiming for her own will, not God's. But she couldn't let go of the control she thought she had. Not yet. Not until everyone was safely back on shore.

The service ended, and on the way to lunch at Pie in the Sky, the kids were unusually quiet. Maya spoke first.

"Do you think we can really just hand our problems over to God and just walk away?"

After a few seconds, Winnie answered. "Yes, I do. That doesn't mean that God won't give us assignments. But He is the General. We hand the mission over to Him and wait for orders."

Maya clapped her hands. "Wow, Win! That was brilliant. I've been asking God to bring Hunter back, but now I realize that I've been demanding Him to put my life back rather than asking Him to work His will. That changes everything. I feel so much better about it. Pastor Ed was right. We must give our shipwrecks to God."

"I feel a little better too," Jan added. "I'm going to ask God to work on my future and tell me what I should do. It seems so simple."

"It does," Maya agreed.

When the pizza was delivered, Winnie offered a heartfelt prayer of thanks for God's provisions and trust for His work in their futures. Anna remained quiet. She was grateful that her children felt lighter, but she wasn't ready to turn the steering wheel over to God yet. He might take them off-roading, and she couldn't risk that.

1851

Sarah felt extra fancy as she dressed for her first service at Ash Hollow Canyon Church. Each member of her family had brought only two changes of clothing on the trail, so they all felt like royalty when Mary Miller brought new outfits for everyone yesterday. The 265 residents of their new town had pulled together to provide enough for the Wilkes and Dewayne. Fidget was especially proud of his brown leather shoes.

Dewayne knocked on the barn door early. He was there to escort the family the one hundred yards to the church sanctuary.

"Come in, Dewayne!" Jade yelled.

"Goodness, girl," Sarah scolded. "Make sure we are decent before you yell for him to come in." Jade and Jewel giggled in unison.

"I am eager to show you the sanctuary. It has plenty of windows and a working toilet in the back."

"Will you show us?" Fidget asked.

"May we use it now?" Trenton followed.

"I don't see why not. Let's go." The family followed Dewayne, who was nearly skipping the entire way. Sarah realized that she had never see him in his working environment. He must be thrilled to be back in a church building again.

When the family arrived at the church, the entire congregation was outside, ready to greet them. Some were holding casseroles or pies as gifts. The children ran ahead and blended into the thirty or so smiling people. Sarah stopped in her tracks and watched the scene unfold. God was providing for her family right before her eyes. Not only had He provided food and shelter, but He also provided a church home. Tears began flowing from her eyes.

How does He do it all?

As Sarah began walking, a tall woman with jet-black hair approached. The woman had Native American features and was likely related to the nearby Sioux Indians.

"Good morning," the woman said succinctly.

"Yes, it is a good morning."

The woman smiled. "I am Whichapi, which means *star* in English."

"That's beautiful. My husband calls me Star." Sarah caught her mistake and respoke. "My husband *called* me Star."

"Then we are meant to be best friends. Please, sit by me today." Once again, God had provided. Sarah had a new church and a new friend. What else would the day hold?

After everyone was seated, Mary Miller led the congregation in two hymns. She played the piano very well but sang with less skill. The music was a salve to Sarah's soul. She found it difficult to sing because of a lump in her throat. Yet she thought the words in her mind straight to Jesus.

When the music was over, Mary found a seat in the back pew. Sarah thought that odd but didn't worry on it. Pastor Miller began to speak and greeted the parishioners and welcomed the guests first. He shared the tragic loss of the Wilkes family one week earlier. And he preached a message on shipwrecks in the lives of Christians.

"Paul knew about shipwrecks, both literally and figuratively. Did you know that he was stoned to near-death during his first missionary journey? But that did not stop him. Despite being thrown out of town after town, he turned right back around and preached in the very same towns again. Why would he do this?"

Sarah wondered to herself why a man would deliberately seek harm. The pain she was feeling was too much to invite intentionally. She wouldn't have the strength to face this again.

The pastor continued. "Why did Paul continue to face rejection and harm? Why did the apostles leave their homes for conditions they could not control? Why would Jesus accept death on a cross? I give you three reasons. The first and most important reason is love."

Sarah was surprised to hear that love was a reason for such risky behavior.

"Paul and the apostles loved Jesus. They loved Him so much that they were willing to die for Him. And they loved their fellow man."

As Brother Miller continued, Sarah pondered the idea of love. The only reason she was carrying on was her love for her children. Or was it? Her love for Asher and Luke also gave her strength. And her love for Jesus was the most important reason. God had not caused the deaths, but He was with her. And He sent Jesus to take her punishment of death. Without Jesus, she would never see Asher and Luke again. Yes, love was the reason she would continue living—abundantly.

The pastor continued his message by sharing that Paul and the others were also willing to face harm because of "trust" and "obedience." Sarah listened carefully to Davey's words. She would have to trust God with her future. He had already provided so much in one short week. Why wouldn't He continue to provide? For the first time since the tragedy, Sarah began to feel hopeful. Really hopeful.

Before he finished, Brother Miller made a surprise announcement. "After much discussion with our Lord, I have decided to retire as pastor of Ash Hollow Canyon Church." The crowd gasped. "Mary and I have been praying for God to provide my replacement, and I believe that He brought the right man to our church."

Looking straight at Dewayne, he continued. "A man who gave up his own sister and his own plans to care for another's man's family must be living in the Spirit. I believe that Brother Barton is the right man to replace me, and I look forward to discussing this further with the elders. Next week will be my last sermon. And it will be a doozy." The congregation laughed and stood at once. A crowd formed around

Dewayne. Sarah noticed that Jade was right beside him, beaming with pride.

PART THREE

Calm Seas

Many are the plans in a person's heart,
but it is the Lord's purpose that prevails.
—*Proverbs 19:21*

CHAPTER EIGHTEEN

Saturday, June 14

2025

Today is the day! Anna would fly with Maya to Miami in three hours. Jan was loading their luggage into her car. She expected the day to be blue, but it was surprisingly upbeat. The bridesmaids came over for brunch, and the canceled wedding wasn't even mentioned. As far as Anna knew, Hunter hadn't even texted Maya today.

While Anna would be on the cruise, Winnie and Jan were going to camp out at Jude's apartment. They would go back and forth from house to bachelor pad as needed. Another pleasant surprise was that none of her friends had asked about Jude's move—not even Meg. Anna had planned to stretch the truth and claim that he was allergic to something in the foundation of the house. She knew that was a ridiculous stretch but didn't want to tell anyone the truth. Thankfully, no one had pried.

Jude seemed to be content living in the small apartment. He had lost a little weight but was otherwise healthy. Anna wasn't quite ready to give God control over the situation. But she did accept the fact that she had to wait Jude out. He would only come back home after his midlife antics were over.

As Anna was putting her shoes on, she noticed her grandmother's diary. It had been sitting on her dresser since she brought it down from the attic nearly three weeks ago. She hadn't opened it but knew that it detailed her distant relative's life journey. On a last-minute impulse, she grabbed the diary, then rushed out to the car and asked Jan to help her fit it into her suitcase. Perhaps the boring days of her grandmother would provide inspiration for her novel. The manuscript deadline was six weeks away, and Anna was still way behind schedule.

As Jan was closing the back of the car, his friends drove up. Caleb and Manny were holding matching, king-size fountain drinks from a nearby gas station. Anna couldn't help but think that they were setting themselves up for an extra bathroom stop or two but didn't say anything. Their young bladders were probably more reliable than her aging one.

"Ready, Mom? Everything is packed." Jan was dangling the keys from one finger.

"Yes, I think so." Anna found Winnie and gave her two extra hugs. "Promise that you will head over to Dad's before it gets dark. Jan should be back by then. But if he isn't, I don't want you here alone."

"Yes, ma'am," Winnie groaned. "I'll be fine. You really need to enjoy this week and get your mind off of everything. We can handle things here without you."

That last comment stung a little.

"I know. But I still don't want you driving at night while I'm gone. Have fun at work, and I'll see you in eight days." Winnie hugged Anna for an extra second or two. Anna noticed and was grateful.

Once everything was loaded, the caravan of Anna, Maya, Jan, Caleb, and Manny took off for the Birmingham airport. The group was in good spirits, and Anna was once again grateful. Today could have been a melancholy disaster; instead, it was the beginning of a grand adventure.

In the first ten minutes of the drive, Jan's phone buzzed four times. He didn't look at it but clearly wanted to.

"Don't worry Ms. Anna," Caleb spoke up. "That's just Jan's girlfriend checking up on him. She texts like that all the time."

Anna laughed until she realized that Caleb was serious. "Girlfriend? Are you serious?" Suspiciously, Maya didn't seem surprised.

"She's not really a girlfriend. We just text a lot. We met in a chemistry lab and keep in touch."

Manny snickered. "Way to downplay your girlfriend, dude."

Anna knew she should let it go but had to pry. "Does she live around here?"

"No, Mom. She lives in Weaver, a little town near Oxford. She's going to pharmacy school at Auburn in August. You remember her. Katelyn. Her family had the big sign at graduation."

Anna's eyes bugged out a little. She hadn't even met this young woman and already had two strikes against her. She came from a rude family. And she had the nerve to attend Auburn University. Anna hoped this was just a "text fling" as Jan had suggested.

"Why don't you invite her to the Fourth of July cookout? I guess we aren't watching the fireworks on Stone Mountain anymore?"

Maya's words sent chills down Anna's spine. She had to nip this in the bud. "Weren't you going to invite Sam and One-L to the cookout? That would be too many people."

"Nonsense," Maya replied. "It would be great. I'd like to meet Katelyn. Jan can stay at Dad's, and she can stay in his room. We can have a girls' weekend."

Anna noticed the smile on Jan's face. She didn't have the nerve to say no today. She'd wait until after the cruise and come up with a reason that Katelyn Wright could not join the family event.

At the airport, Jan pulled into a temporary parking spot at departures and helped his mother and sister unload their suitcases. Hugs were shared all around, and Anna and Maya hurried inside the terminal. As usual, the place was hopping with activity. The ladies found that their flight was on time as they checked their suitcases and made their way to the security check.

There were about twenty people at the security que, and Anna and Maya fell in line. At the conveyer belt, Anna took a plastic bin and put her backpack and fanny pack in it. As she was taking her shoes off, an older woman turned to ask a question. The woman was clearly nervous.

"Do we all have to take our shoes off?"

"Yes, ma'am. I think so," Anna replied kindly. "That's a rule. And you must put everything with metal in one of these bins."

The woman seemed flustered but tried to oblige at the rapid pace of the other passengers. She removed her orthotic shoes quickly and then opened her oversize purse. Out of the bag, she removed six cans of green beans and put them into the bin. Anna looked at Maya, whose eyes became large.

"I wasn't sure if Miami had canned green beans, so I brought my own. Better safe than sorry." Anna smiled and pushed her bin toward the scanner. As she moved forward, she noticed the woman remove half of her front teeth and place them into the bin. That was enough to give Anna the giggles. She tried to stop laughing but couldn't.

"Please move forward, ma'am." Anna tried to make a straight face but continued to laugh. Maya came up to help her mom, but the security officer ordered her to step back. Anna should have become serious at this point but didn't. A month of stress was instantly unloaded in the airport security line.

Anna—still laughing—was moved to a separate area and a very tall woman ran a beeping wand over her body and her backpack. Thankfully, she checked out and was able to move on to the correct gate.

Maya was waiting for her a few feet after the security area. "What happened back there?"

Anna started laughing again. "Did you see the woman put her teeth into the bin? No case or baggie."

"What?" Maya started laughing too. "I didn't see that. But I did see the green beans."

"She must not fly very often. Security is so fast-paced. I feel sorry for the newbies."

"Newbies. That's a funny way to put it. I don't think senior citizens have to take their shoes off, but there wasn't time to ask. C'mon. Let's get to our gate. I want to get some coffee before we board."

Mother and daughter found two seats at their gate, and Anna sat with their backpacks while Maya went for an overpriced coffee. When she returned, she gasped. "Mom! Where are your shoes?"

Anna looked down and realized that she was wearing only socks. "Watch my bag!" Anna ran back to the security gate and found her tennis shoes on the floor under the scanner. She grabbed them without attracting attention and put them on. As she was walking back to the gate, she heard an announcement that boarding was beginning on their flight. The first hour of the trip had been stressful. No. Anna thought for a few seconds. The first hour wasn't actually stressful. It was fun. She was already having fun with her daughter. They had their first story to share with the family when they returned. For the first time, Anna was excited about the week ahead. She might have more fun than she expected.

1851

Sarah still couldn't believe it. Jade had just married Dewayne Barton. The ceremony was beautiful, and now the couple was sitting at the head table at their outdoor wedding reception. Pastor Miller officiated the ceremony, and Mary Miller provided her own wedding dress for Jade to wear. Of course, Sarah cried throughout the entire event, especially when Trenton and Fidget walked Jade down the church's aisle together. Jewel looked beautiful in a sage-green dress loaned to her by one of Whichapi's friends.

Asher should have been there. He should have escorted Jade down the aisle. And he should be dancing with Sarah throughout the night. But he wasn't. Neither was Luke. Sarah and her family lived in a fallen world. Each day she vowed to trust God's plan for her family, even when it didn't make sense. Even when it didn't seem possible.

Davey and Mary Miller had moved into her mother's boarding house in town. They would oversee that property and the business. Dewayne had officially moved into the parsonage on Monday. Jade would move in tonight. The rest of the Wilkes family was still living in the barn. Dewayne was debating whether they should convert the barn into a suitable dwelling place or build a new house beside it. Fidget voted to keep the barn and its loft. Sarah trusted Dewayne and waited for his decision. Either way, the construction would not begin until the spring. In the meantime, she would continue to wash clothes and sell bread. God was good.

Trenton had found part-time work at the local school. Without a permanent building, the town's children met in different homes on a strict rotation. Justin Timmons served as the schoolteacher, and Trenton helped him teach penmanship and writing. Sarah could see God working in his life, preparing him to be a teacher one day. He continued to help transcribe Sarah's thoughts into the diary, but the entries were slowing down. Sarah's quest to document her family's experiences on the Oregon Trail was nearly complete.

Fidget was still full of vim and vigor, and he thoroughly enjoyed attending town school. Trenton reported that his brother was excelling in arithmetic, but also in talking too much. Sarah tried to keep him busy with chores and asked Jesus daily for an extra portion of patience to mother her youngest.

All the children were thriving, except Jewel. She was lost without her sister and did not like the responsibility of being the oldest child at home. Sarah tried to spend extra time with her daughter by dreaming about her future and her wedding. But the girl could not see her own fairy-tale ending.

Lively fiddle music snapped Sarah out of her thoughts. She was delighted when Trenton asked her to dance. The night was turning out to be lovely. God had taken her tears and planted new flowers. Sarah vowed to appreciate the flowers she was given today while remembering the flowers she loved in the past.

During the second dance, a loud crack rang through the field where the reception was being held. The music stopped, and a loud boom sounded behind the barn. Half of the crowd rushed to the barn.

Sarah was panicked when she saw Fidget on the ground crying. Beside him was Jonathon York. Both had blackened arms and shirts.

"What happened!?" Sarah asked as she ran to the boys.

Fidget spoke through his tears. "We was just playing with some gun powder. It went off." Just then, he lifted his left arm and a dollar-size section of skin was hanging down. Sarah crumbled, and the crowd stepped back.

As the wedding guests were staring at Fidget, Jewel stepped into action. "Stuart, get some clean water. Marybell, find some clean cloths. We have some in the chest in the barn. Trenton, take care of Mama."

As Jewel was barking out orders, the town physician arrived. "I'm the doctor, Vincent Morgan. You are doing a fine job. May I help?"

Jewel was embarrassed by her previous outbursts. "Of course. I'm sorry for taking over."

"No, you were acting appropriately. Are you a nurse?"

Sarah looked up. *How do you do it all, God?*

CHAPTER NINETEEN

Sunday, June 15
2025, Embarkation Day

Anna woke first and quickly showered and dressed before she woke Maya. Their Uber driver would pick them up at ten a.m. at their Miami hotel for their eleven a.m. check-in time at the cruise port. For the first time in three weeks, Anna was excited for the future. She had no idea what to expect on the cruise but was eager to find out what sailing at sea was really like.

When Maya was dressed, the two went downstairs for the continental breakfast. Anna was too nervous to eat but did want a cup of hot tea. She also wanted Maya to eat something filling. She had no idea when they would eat again.

As they walked into the makeshift dining room, Anna and Maya immediately noticed a couple sitting very close together. After only ten seconds, the woman shared that they were on their honeymoon and were spending it in the Florida Keys. Anna prepared for a teary reaction from Maya but was pleasantly surprised when she congratulated the couple. She even shared that she would have been honeymooning also if her fiancé hadn't bailed on her.

While the two women discussed venues and color schemes, Anna poured hot water in a disposable cup and searched for an English Breakfast tea bag. As her tea was steeping, she decided that a bowl of dry cereal would be a good idea. There may not be much food on the first day, and she didn't want to be hungry.

Anna heard Maya telling the newlyweds about the mother-daughter cruise and smiled. The week was going to be a blessing for her. She turned the knob to dispense the cereal, but it would not turn off. Cereal filled her bowl and began overflowing onto the floor.

"Mother! What are you doing?" Maya rushed over to help. The cereal dispenser completely emptied onto the floor. Maya was astonished that her mother could not shut off the spout, so she showed her on another container of cereal. "See. You just turn it back to the right." But the second handle did not close either.

Cereal was now all over the counter and floor. The breakfast attendant came out and stared at the mess.

"My bad," Anna said sheepishly. Maya burst out laughing, and the worker went to find a broom.

"Really, Mom? *My bad*?"

"That's the first thing that popped into my head. Now I miss your father."

Maya put her arm around her mother. "Yeah, I miss Hunter too. We would be married right now if he hadn't wigged out."

"Well, I'm married, but my husband is still wigging out. Let's help clean this up and eat something. I'm worried that we might not eat again for a while." After helping scoop up the wasted cereal, Anna chose two bananas for her breakfast. Maya made a plate with a toasted bagel and strawberry yogurt cup.

Maya spoke while looking at her plate. "You know, we're in Miami, seven hundred miles from home. There's not much we can do here, especially when we're out to sea. I say that we enjoy the week and deal with the fallout back home a week from now. I don't want to even think about Hunter for the next seven days."

"That's a good idea for you, Maya. But I plan to keep in touch with Jan and Winnie," Anna responded quickly. "I want to know what's going on and what I'll be facing when we get home. Dad could move back home soon. And we need to come up with a plan for Jan. I can't take the week off but do think that you should enjoy yourself." Anna noticed Maya's smirk, so she changed the subject. "Don't let me forget to send a thank-you note to Grace and Gene for this trip. I want to get them some sort of souvenirs from the ship. Maybe T-shirts?"

"Good idea. We need to get Jan and Winnie shirts too. I bet they have cute pirate souvenirs."

"Definitely!" The couple finished eating just as a large group of school-aged baseball players arrived. Maya felt guilty that half of the cereal containers were empty, but noticed that most of the boys were in line for the waffle maker.

"There it is, Mom! The white car." Maya drug her bags to the approaching car and waved for her mother to follow.

The driver, named Rover, helped the women load their suitcases into the back of his minivan. Anna couldn't help but ask about the origin of his name.

"Apparently, my father wanted a dog instead of a child, so my mother let him name me. My middle name is Buddy, so I go by Rover. I hated my name when I was a child but am used to it now."

Anna blurted a response before she could think. "Just remember that you can legally change it if you want." Maya tapped her mom on the knee to get her to retract her comment, but Anna said nothing else.

"Are you sailing on one of those pirate ships today?" Rover asked with a smile.

"Yes, we are," Maya replied. "I'm getting excited."

"I drive people to and from those ships every weekend. I haven't heard one complaint yet. I'm sure you will have a great week." Rover drove through the Miami traffic like an expert. He quickly fell in line for the appropriate ship.

As Rover approached the terminal, both women gasped. *Plunder* was much larger than either one of them had expected. Shockingly, it looked like an authentic pirate ship. Rover followed the traffic to the luggage drop-off where mother and daughter exited. Anna placed her oversize sun hat on her head and checked the car twice to ensure they hadn't left anything behind.

As they were walking toward the entrance of the terminal, Maya put her arm around her mother. "Here we go. Our first big mother-daughter adventure. I will try not to get eaten by sharks, if you try not to suggest that people change their names."

Anna did not smile. "Rover, Maya. His name was Rover."

"Drop it, Mom." Anna smiled and led Maya to the check-in area. With their paperwork in order, they proceeded to the security checkpoint. Anna remembered the woman with the canned green beans and smiled to herself.

"Ma'am, is this your backpack?" A security officer was holding Anna's navy-blue bag. She had borrowed it from Winnie.

"Yes, sir."

"Please follow me." Maya watched as her mother was taken to a nearby table. Both looked down to make sure Anna had her shoes on.

The man told Anna that she had two suspicious items in her bag and needed to investigate them before she could embark. Anna agreed, and the officer began removing items from her backpack. When he reached the bottom, he pulled out a loaf of banana bread.

"What exactly is this, ma'am?"

"That is homemade banana bread. I have three loaves in my suitcase and one in this backpack. I made it before I left home and don't want to go hungry."

The worker laughed. "I don't think anyone on that ship will go hungry. We will have to keep this—and the knife. Homemade food is not allowed. You can expect the other loaves to be confiscated also."

"That doesn't seem necessary. But I understand. Thank you." Anna repacked her backpack and walked toward a smiling Maya.

"What is it with you and security lanes, Mom?"

"They don't allow banana bread."

"Oh, my goodness! I thought you were making those for Jan and Winnie."

"I did make some for them. But brought some for us too."

"I have a feeling that we will have plenty to eat for breakfast. Don't worry about going hungry, Miss Banana Bread."

With their carry-on bags secure, the two made their way to the gangway. "This is it. No turning back. Say goodbye to land for two days. Our first island stop isn't until Tuesday."

"Stop being so dramatic, Maya. You're scaring the children," Anna said with a twinkle in her eye. Maya looped her arm through her mother's as they walked onto the bustling pirate ship.

Anna felt the usual anxiety that happened when doing something new. But today's stress was different. She was literally leaving the country—land and all. Her only contact with home would be through email messages with Jan and Winnie. If something happened to them, she wouldn't be able to reach them for at least a day. Anna looked at Maya with a panicked expression and stopped walking.

"Nope. You're not stopping," Maya declared. "We will be safe. Jan and Winnie and Dad will be fine. You can email them whenever you want. And we will be right back here in Miami before you know it."

"I know. I know. But there is so much going on right now. How can I just turn my back on everyone for an entire week?"

The couple was slowing down others trying to enter the boat, so Maya gently pulled her mother along. "Come on. Think of this as a writing retreat. You admitted that you are behind on your book. You will have plenty of time to write this week. Then we can go home and see how things went without us."

"You're right. It's too late now. And I am curious to see how Dad gets along without me for so long." Maya chuckled at the last comment and was relieved that her mother resumed the march up the gangway.

The end of the gangway opened directly into Shipwreck Boulevard on Deck Seven of *Plunder*. Maya rushed forward and turned back toward her mother. "It's awesome! I love this ship already."

Anna looked around and saw a live band of pirates playing jaunty music. She and Maya fell into the line to greet three of the crew members. They shook hands with Poppy Lane, the cruise director; Janari Woods, the staff captain; and Scott Clemmenson, the ship's captain. He had been a captain on another cruise line for fifteen years and was the inaugural captain when *Plunder* began sailing last year.

"Welcome aboard," Captain Scott said as he shook Anna's hand. "I will be your designated driver for the rest of the week, so have fun. And be sure to look under the ship." Anna was a little confused by the comment but promised to look where he suggested—if she could figure out how.

"C'mon, Mom," Maya urged. "Let's find our cabin and put our stuff away. Then we can go to lunch. Want to try the buffet? I think it's called Blackbeard's Fortress."

"Sure. We don't have to rush though."

"Yes, we do. I don't want to miss anything. We only have seven days to do it all."

Anna and Maya scurried to the rear elevators and got in line. They were booked in a Scallywag cabin on Deck Ten. They would have a balcony, which Anna had planned to use for her morning tea.

"I hope they don't take the food out of my suitcase like they did with my carry-on. We might get hungry," Anna announced. Every person in the elevator lobby turned toward Anna with wide eyes.

A middle-age lady with a personalized shirt stating that the Cooper family was celebrating Papa's seventieth birthday put her hand on Anna's shoulder. "I promise that you will *not* go hungry this week, sweetie. In fact, you will be 'Thanksgiving full' the entire time." Others waiting for elevators laughed softly at the Cooper woman's comment. Anna felt slightly foolish but knew that she was prepared if any sort of catastrophe happened with the ship's food.

While she and Maya were waiting, Anna noticed at least twelve other people wearing shirts celebrating "Papa's" birthday. They were bright blue and clearly identified the traveling group. Anna made a mental note to have matching shirts made if she ever went on another cruise with family or friends. Of course, her family was falling apart. This would surely be her only cruise. And she had missed a golden opportunity to wear matching shirts with Maya.

The ladies found their cabin easily. Maya used one of the rubber bracelets attached to their door to open it. "Age before beauty."

"Very funny." Anna laughed. As she walked into the cabin, she was surprised by its efficiency—and its pirate-themed decor. There was a compact bathroom near the door and a decent-size closet behind the bathroom. The cabin had two full-size beds, a sofa, and a desk with a lighted mirror. Anna noticed plenty of plugs and USB Ports. The walls were decorated with sailing memorabilia and a large treasure map. Anna was relieved. She would be able to write in this space easily. At the far end of the cabin was a sliding glass door. Maya was already opening the locked handle.

"Look at our balcony, Mom. Isn't it adorable? We have two chairs and a table. Let's order room service one morning."

Anna centered the table more perfectly between the chairs "Do we get room service with our cabin? Isn't that for the fancy suites?"

"Oh, no. Everyone can order room service twenty-four seven." Anna suddenly felt silly for packing food but was still glad that she brought it. *One never knows.*

The two stepped back into the cabin from the balcony. Anna sat her backpack down on the couch. "When will we get our suitcases?"

Maya looked around. "I'm not exactly sure. They should be delivered soon. Wanna go exploring and then get some lunch?"

"Sure. That sounds fun. I'm a little overwhelmed right now. This ship is so huge. What if I get lost?"

"Don't worry about that. There are thousands of people aboard. Just ask for help. Our cabin is number 1004. Remember that we are on Deck Ten." Maya smiled and turned around while on her tiptoes. Anna hadn't seen her do that since her last dance recital her senior year of high school. Maybe this trip is more important to Maya than Anna realized.

While Maya strong-armed the lock on the balcony door, Anna noticed a bright-blue card with a white starfish design on it. "This is odd, Maya. Is it a postcard?"

Maya came over to look at the card. "That's a clue! That's our first clue. I completely forgot about the treasure hunt. The travel documents stated that we would find our first clue in our cabins when we embarked. Let's be sure that there isn't something else that is the real clue." The two ladies looked over the cabin and concluded that the starfish picture was indeed the first clue. Maya took a picture of it with her phone. "Let's find the buffet and try to figure out the clue while we are eating."

"Good plan, matey." Anna was starting to feel relaxed. A week with her daughter might just be God's plan to set her mind at ease and to get some writing done.

Blackbeard's Fortress, the ship's buffet-style restaurant, was on Deck Twelve. Since it was only two decks from their cabin, Anna and Maya decided to walk up the stairs instead of waiting for an available elevator. There was a buzz of excitement in the air. People were smiling and children were dancing around their parents. Anna figured that the first few minutes on the ship must be the most exciting.

The entrance of the restaurant was designed to look like an entrance to a galley on an authentic pirate ship. The opening was circular and looked like it was made of rustic wood. The walls were covered in faux concrete, and the signage was written with an old-world font. Maya suggested that they split up to gather their food and find a table on the starboard—or right—side of the ship.

Anna turned toward the food and was amazed at what she saw. There were entire sections for salads, pastas, sandwiches, soups, pizza, and stick-to-your-ribs entrees. Toward the middle were Asian, Greek, Italian, and Mexican stations. Anna laughed to herself when she thought about the banana bread in her still-missing suitcase. She went straight to the Italian section and served herself some sort of white lasagna dish with Caesar salad and fresh breadsticks. On her way to the starboard tables, she noticed the vast display of desserts. *Oh, my goodness. I should have brought more stretchy pants.* The sweets looked too delicious to resist.

When mother and daughter had finished gathering their food and matching glasses of ice water, the looked at each other and laughed. "I've never seen so many food choices," Anna declared. "I got panicked and grabbed an enchilada to be safe."

"I know what you mean. I never eat fish, but that grilled halibut looked so good."

Anna said a blessing and got choked up. She thanked God for the plentiful food and her beautiful daughter. She asked Him to protect the rest of their family and to restore their lives to the way they had been.

When Anna was finished with the prayer, Maya put a hand on her mother's arm. "It's never going to be like it was, Mom. You need to accept that."

"God can do miracles, Maya. I'm praying for five of them. That Dad will move back home. That Hunter will come back to you. That

Jan will get his internship back. That Winnie will make a plan for next year. And that I will write a best-selling book by my deadline. Why wouldn't I pray for that?"

"It looks to me like God has another plan. Maybe you should pray for Him to work His plan in our lives. Pastor Ed calls it 'writing a blank check to God.'"

"We aren't robots, Maya. We have feelings and passions. And I know what's best for my family." Anna noticed her daughter smirk slightly at her comment. "Of course, God knows what's best. But I think He lets us be part of the planning."

Maya got serious. "Face it, Mom. You are a control freak. And you can't fix everything."

Anna looked down at her lap. "I know you are right, Maya. But I can't just let go of my family. You all are the most important people in the world to me. I just can't shake the game board and start all over."

"You don't have to change all in one day, Mom. Take baby steps. This cruise was a big step for you. Let's try to have fun. When we get home, we'll come up with a plan for you to slowly loosen your grip on us." Anna felt foolish at Maya's last comment, but knew she was partially right. Maybe she could let a little bit go for now. She silently thanked God for her wise daughter and started eating the heavenly lasagna.

After sampling three types of cake, Anna declared herself "Thanksgiving full." Maya went for a scoop of ice cream. When she returned, talk turned to the mysterious starfish clue.

"There must be a million starfish on this ship," Maya lamented. "Where would we even start?"

"Maybe there aren't that many starfish. Can you pull up the Jewel Cruise Line app on your phone? Maybe there is a 'starfish lounge' or something like that."

"I don't remember anything with a starfish in the name but will check." After a few minutes, Maya confirmed that none of the major venues had starfish in the name.

Anna sighed. "Our only option now is to scour the ship." She meant the comment with sarcasm, but Maya loved the idea.

"We were going to tour the ship anyways. We can just keep our eyes open for starfish. Of course, do we look under them? Or do we take the starfish to the captain? The clue is so vague. They should have told us where to start with that."

"Wait!" Anna gasped. "The captain said something about looking under the ship. Maybe he was helping us with the first clue."

"You're right. He kept saying, 'Be sure to look under the ship.' I thought he was talking about some camera that showed the bottom of *Plunder*. Maybe he was talking about the clue."

"Good thinking," Anna squealed. "I bet there is a screen somewhere that shows the bottom of the ship. Some sort of clue must be written on the bottom of the ship." As soon as she made the comment, she knew how foolish it sounded. "I'm guessing someone didn't actually write on the bottom of the ship. But there must be something."

"It's all we have to go on. Let's go exploring and look for some starfish under the ship." The ladies locked arms as they exited the venue. Anna noticed all the "intact" families enjoying lunch together. Mother *and* fathers were enjoying a weeklong vacation together. She suddenly missed Jude. *How could he walk away from their lives? What if he never comes back?* Anna could not imagine that scenario.

She decided that she would devise a plan to get her husband to move back home. The nonsense had to stop. She would have him back in time for their annual trip to the Gulf in July. Her whole family would enjoy time together again at the beach.

Maya suggested a "top down" approach to exploring, so the two walked up one flight of stairs to Deck Fourteen, the top deck. As they exited the stairs, they were immediately blinded with bright Miami sunlight. "We should have brought our sunglasses," Maya noted.

"Yep. It's a little warm too. But the breeze feels nice." Anna followed her daughter as they made a loop around the top deck, walking forward on the port—or left—side. They saw a movie screen at the front—or forward—of the ship. It was surrounded on one side with comfortable chairs and hammocks.

"This is the Parrot Perch," Maya said. "I think they have movies and performances throughout the week. When we get back to our cabin, we can look at the schedule on the app."

"There's a schedule on the app?" Anna hadn't even downloaded the app. She thought it was only for booking the cruise. "Let's stop so I can download it. We should have made a schedule weeks ago."

"Slow down, Mom. We're on vacation. We can just *go with the flow*." Maya laughed.

"Even I know that I don't *go with the flow*, dear Maya. I'm not built that way." Anna wasn't budging.

"Trust me, Mom. Take a break from controlling everything. Plus, we need to see the entire ship before we can make a week's worth of plans." Anna surrendered and continued to follow Maya. They left the Parrot Perch and walked on the starboard side to the ship's massive pool.

"Do you remember those people who went overboard on *Golden Fortune?*" Maya asked.

"Of course, how could I forget that. Weren't they all saved? The captain was a hero."

"That's right. Well, they fell off some sort of pirate plank that was in this area. It has been removed from *Fortune* and was never added to *Plunder*. I'm guessing that it was where this telescope is now." The two walked over to a large spyglass set up on the side of the ship. It was secured to the rail and had a sign that read "Land Ho! Looking Glass."

Anna looked through the scope and was amazed to see nearby palm trees magnified. "Remind me to come up here when we are at sea. I would love to see a dolphin or whale up close."

"Oh! Me too." Beyond the looking glass was the official splash zone of the ship. In the center was a large, rectangular swimming pool. On either side of the pool were round hot tubs. Past the pool was a colorful splash pad and spray area. Children were already running through streams of water. Anna was impressed that their parents had thought ahead and packed swimsuits in their carry-on bags. The rest of the top deck held a mini-golf course, enclosed basketball court, and quick-serve food court.

Next, the two walked down one flight to Deck Twelve. Ships traditionally omit a thirteenth deck to appease superstitious passengers. They had seen Blackbeard's Fortress minutes ago when they ate, so they walked past it toward the front of the ship. The rest of Deck Twelve contained the Ahoy Kid's Club. Children under eighteen could visit the club to play and socialize. It had a colorful pirate theme with age-appropriate activities, including an art studio and science lab. In the front area was an imitation pirate ship complete with a plank that the children could walk off into a ball pit.

Anna and Maya peeked in the windows at the kid's club. Anna was amazed at the attention to detail given in each area. "This is so cool. You kids would have loved this. There is even a journaling station for Winnie."

"It's perfect for parents wanting a romantic dinner. Or an afternoon at the pool." Maya became choked up at the last few words. Tears rolled out of her eyes. "I'm sorry. It's still hard. He was supposed to be here. We were supposed to have romantic dinners. It hurts, Mom."

Anna hugged her daughter. And she felt ashamed for not considering how difficult this would be. Maya had been in such good spirits so far. But her feelings were obviously still raw. "Let's finish our tour quickly and get back to our cabin. I would love to put my feet up for a few minutes." Maya didn't speak but nodded in agreement.

Mother and daughter walked down to Deck Eleven, which held cabins and the Heave Ho Gym. Anna noticed the spa and asked about the lovely scent enveloping it. One of the staff members showed her a candle with the scent, and she made a mental note to come back and purchase a few candles for gifts. Maya showed Anna the outdoor walking track, and both agreed that they *should* walk a few mornings to keep from gaining too much weight. Anna noticed that Maya still had tears in her eyes.

Decks Nine and Ten held only cabins, so Maya skipped those and led her mother to Deck Eight via an elevator. As soon as the elevator doors opened, Anna heard loud pop music and smelled fresh pizza. She and Maya walked into a lively pizza restaurant, named

Oro—or *gold* in Spanish—that spanned one third of the deck. There were plenty of tables and chairs and even room for dancing.

Maya walked toward the serving line. "That smells good. Should we get some pizza?"

"We just ate," Anna responded. But she saw the disappointment in her daughter, so she changed her mind. "You know, I'm not 'Thanksgiving full' anymore. Let's get some pizza. Why not?"

"Thanks, Mom." Maya rushed to the end of the line and started eyeing the choices. Anna fell in behind her and smiled to herself. She realized that the week was going to be more exhausting than she expected. But the opportunity to spend time with her wounded daughter was priceless.

After selecting their pizza, the two found a table as far from the music speakers as possible. They were quiet for a while before Maya spoke. "I don't think I will ever get over Hunter. I still love him. How do I make myself stop? How did you get over Dad? You've been married twenty-five years."

"My goodness, Maya. I'm not over Dad. He will come back to his senses and come back home. This is just a mid-life crisis. Really, it could be worse."

Maya seemed surprised by her mother's response. "I'm not so sure about that, Mom. He seems happy right now. Like he just doesn't want to be married anymore. I guess Hunter feels the same way. I don't even know if he has moved to Nevada yet. We were supposed to be soulmates, and now we don't even talk. I hate this." Maya put down her half-eaten slice of pizza and covered her face with a napkin. The tears began to fall again.

Anna kicked into mom mode and patted Maya on her back. "Look, we're on this ship now. We can't do much from the middle of the ocean. Let's finish exploring and get back to our cabin. You can still text Hunter while we are in port. Would that help?"

"No. I refuse to text him first. He knows I'm going to be gone for a week. If he doesn't text, he really doesn't care. I just need to get past him. Like a hurdle. I just need to jump over him and move on."

"That's a great attitude. I have so many ideas of how to handle this, but I'm going to try to keep them to myself. You are so smart, Maya. So mature. And so brave. I'm proud of you for going on this trip. We can make a plan when we get home if you'd like. I say we enjoy ourselves this week. We might even find the treasure."

"Thanks. You are right. I thought I was okay. It just hit me. What if I never get married? What if I'm alone the rest of my life?"

Anna side hugged her daughter as they stood. "You will not be alone, my dear. I promise you that. And remember, you are only twenty-three. You are still very young. God has given you a chance to spend time with your friends. To have fun as an individual. I'm sure some perfect man is going to come into your life when you least expect it." Anna didn't really believe in that last part. She was a planner. Maya needed a plan to find a husband. But she couldn't design a plan right now. They would work on that when they got home.

After discarding their pizza trash, the two toured the rest of Deck Eight. They passed a large game room on their way to the ship's ice-skating rink. The venue was designed with tiered seating in a circle and the round rink in the middle. On each side of the entryway were digital screens displaying the name of the show and upcoming showtimes.

"These screens are cool," Anna observed. "I'd like to come see the *Waltzing Sharks* show. Is that one on the app?"

"I'm sure it is. I want to see it too. I have no idea what to expect with that." As they were turning to leave, Maya remembered the clue. "The screens. We're supposed to be looking for a live shot of the bottom of the ship. Are these screens showing anything. Do you see a starfish?"

Anna and Maya watched the screen displays for a minute and determined that they did not offer any help with the starfish clue. They continued to Deck Seven, which landed them at Shipwreck Boulevard at the aft, or back of the ship.

"Wow!" the duo said in unison.

"This is amazing," Maya added. "I can't believe we are on a ship." Shipwreck Boulevard held a large mall-like shopping area. There were high-end stores as well as eating venues and a coffee shop. Excited passengers were bouncing from venue to venue. "Should we eat again, Mom? We could sit and people-watch."

"Ha! I am officially embarrassed that I packed food for the week. We might be eating fifteen times a day. I'm not complaining. But I only packed one pair of stretchy pants. I need to be careful." The two walked through the area and found a choice of four garden paths. Each would end at the ships two-story theater. The paths were lined with tropical foliage and dim lighting with relaxing music. They were such a contrast to the spirited Boulevard.

Mother and daughter took one of the middle paths. Maya oohed over the beautiful ivy climbing around the entrance. Anna wondered if one of the café tables would be a good spot to write one morning. The idea was worth attempting. As they exited the path, they found the entrance to the upper level of Swashbuckler Theater. The doors were flanked by digital screens like those by the ice-skating rink.

"Do you see anything on these screens?" Anna asked. "Anything that helps with the clue?"

"Nope. To be honest, this treasure hunting isn't fun yet. I bet half of the passengers don't even solve the first clue."

Anna laughed. "I have a feeling we will be in that group." Maya chuckled and walked into the theater.

During the week, Swashbuckler Theater would host two production shows. *Aurum*, which means "gold" in Latin, was a tribute to the American gold rush of 1849. The other show was a high-energy, circus-style show named *Big Top Under the Sea*. Many reviews of the cruise mention the mind-blowing jump that an octopus character makes from four trapeze bars to four others.

"Add this to our calendar," Anna requested. "Both shows sound interesting."

"I agree. I will put them on your schedule, Mrs. Yearling."

"Thank you very much, Miss Yearling."

The two carefully walked down a golden spiral staircase to the lower level of the theater. Anna was amazed at the amount of seating available. And the crisp video of a pirate battle displayed on the oversize LED screen.

Maya recognized that her mother was slowing down, so she grabbed her hand and rushed her through the rest of Deck Six. They passed a large dance hall and two specialty dining restaurants. At the aft of this deck was the upper level of the main dining room, or the galley. Anna and Maya entered the area and looked down onto the lower level.

"Oh, this is pure elegance," Anna said. "I can't wait to get dressed up fancy for dinner. Will you pin my hair up for me like you did for the anniversary party?"

"Of course, Mom. That will be fun." They walked out of the dining room and looked around. "I think Deck Five only has the bottom of the dining room. Plus, those famous Torpedo X launch sites." On the inaugural sailing of *Golden Fortune*, an inflatable life raft was deployed to save the three passengers who fell overboard. Other cruise lines were now employing similar technologies on their ships. "We don't need to see those. Want to head back to our cabin?"

Before Anna could respond, an announcement was made over the ship's sound system. *Welcome, passengers! This is Poppy, your cruise director. Please be sure to check in at your designated muster station immediately. We cannot sail until everyone checks in. You can find your muster station on your cabin doors or on the app. You will also find a complete list of our restaurants, shows, and activities on the app. Have a great week, everyone. And ahoy, mateys.*

Anna looked at Maya. "Do you know our station?"

Maya was looking at her phone. "Nope. But I am looking right now." In a few seconds, Maya announced that they were to report to the ice-skating rink on Deck Eight. "That's easy. Let's head up there and then get back to our cabin."

At the rink, Anna and Maya watched a short safety video and offered their key bracelets to be scanned. A petite woman read their wristbands with a hand scanner. Her nametag revealed that her name was Keyata, and she was from the Dominican Republic. Anna found out that she was one of the acrobats in the circus show. "We will look for you at the show," Anna said warmly. Keyata grinned and gave the two a dainty wave.

When the two finally returned to their cabin, Anna placed her shoes neatly beside the closet and collapsed on the couch. "Whew! It's only two o'clock, and I'm already pooped. I'm going to have to pace myself."

"Don't worry. We'll be relaxing soon. The first day is probably the most hectic."

"I hope so. Let's go through the activities and set up some of our calendar. And I need to download the app."

"No worries. Hey, we still don't have our suitcases. Did you see any out in the hall?"

Anna stood and looked around. "You're right. Should they be here by now?"

"I have no idea. The reviews I read didn't mention suitcases. Maybe we have to go find them. I could be wrong about them being delivered."

"Can you look on the app?" As Maya looked at her phone, someone knocked on their cabin door. She got up and opened the door.

"Good afternoon, milady. I am Delroy, your room steward. I have two luggages to give you. We apologize for them being a little late. Security had a problem with the blue one." Maya thanked the man, whose nametag indicated that he was from Jamaica, and pulled the suitcases into the cabin. She laughed when she saw a large, neon-green sticker on her mother's suitcase. The sticker had one word typed on it: VIOLATION.

"Goodness, Mom. You are an official criminal. It looks like the banana bread was confiscated from your suitcase also."

"How embarrassing." Anna quickly removed the sticker from her suitcase. She placed her bag on the couch and opened it. On top of her clothes was a form letter. She read it to Maya. "After a routine scan of your items, one or more prohibited items were found. You may retrieve your item(s) at disembarkation in the "Item Retrieval" section of the port." She added, "Below that is handwritten 'Bread and Honey.'"

"Are you serious, Mom? You packed more bread? And honey?"

Anna closed her eyes. "Yes. I did. I can't believe I thought we might be hungry. It looks like we will be eating at least ten times per day on this ship."

Maya laughed. "Yeah, we won't be going hungry. I'm just glad we got our bags. Wanna unpack?"

"Sure. I think I will feel better when we get more situated." The two took about twenty minutes to unpack their clothes in the dresser drawers and closet. They arranged their toiletries neatly in the bathroom, placed the empty suitcases under their beds, and then sat for a break. Anna laughed at her grandmother's diary. "I can't believe I brought this thing. Maybe I can skim read it in the evenings before I go to bed."

Maya looked at her phone. "I think it's cool. Wanna go through the activities? I can mark the ones we like on my calendar. They will show up on yours."

"Yes. That sounds fun," Anna said. Maya went through the events for the week. Both women became excited for what was coming. "Napkin folding? Are you serious? I don't want to miss that."

Maya wasn't as excited about the folding of napkins. "I may skip that one, Mom. But it's on our calendar. What about the belly flop contest? Should we go to that?"

"I'm game. And that outdoor movie on the pool deck sounds fun. What about pickleball? I've always wanted to try that."

"Let's try it. But only once. I don't think I will like it, but I can add it to our schedule."

Anna smirked. "That sounds like a challenge." She checked the app on her phone and saw the marked events on her calendar. The week was set. "I'm going to text Jan and Winnie before we leave Miami. You know, I didn't take one picture of the ship while we were walking around. Please remind me to take some tonight."

"Will do. I texted them during lunch, so they know we made it onto the ship. We need to work on the clue before sailaway."

"What exactly is sailaway? It sounds a little serious."

"Obviously, that's when the ship starts to move. But there will be a big party on the top deck. Music and dancing. If you aren't up for that, we can just watch from our balcony."

"No. Let's see the party. This is probably the only time I'll ever get to do this."

"Don't say that, Mom. We may do this again next year." Maya regretted her comment as soon as she said it. "Don't worry. Dad will come back."

"I know, honey. I just wish everything would go back to normal." Anna put her phone down and finished her unpacking. She placed some magnetic hooks on the walls, which were always metallic, and hung her beach hat on one of them.

"You must accept that this is your normal now. Things change. It's like a video game. Sometimes God closes a path. We can't just stop. We have to find a new path to keep moving. The best path of the choices we have given."

Anna's eyes started tearing up. "That sounds good. But I don't think that God has closed our paths yet. I'm still praying that He will restore everything like it was."

"Let's just crash for thirty minutes and then head to the sailaway party." Maya adjusted her suitcase under her bed and lay back on the bed with a sigh. "Don't let me miss it if I fall asleep."

"Okay. I won't." Anna lay on her bed as well. She suddenly missed Jude terribly. He moved out three weeks ago. She hadn't been able to share her days with him or ask his advice about her book or the children. She hadn't cooked for him or even held his hand. The thought of being without him was too much to take. Anna decided that she would do whatever it took to knock down the new wall blocking their path. She needed Jude. And she would get him to move home next week.

After half an hour of overthinking everything in her life, Anna nudged Maya. "Time to go, My. We don't want to miss the excitement." Maya jumped up. Both women freshened up and walked out of the cabin toward the elevator area.

"We forgot to talk about the clue," Maya remarked. "Keep your eye out for an image of the bottom of the ship."

"Could there be another ship? Is there a mock ship in one of the shows or something like that?"

Maya's eyes widened. "Oh, good thinking." She scanned the app while the elevator was travelling to Deck Fourteen. "Hey, there was a pretend pirate ship in the kids' club. It's in the common area, so anyone can play on it. We can run down one deck and check it out before the party."

"Let's go. I'll follow you. I'm so confused by the layout of this place."

"Ha! I've got it in my head already. Must be a logistics thing." Maya led her mother to the kids' play area. There were at least a dozen children playing on the pirate ship, and their parents were standing close by. As she scanned the ship, she noticed a man discretely looking underneath it. He appeared to notice something interesting and walked away quickly. "Wait here."

Maya walked to where the man was looking and instantly saw tiny letters written on the mock hull, which had a large starfish painted on it. She read them quickly and then rushed to her mother. "It's the clue! Let me put it into my phone before I forget."

Anna loved seeing her daughter so excited. How had she and Jude managed to raise such a resilient young woman? She silently thanked God for her three amazing children.

Maya finished typing and took her mother by her arm. "Let's get out of here so I can tell you what it says."

"I can't wait to hear it."

"There were tiny words handwritten on the bottom of the ship near the starfish: 'Here you can walk, run, or hop. But make sure that you do not stop.'"

Anna thought for a minute. "That's a strange clue. You can walk everywhere on this ship."

"Not in the pools," Maya added quickly. "What do you think of when you think of walking?"

"The track!" the women answered in unison.

Maya was excited. "I'm not so sure about hopping on the track, but it does sound like the walking track. Which deck was that?" Maya checked the app and announced that the track was one deck down, Deck Eleven. "If we go now, we'll miss sailaway. But it's not far."

"Let's go have fun, sweetie. We have all night to check on the next clue." Maya agreed and the two walked back up to Deck Fourteen. When they came through automatic doors to the pool deck, the were greeted with loud music from a live band. A large group of people were doing an organized line dance to the music.

Maya tugged on her mother's arm. "C'mon! Let's dance." Anna would normally never join in the dancing mob. Jude would be too embarrassed. But she couldn't resist her daughter's exuberance. As they were fitting into the group, Anna realized that Hunter should be doing this. He should be dancing with Maya at the ship's sailaway. But he wasn't. He was on the other side of the country. How did that happen so quickly?

As the dozens of people were dancing to another line dance song, the ship's horn blew. Everyone cheered. Anna figured they were about to move. After the next song, she asked Maya if they could go look over the side of the ship. Maya agreed and followed her mother to the port side. They were shocked to see that they had already left the port and were about a mile out to sea.

"I can't even tell we are moving," Anna said. "This is so cool!"

"It is! Can you see all the people on the beach. This is a different perspective." Maya waved at three people on a nearby fishing boat. She was grinning from ear to ear. "Okay, Mom. The clue is driving me crazy. Can we go look at the track? Then we need to get ready for dinner. Our reservations are for seven o'clock, so we aren't in a huge rush."

"Lead the way, matey." Anna giggled. "But just know that I can't keep this pace up for an entire week. I will need to take breaks at some point."

"Don't worry. We will get plenty of rest. The first day is always crazy." The women walked to the elevator bank and went down to Deck Eleven. They exited near the spa and found the entrance to the track.

The ship's walking track went around half of the ship and was open to the air, except for a tunnel that led walkers and joggers from one side of the ship to another through the gym. It was clearly marked with arrows to ensure that everyone traveled in the same direction. There were a few serious walkers on the track and a handful of people watching land get farther and farther away.

"This is another cool perspective," Anna observed. "We are really out to sea now."

"Yep, no turning back," Maya said with a smile. "Let's walk a lap and look for a sign or something." Maya and her mother started walking in the designated "walker" lane. They looked for writing, especially small writing, but found nothing.

"This is impossible," Anna groaned. "I don't see anything. Let's finish the loop and give up."

"Can we do one more lap? It must be here. We just aren't looking close enough."

"Sure. And if we don't find it soon, we can come back after dinner. The clue might not be out yet."

"It has to be out." Just as Maya spoke, she noticed a sign above her head that read "Yellow." She walked a few more steps and saw a sign with a plus sign. "That's it," she whispered to her mother. "Look up." Anna noticed the words, also.

"Where do we start?"

"I'm not sure. Let's read them all. I'm sure it will make sense after we have all the words." The two kept walking and discretely noted the signs above them. One of the signs read "Start," which was also the point someone could start measuring his or her distance on the track. Maya typed the rest of the clues into her phone. When they returned to the starting point, they left the track and returned to their cabin.

"Whew! This is a lot of work," Anna said as she collapsed on her bed.

Maya laughed. "I think it will calm down, but I admit that I could be wrong. Let's see what we have: 'START, COUNTING, MERMAIDS, YELLOW + PINK + GREEN = BOW.'"

Anna listened closely. "Is that all ten of them?"

"Yep. That's all. I think this is easy. We are going to Mermaid Cove tomorrow. We must add up the number of yellow, pink, and green mermaids. That will probably give us a deck number. Then we look at the front."

"You are a genius! I wouldn't have gotten that. How do you know the front?"

"The bow of the ship is the front."

Anna smiled. "Your mind is built for this type of stuff, Maya. I'm really proud of you."

"Thanks. Take a break, Mom. You've earned it. We can start getting ready around six o'clock. Tonight is casual night. I think I'm going to wear that romper I got for the couple's shower.

"I can wear that yellow sun dress I wore on Easter."

Anna was amazed when Maya woke her. She had fallen completely asleep and had a sweet dream. All of her family, including Jude, was walking on a beach boardwalk. The kids were little and holding ice cream cones. Of course, Anna was wiping their arms to keep the drips off them and their clothes. She wasn't eating ice cream of her own because she was constantly wiping the drips.

Listening to Maya blow dry her hair in the bathroom, Anna awoke and thought more about her dream. Is that how she has lived? Never enjoying the moment. Always focusing on the messes. She opened the closet to pull out a yellow-printed dress. She noticed that all the clothes were neatly hung in order of length. Anna wouldn't have them any other way. Is that wrong? No. It couldn't be. God is a God of order. He doesn't like chaos. She quickly dismissed her questions about her attention to detail. If anything, she resolved to do a better job of cleaning up the messes. She decided that she would call Jude when she got home and insist that he come back. He could choose the day, but he would come home.

Dinner was in the galley dining room on Deck Five. Maya had signed them up for a group meal, thinking that it would be fun to meet new people. The cruise line promoted the group meals on the first day to encourage friendly interactions. The idea didn't make sense for a honeymoon, but now it seemed appropriate. Thanks to Anna's insistence on arriving twenty minutes early, they were the first to arrive at their table. It was a round table set for eight people.

"This is so fancy," Anna said with wide eyes. "I never expected the ship's restaurant to be so nice. I'm glad I brought those dresses."

"I'm so glad you taught me table manners." Maya laughed. "I think I know which fork to use first. But be sure to elbow me if I'm eating my salad with a dessert fork."

"You got it." Just as Anna spoke, a family of six arrived at their table. The parents were Anna's age, and the four "children" were close in age to Maya.

"Good evening," the father said. "You must be our table mates. We're the Weeks family. I'm Mick, and this is my wife, Leah. Our son is Whit, and this is Courtney. The twins are Sandra and Amanda." The entire Weeks family smiled and waved as they sat around the table.

Maya immediately perked up. She hadn't even thought about making new friends on this trip. She expected to spend all her time with her mother and enjoying a light beach read. "Hi! I'm Maya, and this is my mother, Anna. We're new at this, but we've had a lot of fun so far."

"I'm already exhausted!" Leah sighed. "The twins are really into the treasure hunt, so we have been running all over the ship. They promised we will slow down for the rest of the evening."

"I feel the same way," Anna added. "So where are you from?"

"Columbus, Georgia," Leah replied. "Mick and I own an antiques store in the middle of town. All the kids have worked there, from high school to college. Whit and Courtney have finished, but Sandra and Amanda have two more years to go. All six of us have been students at Auburn. War Eagle!"

Anna choked on the water she was sipping. She made a mental note to ask Dr. Ross about the sudden choking spells. "I'm sorry."

"Mom!" Maya scolded. "We're an Alabama family. My brother just graduated from Bama last month. So we can no longer speak to you." Whit laughed out loud. "Seriously, we will be cordial. But that's it." Whit made eye contact with Maya, and she stopped talking.

Mick broke the ice. "Now that we have established that we are mortal enemies, I'd love to hear more about your day. We are new at this also."

The conversation around the table was easy and friendly. Anna marveled at how cheerful Maya had become. She was thankful that God placed them on this ship this week at this very table. The Weeks children were very polite, especially for Auburn fans. Mick said a heartfelt blessing when the food arrived, and everyone began eating with the proper forks. To top everything off, Anna's prime rib was cooked perfectly. She could not have asked for a better dinner.

When dessert was served, Maya asked what the Weeks children had planned for the evening. They revealed that they had reservations for the *Aurum* show. "Rats! Mom and I are booked for the ice-skating show. Would you like to meet afterwards?" All agreed, and the young people exchanged contact information. "There is so much to do. Maybe we can meet at the soda shop on Deck Eight and go from there."

"Sounds like a plan," Courtney confirmed. "We'll see you there."

A waiter dressed like a pirate offered the group coffee. Anna groaned. "For the second time today, I am 'Thanksgiving full.' I will pass." The rest of the party agreed. "And I am looking forward to going to bed early tonight. I have a feeling that tomorrow will be another eventful day."

"I'm with you, Anna," Leah agreed. "I'm feeling my age already. If we don't see you at breakfast, have fun at Mermaid Cove." The four Weeks children smiled when their mother said "Mermaid." Anna figured they had found the walking track clue.

After goodbyes were said, Maya and Anna took an elevator to Deck Eight. They smelled pizza as soon as the doors opened. Both laughed at the overabundance of food on the ship. "We're a little early," Maya declared. "Do you want to check out the pizza area or find some seats for the show?"

"Let's get our seats. I wouldn't mind sitting in the rink for a while. And I need to email Jan and Winnie."

The couple were surprised to see that the seats were nearly half filled. They found a spot near the middle and settled into them. Anna wished that she had worn a sweater but was warmed by the energy in the area. Children were giggly, and parents were smiling widely. Anna had seen one ice-skating show in Birmingham when the children were small and was looking forward to seeing the acrobatics on a moving cruise ship.

Maya looked up from her phone. "I'm meeting the Weeks at the soda shop after the show. Are you okay with that?"

"Sure, honey. Have fun. Just be safe. Don't go into anyone's cabin."

"Oh, Mom. I know better than that." Maya side hugged her mother in her seat.

"I know you do. But that Whit boy is awfully handsome." Maya's face turned red. "I'm just saying. It's good to make new friends, but don't get too attached to them. We can't go around making Auburn friends."

Maya laughed. "Yep. Dad would never forgive us." The comment was awkward, and the women became quiet as they waited for the show to begin. Anna emailed Jan and Winnie with her phone. She shared with them the layout of the ship and ever-present food. And she avoided asking about Jude. This week would be about Maya. Next week would be about recovering her marriage.

The *Waltzing Sharks* show was amazing. Elite skaters zoomed around the rink in elaborate costumes. They made the choreography seem effortless. And the storyline of four sharks being invited to the Aqua Ball for the first time was charming. Anna was awed with the creativity of so many people involved in the show. From the male sharks' tuxedos to the flipping dolphins to the swimming orchestra, the show kept the audience entertained. Bubbles rained down upon the audience when the musical ended. Anna joined the crowd in a standing ovation.

"That was great," Maya exclaimed as she and her mother were making their way out of the arena. "I wasn't expecting such a top-notch performance."

"Neither was I. Can we see it again?"

Maya thought for a few seconds. "Yes, I think we can. We have three other shows scheduled, but I will check the app to see if we can fit this in again."

"We don't have to see it again. But I really did enjoy it." At the elevators, Maya offered to escort her mother to their cabin. "No worries. Go find your friends. I can make it back by myself. Wake me if I'm asleep when you get back. I want to know you are safe."

"Sure thing, Mom. I won't be that late. We'll probably just find a place to watch a band or something. And you can text me with the app. I'll check my phone."

Maya showed her mother the chat feature on the ship's app before darting off to the soda shop. Anna took an elevator to Deck Ten. She shared the car with eight other people, and all of them were marveling over the *Waltzing Sharks* show. Back in her cabin, Anna opted for a quick shower and dressed in a comfortable T-shirt and shorts rather than pajamas, just in case Anna brought her friends back to the cabin. She dug a book out of her backpack and sat with her legs crossed on her bed.

Before reading, Anna prayed to God. She thanked Him for their safety and for the fun day she had with Maya. She asked Him to protect Jude, Jan, and Winnie and to make her husband come back home. "Please put my family back together, God. Please."

Before she opened her book, Anna checked her phone. Surprisingly, Winnie had already responded to her earlier email message. With a smile, Anna opened it.

I'm glad to hear that you are having fun. You sound happy. Send pictures of the food. Dad took Jan and me to the new Italian restaurant in Tullah. Brandee came with us. She's really nice. Tell Maya we miss her, and don't fall off the ship. LOL! Love ya, Win.

Brandee? What? Anna couldn't breathe. She literally couldn't breathe. She stood quickly and wasn't sure what to do next. The room began spinning, and her vision became foggy. Her only thought was Maya. She had to get to Maya.

Anna found her room key and rushed out of her cabin. As she turned left toward the elevator bank, her vision went cloudy, and she collapsed to the ground.

"Ma'am. Ma'am?" Anna's eyes fluttered open, and she saw two women dressed entirely in purple kneeling beside her. A room steward was standing behind them and speaking on a walkie-talkie.

"Where am I?" Anna asked softly.

"You passed out in the passageway," a sweet older lady said. "Have you eaten anything today?"

With that question, Anna began laughing. She laughed so hard that tears began streaming down her cheeks. She had officially lost control of everything. If Jesus had the wheel, He was taking her through a ditch and into the woods. She wouldn't survive this day.

The steward looked very concerned and took off for help. "Yes. I've eaten plenty today. Thank you for asking. I'm fine. I just read an email message from my daughter."

"Oh dear," the woman said. "Was it bad news?"

"Yes. I can't talk about it."

"Then we will sit right here with you until you calm down. We've all be there, sweetheart." The two women sat beside Anna and began patting her back. Anna was speechless. "I'm Dovie, and this is Kate. We're part of the Amethyst Bunch." Anna began giggling as she imagined the Munchkins introducing themselves to Dorothy. Yes, she had lost it.

"Every year, we take a cruise together," Dovie continued. "We dress entirely in purple and go by purple names. On the ship, I am Lavender. And Kate is Lilac. We also have Orchid, Magenta, and Mauve. Violet couldn't make it this year. She had a knee replacement three weeks ago. We just watched the ice show and were going back to our cabin when we saw you run out of your cabin and collapse. Are you hurt?"

The three women were now sitting side by side with their backs to a wall. As Anna was about to speak, the room steward rushed to them with the ship's doctor in tow. "I'm Doctor Finch. Are you okay?"

Anna was embarrassed and tried to answer clearly. "Yes, I'm fine. And I apologize for the scare. I received an upsetting message and felt faint. I seems that I did faint, and these lovely ladies took care of me. Please, go help someone in serious need."

"I'd like to check your vitals to be sure before I leave." Anna agreed and patiently waited for the doctor to check her heartrate and blood pressure.

"You do seem a little agitated, but otherwise fine. May I help you to your cabin?"

Anna shook her head. "No, thank you. I'm fine. I actually feel more peaceful out here than in my cabin. When my mind clears a little more, I will message my daughter and let her know what happened. Thank you very much for your time." Before Dr. Finch left, he asked the steward to bring the ladies bottles of cold water.

Dovie, aka Lavender, spoke first. "You don't have to tell us what was in the message, but we have a pretty good idea of what it was. We've been around more than seventy years, dear. We know that life is messy. But you need to know that God is in control. He sees everything."

Anna didn't speak. God wasn't watching over her life. He couldn't be. Her life wouldn't be spiraling out of control if God were paying attention. Anna felt numb. Normally, she had a plan. But tonight, she just felt like she was stuck in neutral.

"My husband walked out on me," Kate blurted, aka Lilac. "My girls were four and two, and he decided that he wasn't 'himself' anymore. So he just left. I was numb. And I didn't see a way out." Anna listened to the sweet woman's story. Did Lilac know what happened? Had Anna mumbled her troubles after she fainted?

"I was lost," Lilac continued. "My grandmother figured out what happened and came over. She sat at my small table and helped me come up with a plan. We began by praying and giving everything to God. Then we asked Him to make my next move clear. She shared with me that something similar had happened to her."

Lavender spoke up next. "Yep, sweetie. This is life. Eve lost a son at the beginning of time. My mother lost her husband to a massive heart attack at age forty-two. My husband lost his job right after our third son was born. We had to move in with his parents. That is life, my dear. The seas aren't always calm."

"Why does it have to be like this?" Anna asked through soft tears.

"It's not for us to know why," Lavender replied. "Not now. We are in a battle on this planet. We are to ask, 'What next?' That's the question. Keep moving forward. One day at a time. One hour at a time if you need to. And ask God for His guidance."

As the women were talking, the room steward arrived with a room service tray. He lifted the lid to reveal three water bottles and a plate of warm chocolate chip cookies. The three women, still sitting on the ground, began laughing.

"What is your name, dear man?" Lilac asked.

"I'm Bennie. And I have a wife. She eats sweets when she is unhappy."

"You must be a wonderful husband, Bennie," Lilac gushed. "We will be fine. Thank you very much."

Each woman took a cookie and a water bottle. They were silent for a full minute. Anna's mind was whirling, but she did not have the knot in her stomach anymore. She was surprisingly at peace.

"Brandee!" Anna blurted. "Her name is Brandee." Lavender and Lilac nodded in agreement.

"I had a feeling it was another woman," Lavender said. "How long has it been going on?"

"Well, I don't know that anything is really going on," Anna admitted. She explained that her perfect world had recently fallen apart. Sitting in a passageway on a modern-day cruise ship, Anna shared her story. She included Jude's new apartment, Maya's cancelled wedding, Jan's lost internship, and Winnie's yearbook accident. She opened her heart to the strangers and even included the dreaded poop socks.

"My my, sweetie," Lavender consoled. "You've had a time. I'm a little nervous about you being on this ship. You may cause it to sink."

"Oh, Lavie, don't say that," Lilac scolded. "You have had a rough time. Don't blame God for the bad times. Never do that. But remember that He has been there. It seems to me that He has blessed you with a week to spend with your daughter. And the younger children have a week to spend with their father. God is doing something. I can feel it. Listen for Him to tell you what to do next. That's your assignment."

Lavender nodded and looked Anna in the eyes. "And be ready to share your story when you find a woman collapsed in despair. We must lift each other up." She hugged Anna and reached for another cookie. "And don't give up on your marriage yet. I have a feeling there is some sort of misunderstanding with *Brandee*."

Anna felt lighter. She couldn't explain it, but she felt lighter. "I think I will email Jude and let him know that that I know she went to dinner with him."

Lilac interrupted. "No! Now stop that! Let it go. You must let it all go. Give it to God and let Him handle it. He sees the big picture. Let it go tonight and sleep well. Have a fun day at the tropical island tomorrow, and wait to see what God tells you do to."

Lavender spoke next. "Don't go over this in your mind. That's what Satan wants you to do. Just ask, 'What's next?' That's it."

"I don't know if I can do that," Anna admitted. "But I will try." As she was talking a young couple passed by. They asked if the ladies needed help and were relieved to hear that the women were just chatting.

"We're gonna get to bed now," Lavender said. "It's pretty late for us old people. We have to count mermaids tomorrow." Anna smiled knowingly. "We are doing the ballroom dance lessons with the cruise director on Tuesday morning. It's in the app." Anna made a mental note to look at the app more closely before she went to bed tonight. "I hope you can join us. We'd like you to meet the rest of the Amethysts."

"And we'd like to know that you are okay," Lilac added.

Anna smiled. "That sounds like fun. I've always wanted to try dancing lessons, but my husband doesn't enjoy that kind of thing."

"You'd be surprised," Lilac joked. "Sometimes there are some dashing gentlemen at these lessons. I'm always hopeful." The three women laughed and began standing.

"Mom! Are you okay?" Maya was rushing down the corridor toward her mother.

Anna hugged her daughter when she approached. "Yes, dear. I was having a 'moment,' and these dear ladies helped me. They were sent straight from God." Anna introduced the women and asked Maya to add the dance lessons to her calendar. Maya grabbed the last cookie as she was looking for the lessons on the app.

Back in her cabin and settled for bed, Anna listened to Maya sleep soundly. Her daughter was handling life's curveballs better that she was. And she never even asked how the evening with the Weeks kids went. Anna decided to take the Amethysts' advice. She would start with a baby step and try to step out in faith further each day.

God, my boat is drifting out of control. Please take the wheel—or the helm. I'm sorry I don't know the terminology. But please take my mess and fix it the best way possible. I will try to stay out of Your way and listen for Your orders. Please make them clear. You know how I like to get ahead of You. Thank You for sending Lavender and Lilac just when I needed them.

"It itches!" Fidget was begging to remove the bandages on his arm.

"No," Sarah scolded. "You must leave them on for a week. Dr. Morgan said that you might get an infection if you take them off too soon." The two boys' careless accident ended the wedding reception early. Sarah figured that Jade and Dewayne didn't mind. Jewel tended to Fidget while Sarah helped put away tables and chairs. She saved a large piece of the cake for the newlyweds and offered the rest to guests.

Sarah did not attend church services this morning so she could tend to Fidget. He was in too much pain to sit through a sermon. Charles Bishop was filling in for the newly married pastor, and Sarah had been looking forward to his message. Jewel promised to share the highlights.

A few minutes later, Fidget was breathing softly. Sarah was thankful that he had fallen asleep. She took her Bible outside and sat in one of the chairs by the door. This morning was a perfect time to read Psalms. It wasn't the same without Asher reading. But the message was the same, and that provided her some comfort.

Before she could open her Bible, Jewel came skipping out of the church. She headed straight to the barn. "You'll never believe it, Mama. Dr. Morgan asked if I would like to work as a nurse apprentice with him. He doesn't have anyone helping him and liked the way I took care of Fidget and Jonathon." Sarah had asked around and found out that Vincent Morgan was not married. He returned from medical school in Lincoln only six months ago. Could God be blessing her family again? And so soon?

"I think it's a fine idea. Would you have to go to Lincoln?"

Jewel wasn't sure. "I think I might have to go to the hospital in Fort Laramie for a few days. But that would be it. Trenton could take me. We'll be fine."

Love. Trust. Obedience. These were the words that Sarah lived by now. "Of course, dear. I couldn't be happier."

CHAPTER TWENTY

Monday, June 16: Mermaid Cove
2025

Anna woke first. She quietly dressed for breakfast and went to the balcony. The ship should be docked at Mermaid Cove by now. Anna and Maya planned to spend a relaxing day on the beach with two books and plenty of sunscreen. When she opened the balcony door, Anna was surprised to see the beautiful island just outside of reach. If she had Jan's strength, she could have thrown a rock to the shore.

Mermaid Cove was beautiful. Passengers were not leaving the ship yet, so Anna got a pristine view of it. Palm trees covered the entire island. She noticed a large beach area with rows of chairs on the left side. *Do islands have a port side?* And she saw colorful splash areas for children on the right. The slides and pools looked like welcome venues for weary parents to let their children swim and play.

Anna sat in a chair on the balcony and spoke with God. *How did You make all of this? It's so beautiful! Thank You for providing me with sleep and this peace that I do not understand. You know that I would like for my family to be restored to the way it was two months ago, but I accept what You have in store instead. Well, I'm trying my best to accept it.*

As Anna was finishing her prayer, Maya stepped out. "Wow, Mom. This is so cool. I didn't think we would be so close to the land."

"I know. Thank you for inviting me. I would never have seen anything like this if you hadn't included me."

"Ha! You can thank Hunter. He left me with the extra ticket." Maya sat beside her mother and watched the waves roll back and forth to the shore. The two pointed to a section of the beach they deemed their reading nook for the day and declared that they were hungry again.

Before they left for breakfast, Anna asked about Maya's evening. "I'm sorry that I never asked about your evening. I was too preoccupied with my public meltdown."

"No worries. I understood. Those cookies were really good, by the way. Can we just order them any time?"

Anna laughed. "Yes, I think we can. Now tell me about your evening." Maya shared her fun as she dressed. Only Whit and Courtney showed up at the soda shop. The twins wanted to try pirate trivia with their parents. The others found a table at the Dance Hall on Deck Six. Whit ordered three Sabers, *Plunder*'s signature family friendly drink. Much like the Cutlass on *Golden Fortune*, the Saber was sold in a large, collectible cup. While the Cutlass was made with cherries and limes, the Saber was created with bananas and coconuts. Maya loved the Saber and promised to buy her mother one.

On the way to breakfast, Maya talked nonstop. She gave her mother a rundown of the evening, complete with two semi-slow dances with Whit.

"What exactly is a semi-slow dance?" Anna asked as she entered the elevator.

"We sort of danced together. But we didn't touch." Anna joked that she approved, and Maya continued. "He's really nice. But he went to Auburn. That takes at least ten points from his score."

Ann laughed. "More like twenty points. I'm glad you had fun. You deserve it, My." As soon as the two exited the elevator, they saw the entrance to the buffet at Blackbeard's Fortress. "Oh no!"

"I see it," Maya squealed. The first thing they saw was a huge display of fresh banana bread. There were five types arranged beautifully with a crew member slicing them on demand.

"I've never seen so much banana bread." Anna laughed. "Not even in my suitcase." Maya doubled over with the last comment. "Blueberry, chocolate chip, cinnamon, pumpkin, and Hawaiian. Who knew?"

"I'm getting some chocolate chip banana bread. I'll meet you by that window."

Anna just shook her head with a smile and found a plate. She opted for scrambled eggs, bacon, fruit, and a mango crepe. She couldn't even walk near the banana bread exhibition. Maya was already at a table waiting for her mother when she finished filling her plate. Maya had added a yogurt cup to her plate and smiled when her mom sat down. "Thank you for doing this. I feel like my tank is gassed up again. I'm ready to move forward with my life. For some reason, I feel rested today."

"I'm happy to hear that, and that Whit boy is pretty cute—for an Auburn fan."

"Mom!"

"Don't think I didn't notice that his last name is Weeks. A perfect calendar name."

"Yikes. I didn't even notice that. He is cute and easy to talk to. But another relationship is not on my mind yet. I want to coast and heal for a little while." As soon as Maya stopped speaking, her phone buzzed. "That's Whit. He wants to hang out today."

Anna raised her eyebrows. "I say *go for it*!"

"No!" Maya said quickly. "I want to spend the day with you."

"Oh, I will be fine. Help me find a good spot on the beach. Then you can run off with your new friends." Maya finished her mango crepe and mentally debated if she should get another.

"I don't want to leave you. I'll tell Whit that we'll be on the beach. He can come find us later."

"Sounds good. But I'm gonna read our grandmother's diary most of the day. The purple ladies were talking about women going through trials throughout time, and I suddenly want to read about our ancestors. It never occurred to me that even she would understand."

"That's cool," Maya said. "Is it even legible?"

"Yes, I think so. It's just a hardback journal. It's in pretty good shape. And the handwriting is beautiful. It's amazing how penmanship is becoming a lost art. People made an effort to write so clearly years ago. And on that note, I will be right back. I *need* another mango crepe. That was sooo good."

When Anna came back with the crepe, Maya went for a glass of green "go go" juice. "I've wanted to try this. It's supposed to give you energy." Both ladies agreed that the green color was a little creepy, but Maya was pleasantly surprised at the tastiness of the healthy drink.

When Anna once again reached Thanksgiving fullness, she led Maya back to their cabin. The rest of the ship was still a maze, but the path to and from the buffet was quite clear now.

"Wow. It feels weird to be back on land again." They had only been sailing for sixteen hours, but Anna's equilibrium felt a little off. Thankfully, neither she nor Maya had any sort of seasickness. Just a little whooshing in her ears. The next two days would be spent at sea, so the real test was coming soon.

Anna and Maya marched directly to the spot they had chosen from their balcony earlier. Anna placed towels on two chairs while Maya dug sunscreen out of her bag. Dozens of children were already splashing in the water. A few were building hasty sandcastles on the shore. Energized parents were sitting in nearby beach chairs watching the fun.

"You kids would have loved this when you were that age. Winnie would be building a perfect sandcastle. Jan would be too deep in the water, and your dad would have to get in the water to keep an eye on him. And you, my oldest, would be running back and forth, checking on everyone. I can see it now." Anna looked at her daughter and became teary-eyed. She would give anything to go back to the time when the kids were little. Just one more hug from each of them. One more bedtime story. Or family movie night. Adult children were blessings too. But Anna had no control over them. She could only influence them from afar.

The reason that life seems like it is out of control right now is because it is. You never had control in the first place. Anna remembered Lilac's advice from last night. Could it be possible that she never had control? Giving up her idea of control was going to be difficult, but Anna knew that it was the right thing to do. She would need plenty of help from the Holy Spirit to let go. Today was a nice place to start. She and Maya had no plans until dinner. Anna would enjoy the slower pace and freedom to be unproductive. Tomorrow, she would carve out at least four hours to write. She had to come home with one third of the book written—or more.

Anna thought about Jude. He would be at work right now. With Brandee. What a nightmare. Anna wouldn't know how to fix her marriage even if God handed her both reins. Maya's attention was on a book, so Anna took out her phone and reread the message from Winnie. *Brandee came with us. She's really nice.* Did Jude really bring their kids on a date? Or did he bring a date on a family dinner? That common feeling of dread came back to her insides. What should she do?

Wait on the Lord.

Where did that come from? Anna heard the message as clear as if Maya had said it out loud. Wait on the Lord? How would she do that? Anna was never good at waiting. Doing nothing was a waste of time. Or was it? Could she possibly just wait and do nothing? While some size-four floozy was stealing her husband? Ouch. That hurt. Was he even her husband anymore. Was Jude gone forever?

Thoughts of the unknown overwhelmed Anna, and she began crying. Maya looked over and sat up to comfort her mother. "What's wrong?"

"What if Dad never comes back?" Anna asked while looking straight ahead.

"I really think that he will come back. He wanted to see what it would be like to have his own life. That was totally selfish. But he can't be happy. Just wait it out. And if he doesn't come back, you will be fine. You know how to do everything. Dad is the one who will be lost. It will be okay. Just wait on the Lord to tell you what to do."

Anna got chills on her legs. That was the second time she'd heard the message. The Holy Spirit knew her pain and was telling her what to do. "How do I do that? You know I'm not good at waiting."

"Okay, here's the plan. You enjoy the week. You really can't do anything right now. When we get back home, you call Dad and ask him to meet you to talk. Until then, you focus on the present. And listen for any orders from God. Let Him be the Designated Driver. Let go of the steering wheel."

"You are amazing, Maya. I'm so glad you are my daughter. Get back to your book. I'm gonna take your advice." Anna liked the idea of a divine Designated Driver. She didn't really give up control. She just handed it to Someone else. She decided to make a strong effort to let her troubles go. She would enjoy the rest of the trip with Maya. When they got home, Anna would try her best to follow God's lead. It wouldn't be easy, but it would be the right thing to do.

Anna dug the diary out of her bag. She also found a notebook and pen. Hopefully, it would hold interesting insights that could be used in her novel. She opened to the first page. In a beautiful script, women's names were written as a list. After them were names of husbands and children.

Sarah Wilkes—1816, Husband: Asher; Children: Luke, Jewel, Jade, Trenton, Jeremiah

Jade Barton—1848, Husband: Dewayne; Children: Lilly, Asher, Luke, Berty

Lilly York—1880, Husband: Paul; Children: Gayle, Elizabeth, John, Alice

Elizabeth Washington—1905, Husband: Abe; Children: Victoria, Edward, James, Bettie

Elizabeth "Bettie" Brown—1927, Husband: Vaughn; Children: Karen, Kathy, Stephen

Karen Minor—1948, Husband: Dewayne; Children: Anna

As Anna was about to read the first page, Whit and his sisters walked up. "We found you," Courtney said. They all began talking at once, and the Weeks eventually convinced Maya to take a tour around the island.

"Will you be okay?" Maya asked as she put her book back into her beach bag.

"Yes, honey. I'm fine. I'm gonna read the diary. Take all the time you want. I can smell the burgers from here, so I will be able to feed myself." Anna was surprised that her appetite hadn't diminished with the worry over her family. Maybe she was really giving her cares to God. "If I'm not here, I'll be back in the cabin. I would love a little nap before dinner and the *Aurum* show."

"Sounds good," Maya said as she walked away with the others. "Message me in the app if you need anything."

Anna sighed. God was solving one of her family member's problems right before her eyes. Maya was moving on. The breakup with Hunter must still hurt, but Maya was demonstrating resilience. This week would be good for her daughter. Anna could tell by the way she smiled. As Maya waved goodbye, her smile went all the way to her eyes. Anna hadn't seen that smile from her daughter in weeks. One problem on the way to being solved. *Thank You, Lord.*

Mae's wedding was beautiful. Anna couldn't put the diary down. She forgot to reapply her sunscreen and cringed at her reddening skin. It was after noon, but Anna didn't want to stop reading. She was amazed at the details her distant grandmother shared about her troubles on the Oregon Trail. She and her husband had left their home for a dream of a better life in the Oregon Territory. As she was reading, Maya called out.

"Mom? Are you there, Mom?"

"Oh," Anna answered. "I didn't hear you. I'm caught up with this diary. I can't wait to tell you what I've read so far."

"The Weeks are eating with their parents, so I told them I would eat lunch with you if you haven't already eaten."

"Sure. That would be great." As the two made their way through the sand to the brightly colored pathway that led to Landlubber Café, Maya shared her morning. She and the others explored the small island and spent some time splashing in the water at the farthest section of the beach.

"Did you see the mermaids? They look so real!"

"No," Anna said as she walked beside her daughter. "Where were they?"

"We saw them swim by twice when we were in the water. I counted them. Whit counted, too, so they must have figured out the walking track clue. Let me see . . . There were three yellow mermaids, four green ones, and one pink mermaid. The pink one was difficult to see, but we spotted her. Whenever they came by, children would swarm the area. But we were close enough to get a good count."

"So what does that add up to?" Anna asked.

"Three plus one plus four is eight. So the clue is *eight* and *bow*. I'm not sure if we are on the right track, but we have the number correct."

The two arrived at the buffet and went separate ways to get their food. Anna built a double cheeseburger and added French fries, fruit, and a brownie. Maya had chosen tacos and tortilla chips. They sat at a picnic table painted light blue with a matching umbrella.

"There is something about a beach burger," Anna remarked.

"I know, but these tacos looked so good. I'll get a burger when we get to Treasure Island on Thursday."

Anna laughed. "I'll get another one. This looks delicious." She started a prayer of thanks for the food and stopped as she thought of Jude. The diary and walk to lunch had kept her mind free of worry. God's order to wait was working. Anna thanked God for everything He was doing in her life and asked Him to continue working His will. When she finished Maya gave Anna's hand a squeeze. For the first time in a while, Anna felt that life would be okay.

"So, tell me about the mermaids," Anna asked.

"They just randomly swam by. It was exciting. They never left the water and appeared to have real tails. I'm sure it's some sort of stunt. But they looked real."

"I hope I get to see them before we go back to the ship," Anna remarked. "Tell me about your new friends."

"There's not much to tell. Sandra and Amanda are very close. And they are a little bit younger. Courtney is really cool. She's a dancer. Whit was joking about her joining the circus show on the ship."

"What's the scoop on Whit?"

"Gosh, Mom," Maya moaned. "Let me get over Hunter first."

"Wait. I didn't plan a wedding or anything. I just asked."

"Sorry. He's nice. Jan would like him. He's a science nerd but has been helping with the family antiques business. Oh, he won't eat any foods that are red. Isn't that weird?"

"Even lobster?"

Maya chuckled. "I'm not sure. I'll ask about that."

After lunch Anna read the diary at her beach chair for two more hours. She left Maya with the Weeks and returned to her cabin on her own. In her room, she first took a long shower and then plopped down on her bed. Anna had planned to nap before dinner, but the diary was too intriguing. Her great-great-great-great-grandmother had made it to the California Crossing despite the challenges that came with traveling with five children. The family was about to cross the South Platte River, and Trenton was clearly worried. Anna decided that she would nap once she read about how the family had made it across safely.

The lock on the cabin door opened, and Maya walked in. "Can we eat at the buffet tonight instead of the dining room?"

Anna was startled out of her focus on the diary. "Sure. I don't mind."

"Great! I gonna go hot-tubbing with Courtney and Whit for a little while, but I'll be back to get cleaned up for dinner. We were thinking of eating around seven o'clock. That should give us enough time to make it to the *Aurum* show."

"Count me in. I'm not exactly sure what hot-tubbing is, but please don't get hurt."

Maya rolled her eyes. "I won't. I promise." She threw her beach bag onto her bed and rushed out the door.

How could Maya seem so downright giddy? Had she forgotten Hunter that easily? Was she just masking her pain? The entire scenario was confusing. But isn't that how God worked? He took the leftovers and made a beautiful meal His way. Anna just had to stay out of His way. But she would have to work at it. Giving up control was not in her playbook.

Anna decided that a short nap would be a good idea after all, so she put the diary under her pillow. She didn't want anything to happen to this precious heirloom. She made a mental note to research ways to preserve the journal. At the very least, she could take pictures of the pages. Anna fell back onto her pillow. *I'll read about the crossing tomorrow, Grandma.*

Dinner was lively with the five young adults sharing one table and the three parents sharing another. Anna chose a healthy salad to go along with an unhealthy pasta dish. She was still amazed at her daughter's joyfulness.

"Is she always like that?" Leah asked. "I'll be honest. Our girls are still moody. I'm waiting for that phase to end but am losing hope."

"Ha!" Anna answered. "No, not really. I think she is letting go of a lot of baggage on this trip. This may be the real Maya, and I've just never seen it." Mick nodded. "I'm not sure if you know, but her fiancé called off their wedding a few weeks ago. This was supposed to be their honeymoon."

"Oh, goodness." Leah sighed. "I had no idea. Whit said something about a wedding, but I didn't realize it was that serious. She must have been devastated."

"You know," Anna began, "I'm starting to think that I was more devastated than she was. I have been mourning the loss of her perfect plan. But maybe that wasn't the perfect plan. Or that *isn't* the perfect plan anymore. Sure, Maya was mad. But she immediately stepped into action and moved forward."

"That's wonderful," Leah said. "Amanda has been dealing with some health issues. She doesn't like to talk about it, but I'm like you. I'm more worried about it than she is. She just takes her infusions and carries on like a trooper. We have a lot to learn from our children."

The group at the other table laughed at something Whit said, and Anna smiled. "You're right. And from our ancestors too. I found a diary from my four-times-great-grandmother recently. I can't explain why, but I brought it on the cruise with me. I guess I didn't think there would be enough to do." Mick and Leah laughed. "My grandmother took her five children on the Oregon Trail. That's two thousand miles of walking—with five kids. Can you even imagine?"

"Wow," Mick remarked. "I thought four kids on an all-inclusive cruise was a task."

"Exactly! I can't wait to read more tomorrow. It's so interesting."

"You'll have to tell us how it ends," Leah said.

"Oh, I will. There isn't much more to read."

After two desserts—pecan pie and bread pudding—Anna pried Maya away from her friends. Neither of them wanted to miss the show. Maya made arrangements to meet her new friends on the pool deck after breakfast the next day. She joked that she was forced to spend time with her own mother. Then she put her arm around Anna and led her to the elevators. "C'mon, Bestie."

Anna hoped she heard her correctly. Bestie? She and Maya had always been close. But never besties. Maya always kept a distance from everyone in the family. Was she maturing this summer? Or was Anna relaxing?

"Whit thinks the eight from the mermaids is the deck like I was thinking earlier." Maya brought Anna out of her thoughts. "We have time to check out Deck Eight if you're okay with it."

"Sure. I'm game. I got a nap, so bring it."

Maya laughed and pushed the elevator button for Deck Eight. "The bow is the front, so we can check out the soda shop and the game room."

"Sounds good."

When they landed on Deck Eight, Anna and Maya walked straight toward the soda shop. The electronic sounds of the game room filled the air until they passed through to the Oro pizza shop.

"Where should we start?" Anna asked. "It could be anywhere."

"I know. It's like a needle in a haystack." The couple decided to stick together and start in the game room. They looked at all the machines and the walls near them. Anna checked out the colorful carpet, and Maya examined the red stools stationed at various games. After a few minutes, they left.

"Well, that was a bust," Anna joked. "Where to, Captain?"

Maya noticed an older couple pointing to the menu at the pizza shop. "They may be onto something. Let's casually check out the menu."

"Lead the way,"

Sure enough, one line on the menu had a clue written instead of a pizza or drink item. Maya took out her phone and snapped a picture of the menu. She covered her tracks by adding, "Just in case we get hungry later." Anna laughed and followed her to a café table near the soda shop.

"What does it say?"

Maya read the clue: "If it's treasure you seek before Sunday, Do NOT follow the Captain's Orders on Wednesday."

"That's odd." Anna took Maya's phone and read it for herself. "I think the capital *O* in *Orders* means something."

"I agree." Maya stood. "Let's get seats for the show and think about it." She led her mother down two flights of stairs to Deck Six. The theater was already buzzing with adults and children finding seats. Neither Maya nor Anna knew what the show would be like. They just knew that the title meant "gold" in Latin and that it had something to do with the gold rush.

"What do you think the 'Captain's Orders' means?" Anna asked.

"First of all, his orders will be on Wednesday. So we have tomorrow off from treasure hunting."

"Nice!" Anna chuckled.

"There must be an official order from the captain somewhere. We are missing it. I guess we can keep our eyes out for his official orders tomorrow. Then don't do what he says."

"Sounds easy. You'll be good at that." Anna mock-punched Maya's shoulder.

"Very funny, Mom."

The show started, and Anna was amazed to discover that it was a musical celebrating the gold rush of 1849. In the opening act, actors were walking beside a life-size Conestoga wagon. They were singing Abba's "Money, Money, Money." She saw the scenes from her grandmother's diary displayed before her eyes. According to the diary, westward travelers began together on the trail. Those heading to the Oregon Territory separated from those heading to California at the Parting of Ways in Idaho. Maya still had no idea that her relatives had endured a journey like the musical. Anna laughed to herself thinking of the real pioneers breaking into song every five minutes.

After the show, Maya talked her mother into getting a Saber drink in the dance hall.

"This is good," Anna announced as she tasted her drink. "Very coconutty." She had to speak loudly over the live band performing songs from the 1970s.

"I told you they were yummy. Do you have any plans for tomorrow? I'm just hanging out by the pool with the Weeks. We might play pickleball if a court is available."

"I'm taking lessons in ballroom dancing tomorrow morning, if you want to join me."

Maya's eyes widened. "Are you serious? I thought you were joking about that."

"Don't you remember the ladies in the hallway last night? You added it to my calendar."

Maya took out her phone and opened the app. "Sure enough. You have dance lessons scheduled for tomorrow at nine thirty. I'm impressed. And with the cruise director. Should be fun."

"I hope so. The purple ladies helped me out when I was having a moment." Anna took another sip of her drink.

"Do you want to tell me what happened?" Maya asked.

"No."

"Was it about Dad?"

"Yes."

Maya looked at her mother. "He's just being dumb. He'll move back home. Winnie said that she's ready for us to get back."

"You know, I've been so stressed about our family, but I finally decided to give it all to God. And I'm doing a pretty good job of it. Of course, I still hate those poop socks. But I'm trying. We'll be okay if Dad doesn't come back. I think I will be sad for a long time. But I will be okay."

"That's great, Mom. I'm proud of you. And I'm coming by the dance hall to get pictures of you dancing with the Lavender Ladies."

Anna smiled. "They are called the Amethyst Bunch."

"That's cool—sort of. Do you have anything purple to wear?"

"Gosh. I don't think I do. Do you?"

"Not that I can think of. But I have a light-gray shirt that is sort of purple. You can wear that with your white shorts."

"Thank you," Anna said. "This trip has been way more fun than I expected. And I can hardly feel the ship moving. Your dad might be fine on a cruise. Maybe we can take a big family cruise someday."

"That would be a lot of fun. But don't get your hopes up. Things are kind of crazy right now. But yes. A family adventure at sea would be great. You will have to bring a separate suitcase for all the banana bread." Anna laughed at her daughter and called it a night.

The two headed back to their cabin. Anna found their passageway without Maya's help.

"You know, Mom," Maya said as she was washing her face, "I didn't think about Hunter once tonight. I think my storm might be ending."

Anna, sitting on her bed, raised her fist in the air. "God's working on us." She had taken the diary out from under her pillow and had it opened on her knees. When Maya slipped into her bed, Anna began reading. "You will have to read this someday. Our ancestors were pretty tough. I don't remember anyone from Oregon. They must have moved back to Nebraska sometime after settling near Portland."

"I'll read it when I have some free time. Winnie would like that too."

Anna agreed and continued where she left off. The Wilkes were about to cross the South Platte River. A week after Jade and Jewel's birthday. Maya was breathing softly in a matter of minutes. She had always been an easy sleeper.

Today was a bad day. We lost Papa and Luke. What? How did they lose them. Anna continued to read and was horrified to discover that her great-great-great-great-grandmother lost her husband and oldest child five weeks into their journey. She didn't want to read any further but had to continue. She owed it to her. *Tyler found their bodies and is helping Brother Barton bury them.*

Oh, how awful! What will happen to the family? "This can't be happening." Without realizing it, Anna woke her daughter.

"What's wrong?" Maya asked.

"He died," Anna answered with a catch in her voice. "Sarah's husband died. Your five-times great-grandfather. Remember they were traveling on the Oregon Trail? Well, your grandfather and their oldest son drowned while crossing the river."

"How sad. How did they drown?"

"I'm not sure. But someone is burying their bodies right there. The rest of the family just has to go on."

Maya shook her head. "I can't imagine. Keep reading." Anna continued reading the journal. She and Maya stayed up until nearly midnight reading the rest of the account. They discovered that the family settled in Ash Hollow in the Nebraska Territory. Jade and Jewel married men in the town, and the two boys thrived in their schooling. About a year after the tragedy, the penmanship changed from two different writers to only one. Sarah must have had help with the writing while on the trail but finished it when they were settled in Ash Hollow.

My hope is in the Lord, the Maker of heaven and earth.

"She so easily gave it to God." Maya marveled.

"I don't think it was that easy. But she did have remarkable faith. She gave her family to God. And He took care of them. Like He always does with His children. Why am I having such a hard time with that?"

"Don't be so hard on yourself, Mom."

Anna shook her head. "No. Really. Why can't I trust God enough to let Him have the reins?"

"I don't know, Mom. You like predictability. You want to write the ending that you prefer. But remember, you aren't the best author around. You are my favorite author on Earth, of course. But God is the Author of the universe. He is writing the entire story. Trust Him to write your part exactly how it should go, especially with the world throwing in unexpected plot twists here and there."

"Wow!" Anna looked at her daughter. "How did you get so smart?"

"Ha! I come from a line of strong women."

"It does seem that you do."

"That is an amazing story," Maya remarked. "Someone needs to get that down electronically."

Anna's eyes widened. "My book! I've been struggling with the details. Now I have the story. It's from the 1800s. And it's personal."

"That's great, Mom. Our grandmother was so brave. Her faith could help others."

"And there are more books in the attic. Plus a digital version somewhere. Maybe we can read what happens to the children. Jade is your great-great-great-great-grandmother. And I am eager to see what comes of Fidget. His parents believed he would add to the kingdom somehow."

When Anna finally turned off the reading light to sleep, she spoke to God from her heart. "I am inspired by my grandmother to trust You with my family. Please take care of us. Your will be done. I will try to let You be the Captain. I'm ready for duty. Just give me Your orders."

CHAPTER TWENTY-ONE

Tuesday, June 17
2025

Anna woke with a light heart. She was genuinely trying to trust God with her life. It wasn't easy, but it was best. Her own grandmother inspired her to let Him be the Captain.

"I'm almost ready." Maya was dressing for breakfast in the bathroom. "Don't want to be late for the banana bread."

"Very funny." As Anna was putting on her earrings, she hoped the gray shirt would work for her date with the Amethyst Club.

Anna skipped the banana bread and chose French toast with fruit and bacon instead. She added a little too much syrup, but only because it was warmed. While Maya was waiting at the omelet station, Anna enjoyed a cup of hot cocoa at their table. She added caramel syrup only because it was available.

"No banana bread?" Maya joked as she sat down.

"Not today," Anna replied. "You will never let me live that down, will you?"

"Nope. That will become a family legend. Just like Grandma Bettie walking in front of that train. I never met her, but I still love that story."

Anna shook her head. "So my great-great-great-grandchildren will know that I brought a suitcase full of banana bread on an all-inclusive cruise."

"Yep. And the story will probably grow. By then it will be that you brought monkeys onto the ship." Anna nearly spit out her cocoa. Her spirit was joyful today. Despite what she had always thought, giving God control was simple. She just had to sit back and wait for marching orders. Those came straight from the Bible and the Holy Spirit.

After breakfast, Maya set out for the pool deck, and Anna made her way to the dance hall on Deck Six. She was surprised to hear the big band music as soon as the elevator doors opened.

A group of about twenty people were standing on the dance floor, and the Amethyst Club section was noticeable. Lavender spotted Anna and walked toward her. "You made it! We were hoping you would. Come join us." Anna walked with Lavender to the group and met the rest.

"You already know Lilac," Dovie started. "This is Orchid and Magenta. Mauve is sitting at the table over there." Anna noticed a pretty woman wearing a deep-purple scarf on her head. She had obviously lost her hair from chemotherapy.

Lilac walked up to Anna. She was holding a fluffy purple boa. "This is for you. You are now part of the Amethyst Bunch. What should we call her, ladies?" Lilac turned to the purple-clad women.

"How about Periwinkle?" Mauve asked. "Her eyes are sort of sparkling today."

"Periwinkle it is," Lilac declared.

Anna appreciated the kindness of the women. "This means a lot to me. I will never forget you and how you were there for me at my low point."

Lilac hugged Anna. "We were glad to do it. Women should stick together, especially at our low points."

Before Anna could reply, Poppy Lane began speaking into a microphone on the stage. She was accompanied by a younger man named Carlos. "Good morning, ladies! And gentleman." Everyone looked at the only man in attendance. "Are you ready to shake your tailfeathers?" The grouped hooted and clapped.

"Carlos and I will demonstrate a simple closed hold, so partner up!"

The group quickly formed into pairs. Anna smiled as at least eight women made a beeline to the lone man on the floor. She later learned that his name was John, and he was traveling with his son's family. Somehow, John managed to partner up with three women. He didn't seem to mind. Anna paired with Lilac, who was also wearing a purple boa. Poppy and Carlos demonstrated a basic hold and instructed the dancers to choose a leader.

"You lead, Periwinkle," Lilac suggested softly.

"Okay," Anna agreed. "But I've never done this before."

"We will start with the simple waltz steps." Poppy began calling out steps for the leaders. Anna tried but could not get them in time. "Left foot forward, right foot side, left foot close. Switch weight."

Poor Lilac could only patiently watch Anna stumble. Finally, she offered Anna relief. "Let me lead."

A chill ran down Anna's spine at Lilac's words. *Was that you, God? Am I making a mess of things while trying to take the lead?* He was telling her once again to give Him control. Let Him be her Designated Driver.

Anna smiled at Lilac. "Of course. Lead away." The two did better with Lilac leading but were still not quite master-class waltzers. When the lesson was over, Anna said goodbye to her new friends and returned to her cabin. She wanted to get her thoughts down onto her laptop and sketch out her upcoming book.

With a bottle of water and a leftover cookie, Anna sat on her balcony and typed away for two hours. Around one thirty, Maya found her and asked if she was ready for lunch.

"I think I will stay here," Anna answered. "I need to get my thoughts typed out."

"Are you sure?"

"Yes, I'm very sure. I'm a peace right now."

Maya found a card with the room service menu. "Order in if you get hungry. You can order lunch on the app or with the phone. It will be delivered within thirty minutes."

"Oh!" Anna squealed, "I've never done that." She took the menu and scanned the choices while Maya touched up her lip gloss.

"I'm gonna find Whit and Courtney. They were just going to lunch. We might try ice skating afterwards. There is an open skate session at three o'clock."

"Be careful. And thank you."

Maya sat in the other chair. "For what?"

"For this trip," Anna answered. "You could have taken one of your friends. Or Jan or Winnie. But you took me. I needed this. I needed to get away." Maya began nodding. "I don't think I could hear God in my everyday busyness. I wasn't even listening. But I hear Him so well on the sea. Thank you for this time."

"Thank you for coming. I don't think anyone else would have given up a week of their life for me. Hunter certainly wouldn't." Anna squeezed one of Maya's hands. The two decided that they would dress up for tonight's formal night events. Maya promised to return in time to be ready for their seven o'clock reservation.

Later that night, as Anna was taking off her chandelier earrings, she noticed the daily activity sheet on the vanity. The next day's planner was left by the room attendant each night. "Maya! Look at this!" Maya rushed out of the bathroom and looked at the six-page flyer.

"Captain's Orders," Maya noted. "I never noticed that before. The title of the activity sheet is 'Captain's Orders.'"

Anna smiled at their discovery. "So we must simply find what the captain tells us to do today and do the opposite. The clue said, 'Do not do what the captain says.'"

"Let's see." Maya scanned the activity guide. "I see some information about Treasure Island, the weather forecast, and a huge list of activities and times. What could the captain be telling us to do?"

The two scoured the pages but did not find any order directly from the captain.

Finally, Maya noticed the very first sentence. "Look. Right under the title. 'Today is Wednesday, June eighteenth. Expect calm seas. You won't need safety goggles.' That's odd."

"Safety goggles?"

Maya thought for a minute and remembered. "The science lab. That would have safety goggles."

"So we *will* need safety goggles tomorrow. That should be easy. Which deck is that?"

"Twelve, I think. We can check it out after breakfast."

Anna looked at the activity guide again. "You are very good at this, Maya."

"Thanks, Periwinkle."

Anna could only laugh. Today had been a very good day.

CHAPTER TWENTY-TWO

Wednesday, June 18
2025

Anna was amazed to discover that she had slept until 9:10. She never slept that late. After quietly dressing, she took her laptop to the balcony to check her email, which she hadn't done the day before. Maya was still asleep. They had no plans for the morning, so Anna let her continue to sleep.

After two advertising messages, Anna noticed one from Jan. He rarely sent her email messages, and Anna was relieved to see that the subject was "Miss you."

Hi, Mom. How are you? Maya said that you aren't eating enough. I hope that was a joke. Ha!

I wanted to share my big news. I decided to apply to pharmacy school. Don't be mad, but I plan to apply to Auburn. Another ha! And to Samford. I signed up to take the PCAT at the beginning of July. Applications are due at the beginning of August.

I know this seems sudden, but Katelyn is doing well at Auburn. And I talked with Dr. Manning yesterday. He is going to write one of my recommendations. And someone from Dad's work went to lunch with us after church. Her boyfriend just finished pharmacy school. Dad asked them to come so I could get help with my applications.

Wait. After church? Sunday? Dad's work? Was that why Brandee joined them for lunch? So Jan could seek advice from her pharmacist boyfriend?

Anna closed the laptop without reading the rest of Jan's message. She had to sort the facts. Jan had a new path. Her husband was not dating someone from work. Brandee's boyfriend was helping Jan with his new path. Anna couldn't believe that she had collapsed in the hall over nothing. Of course, meeting the purple ladies was one of the many blessings she had received on this short journey. But the collapse was totally unfounded.

Opening her laptop, Anna read the rest of Jan's message. *Bad news. Pastor Ed gave an update on the orphanage in Honduras. Winnie is trying to figure out how to mail herself to a foreign country. Not joking! Don't eat too much. Love, Jan.*

Maya startled her mother when she stepped out onto the balcony. Her bangs were plastered to her forehead like they did when she was a child. "What are you smiling about?"

"I didn't realize that I was smiling. I just read a message from Jan. It was good news. He's gonna apply to pharmacy school."

"That's cool. He will be great at that."

"And Brandee's boyfriend is helping him with the applications. That's why she ate lunch with them."

"Ouch!" Maya said as she walked towards the bathroom. "Jump to conclusions much?" Anna quickly wrote Jan to tell him how proud she was and then got dressed to eat.

After a late breakfast, Anna and Maya decided to spend the day lounging on the top deck. Anna talked Maya into later watching a movie at the theater before dinner. They walked directly from the buffet to the front of the ship and the Ahoy Kid's Club. Near the entrance of the club was a basket of safety goggles. Anna noticed several adults standing near the basket with the goggles. A few wore the goggles.

"Go check them out," Anna urged. Maya walked to the basket and picked up a pair of goggles. She finally put the pair over her eyes and smiled. A clue must be written on the inside.

Maya rushed to her mother and pulled her arm to make her leave. "I got it. Let's go." Anna followed until Maya stopped near the buffet entrance.

"What did it say?" Anna asked.

"It said, 'Take a walk from the dock.' Then it had three chemical symbols. You know, the ones on the periodic table."

"Which ones?"

"Carbon, potassium, and gold. I remember the Au from the show last night."

Anna thought. "Is that C, P, and Au?"

"No. Potassium is K, not P," Maya corrected. "But I think the numbers matter, not the symbols. The numbers were on the clues. Let me check on my phone to make sure I have them correct." The two walked to a table near the front of Blackbeard's Fortress. "Here's the whole periodic table."

"Jan probably knows it by heart."

Maya rolled her eyes. "He probably does. Let's see. Carbon is six. Potassium is nineteen. And gold is seventy-nine. There were plus signs between the symbols. So I think we add them."

"One-oh-four!" Anna blurted.

"Wow, Mom. That was fast."

Anna smiled. "Your dad isn't the only one who can add numbers."

"Apparently so," Maya joked. "So we walk one hundred and four paces from the dock when we go to Treasure Island tomorrow. That should be easy. And that should give us the final clue."

"These clues have been more fun than I thought. We make a good team."

Maya shook her mother's hand. "Partners in crime—for life."

For Anna, the rest of the day involved reading, writing, and eating. She watched Maya dance with the Weeks kids and enjoyed late-night pizza with them before bed. Another great day with her daughter.

CHAPTER TWENTY-THREE

Thursday, June 19
2025

Anna ordered room service for breakfast, and she and her daughter ate on their balcony overlooking Treasure Island. The third and final island was encircled by white sand. Anna spotted the meandering lazy river and massive saltwater pool that featured two waterfalls. She also noticed young men running jet skis through the water.

"This should hold me over until my beach burger," Anna declared.

"Oh," Maya replied. "I forgot about the beach burgers. They will be the best part of today. I was thinking about the hundred and four steps. Are they huge steps? Or literal foot-sized steps? That matters."

Anna sat her fork down. "We have plenty of time to redo our steps. But I'm thinking that we should just casually walk and keep count. We don't want anyone else to figure out what we are doing."

"Good idea. You are getting into this, Mom."

"I am. And the clue said, 'Take a walk from the dock,' so I think we should start counting at the very end of the pier. The whole pier is more than one hundred steps anyway."

"Sounds good," Maya agreed. "Let's go!"

When Anna and Maya exited the gangway, they were discussing which beach to visit for the day and did not notice the fanfare on the island. Balloons were floating, live music was joining the island's usual pirate music, and photographers were capturing an exciting moment.

The cruise line would later announce that a family from New Orleans was the first to march the correct number of steps from the pier. Rather than another clue, the family with two energetic boys found the treasure chest of $50,000 in gold buried in the sand. In their official press conference, one of the boys yelled, "Jesus is the real treasure." His outburst had gone viral throughout social media.

Anna wanted to watch some of the celebration, and Maya agreed to join the onlookers. Over time a large crowd surrounded the happy family. With the treasure hunt now over, the women spent the rest of the time on the island reading, napping, and eating beach burgers at the Crow's Nest.

The evening was relaxing with dinner at the buffet and attending the *Waltzing Sharks* show for a second time. Maya went to the late-night bonfire beach party on Treasure Island with the Weeks family, and Anna settled herself in the cabin. She wrote messages to Jan and Winnie. She also replied to Laney: *I'm changing the story a little, and you are going to love it.*

The rest of the cruise was full of fun. Anna never saw the ladies of the Amethyst Club again, but she thanked God for their love and wisdom in her time of crisis. She made a vow to be on the lookout for others who might need a word of encouragement.

Anna still couldn't believe that a middle school girl won the belly flop contest, and she loved every minute of the group karaoke sing-along on the last night. Her pants were tighter, and her skin was a little tanner at the end of the week. And her book was one-third written. Maya was invited to visit the Weeks in Columbus. Anna resisted the urge to begin planning a Maya-Whit wedding. She asked

Jesus to show her daughter His will for her life. Maya would do just fine figuring the rest out on her own.

CHAPTER TWENTY-FOUR

Sunday, June 22

2025

Disembarking the ship was bittersweet. Anna had found peace on the ocean but missed the rest of her family terribly. As she pulled her suitcase down the exit gangway, she reminded herself that God would be her Designated Driver, just as Captain Scott had been for the ship's passengers. It would not be easy, but it would be the right way to live.

As she finished her cran-apple drink and biscotti cookies, Anna closed the seatback tray in front of her. The plane landed in Birmingham four minutes early. Anna knew this because she had been watching the time intently as soon as the descent began. Jan and Winnie would be waiting at the airport, and she looked forward to hugging them and hearing about their week. But she dreaded what would happen after the hour-long drive home. Would Jude ever come back? Or was the separation permanent? Anna promised herself that she wouldn't get ahead of God. She would trust Him with any outcome. She would rely on His strength to move forward.

"C'mon, Mom." Maya shook Anna from her thoughts as they exited the plane. "Baggage claim is this way." Anna turned to follow her daughter. As she approached the luggage carousel, she saw Jan standing tall. He was walking toward her. Winnie was close behind. Then she saw him. Jude was walking in her direction. He had come to greet them. Anna hoped this was a good sign but also knew that he missed Maya.

Jude hugged Anna first. "We need to talk."

Anna hugged him back and looked upward.

Take the lead, God.

Epilogue

"Be a tree, Mom," Winnie warned. "Let the sloth hang on you."

"Like this?" Anna was smitten with the animal's adorable face.

"No. Just stand there."

"You know I'm not good at doing nothing." Winnie laughed and patted the animal on his back. She noted that he smelled like fresh popcorn.

Anna's youngest child had been serving as a long-term missionary at the Jeremiah and Catherine Wilkes Evangelical Orphanage in San Pedro Sula, Honduras, for two years. After six months of service, Anna put together the astounding fact that the founder of the facility was Winnie's great-great-great-great-uncle. Affectionately known as Fidget, Jeremiah and his wife recruited volunteers to permanently staff a faith-based orphanage on their third trip to Honduras. They had heard stories of political unrest while the country was prospering economically. The advancement of steam transportation led to greater exports of year-round crops such as bananas. But orphaned children had become unexpected victims to the national prosperity.

Winnie had completed a degree in early childhood education with a minor in Spanish for the sole purpose of teaching small children at the orphanage. She shared with them reading, writing, and Jesus. She also wrote the school's monthly newsletter. Today was Anna's second visit to Honduras. She planned to visit as often as possible and had begun writing children's books about the local flora and fauna.

Jan had also visited the Wilkes orphanage twice. He served as a short-term pharmaceutical missionary both times. With his knowledge of medication selection and drug management, he could help not only the orphanage but also local health care professionals. Jan kept in touch with Katelyn, but their relationship slowly transitioned into the "friendship zone" when he chose to attend Samford University over Auburn.

Winnie's assignment required her to travel home for a respite leave one month per year. Last year, she timed her visit for the birth of Maya and Whit's twin daughters, Leah Jade and Anna Jewel. Whit's mother had passed away from a brief battle with pancreatic cancer the year before, so they named the girls after their grandmothers.

Anna handed the sloth back to the handler. She found her phone and took pictures of Winnie and Jan. They were now in a cage of Capuchin monkeys. One of the animals had stolen Jan's hat and was sitting on it at the top of the cage.

"A penny for your thoughts." Jude put his arm around his wife.

"Thank you for throwing up on me."

"Shipwreck Survival Stories: Violet Jessop in her Voluntary Aid Detachment uniform while assigned to HMHS, *Britannic*," *TidewatterTeddy.com*.

About the Author

Christine R. Whitlock is a wife, mother, Sunday school teacher, and chemist. She and her husband Robert have been married for thirty-five years and have one incredible son. They have also cared for twenty-four foster children. In their spare time, they enjoy traveling-especially to the Caribbean. Christine has a bachelor's degree from Huntingdon College and a doctoral degree from The University of Alabama. Her entire professional career has been as a chemistry professor at Georgia Southern University. Outside of the lab, she enjoys jogging, pizza, and jigsaw puzzles.

Visit her online at ChristineRWhitlock.com.